ALSO BY JILL JOHNSON

The Woman in the Garden

THE
POISON
GROVE

A PROFESSOR EUSTACIA ROSE MYSTERY

JILL JOHNSON

Poisoned Pen
PRESS

For Su

Sourcebooks, Poisoned Pen Press, and the colophon
are registered trademarks of Sourcebooks.

Published by Poisoned Pen Press, an imprint of Sourcebooks
P.O. Box 4410, Naperville, Illinois 60567-4410
(630) 961-3900
sourcebooks.com

Cataloging-in-Publication Data is on file with the Library of Congress.

Printed and bound in the United States of America.
VP 10 9 8 7 6 5 4 3 2 1

1

THERE IS A ROOM IN UNIVERSITY COLLEGE LONDON THAT FEW people know about because it's down a rarely used staircase, along a forgotten corridor, through two sets of fire doors, and at the end of a passage that on first sight looks like a dead end. The room is dimly lit by a permanently curtained window, but there's enough light to see an oak desk, a leather office chair, a glass-fronted cabinet, and shelves sagging under the weight of so many folders and papers and reference books. On the wall beside the desk is a framed photograph of an old man sitting in a faded garden reading a well-thumbed paperback copy of *La Peste* by Camus. He's wearing a Harris Tweed suit and steel-rimmed glasses. A 1950s Rolex glints at his wrist. His hair is neatly combed and precisely parted. He has a kind face. He suits the room, or the room suits him.

Sitting at the desk, marking essays, is me: Professor Eustacia Amelia Rose, head of Botanical Toxicology at University College

London. After a yearlong sabbatical, I've been back in my post for nine months. I can't say it's been plain sailing. There have been times when I've hankered after the precious solitude I enjoyed during my time off. The hours I could fill as I pleased. The research I could undertake free from pointless bureaucracy, petty rules, and officious busybodies. That is, until it was all taken from me. I don't like to dwell on that tragic event, but suffice to say, I lost something very precious last year. Something irreplaceable.

But still, I'm grateful to be back in this stimulating environment, I'm rising to the challenge of interacting with my peers, and, although it isn't the same as it was before my year off, I'm achieving a certain amount of satisfaction teaching this year's cohort of students. At the age of forty-five, I know this is my second chance. The university giving me this opportunity to get my career back on track—to pick up where I left off—is a huge privilege, and I'm absolutely determined that nothing and nobody will knock me off course again. In fact, I intend to remain the head of Botanical Toxicology at University College London until I'm very, very old, indeed.

I finished marking the final essay, took off my glasses, flicked on the desk lamp, and blinked rapidly at its glare, only then realizing how dark it had become. It explained the pain behind my eyes. The absolute silence in the building. I checked the vintage Rolex on my wrist. It was eleven o'clock.

With a soft whistle, I gathered my belongings and put them

into my satchel, but before leaving, I paused in front of the photograph on the wall and studied my reflection in its glass. I was wearing the same Harris Tweed suit as the old man, the same steel-rimmed glasses, and my hair was short, neat, and precisely parted.

I rapped the glass above his face with a knuckle and said, "Goodnight, Father. See you in the morning."

When I arrived in the main university foyer, a student was loitering by the doors. I knew who he was—an anxious PhD student I'd been trying to avoid for months. I've always struggled with remembering names, so over the years, I've developed a strategy of nicknaming people after the plant they most resemble. This student earned his nickname when he was an undergraduate. Giant Hogweed. Latin name *Heracleum mantegazzianum*—a tall, willowy plant with phototoxic sap in its large leaves that causes phytophotodermatitis, resulting in painful blisters and scarring. I'd named him this not only because he was extremely tall, with huge hands and red blotchy skin, but also because he was highly irritating, to the point of causing me physical pain. Headaches mostly, but pain nevertheless. I had no way of knowing if he was waiting for me, but I suspected he was because for the entire time I'd been back at the university, he'd put as much effort into hounding me as I had into avoiding him. I let out a quiet groan, ducked behind a pillar, and peered around it.

Ordinarily, I didn't look at him longer than absolutely necessary, but there was something about him this evening that seemed odd. It wasn't that his trousers were too short for his long legs or that his jacket was too tight. It wasn't the mustard-colored woolen hat clashing horribly with his blotchy skin or the huge headphones that diminished the size of his head. It was something I couldn't put a finger on. Something new. I watched his agitated gait a few minutes longer as he paced the length of the foyer, and then when his back was to me, I turned on my heel and headed for the service exit.

The problem with turning on one's heel on a highly polished foyer floor is the squeal of one's shoe and the resulting echo around the cavernous space. I glanced back in time to see him turn in my direction and pull down his headphones.

"Prof?"

Clearly, I couldn't continue to the service exit now that he'd seen me, so I headed for the stairs as quickly as I could. It was no use. My legs were much shorter than his. He was beside me in moments.

"Are you free for a quick chat?"

A distorted, tinny sound was coming from the headphones, like fingernails on a blackboard. It set my teeth on edge, but I kept up my rapid pace as best I could.

"Not now. I'm very late." This was not true.

"Where're you going?"

"I have to go to the lab." This wasn't true either.

"I'll walk with you."

"I'd rather you didn't. I just have to collect something then dash. I'm very late."

"For what?"

"I beg your pardon?"

"What are you very late for?"

I paused, my mind blank. "That's none of your business."

If I'd thought this through logically, I would not be rushing up empty stairs in a deserted university building with a troublesome student on my heels. I would be outside, surrounded by people who would come to my aid if required. But there was something disturbing about Giant Hogweed this night that had caused my thoughts to scatter.

I reached the floor of my laboratory, pushed open the stairwell doors, and, puffing from exertion, hurried through them. Soon, I was outside the lab, but before I could pull my lanyard and key card from my pocket, he stepped in front of me and took hold of my wrist. I looked down at his huge hand. He dug in his fingers. He was hurting me, but I wasn't going to let him know it.

It wasn't the first time he'd done this, and it wasn't only me he did this to. Many people had complained about this intimidating behavior. Before his PhD supervisor had dumped him, she'd warned him many times that he could be expelled if he continued.

"Let go of my wrist."

His grip tightened. "Ah… Prof… This is driving me nuts. You never want to talk to me. You never listen. I don't want full access to your collection. I gave up on that months ago. I just need ten samples. Ten cuttings. That's all."

I sighed loudly. "I've told you time and time again, that won't be possible."

He gave me a long look. "And I've told you time and time again that I won't tell anyone."

"Let go," I said again, my tone more insistent.

"Alright, alright. Eight cuttings. I'll have to rewrite a chapter of my thesis, but eight could work."

I closed my eyes. "For the hundredth time, there are no plants to take cuttings from. You know this. I've been telling you for months. I've also been telling you that you need to rethink your thesis. So do it. Rethink your thesis."

He took a deep breath and spoke in a lower, almost threatening tone. "You're my supervisor. You're meant to help me."

"I'm not your supervisor."

"Unofficial supervisor."

"Not even unofficial."

"But you're the only person who can help me!" he shouted, yanking my arm upward. "You're the only lecturer in this whole university who's had experience with poisonous plant murder."

I should have been frightened. His wild eyes and unpredictable behavior were menacing. Instead I felt anger—fury that just one of his giant hands around my wrist had rendered me helpless.

"As I've made clear many times, I can't help you, so I suggest you move to a different university." I tried to keep my voice calm. "Imperial and Kings have excellent facilities. You should apply there."

"I did, last year… I didn't get in."

"Then I suggest you rethink your PhD and reapply to a different program."

I glanced up at him. This was patently not what he wanted to hear. His prominent Adam's apple was bouncing. His breathing was fast and hard. His nostrils were flared, his jaw working as he ground his teeth. And this was the difference I'd seen in the foyer. The new thing. He looked almost feral. As if he was ready to hit me.

My phone beeped. I lifted the flap of my satchel with my free hand.

He tightened his grip. "Leave it."

I took my phone out. "I told you—I'm late. Someone's waiting for me. They're probably wondering where I am."

I pressed the screen for the message.

Goodnight, my darling. Sleep well.

The phone beeped again, and three heart emojis appeared.

"I said *leave it,*" he growled, yanking my arm again, making me cry out in pain. Making me drop the phone.

Without warning, the door to the laboratory opened and we spun around to see my lab assistant Carla standing in the doorway. I let out a gasp of relief, thinking I'd never been so pleased to see her in all my life. For a suspended moment, she looked at me and Giant Hogweed, at his huge hand gripping my wrist, then calmly lifted up a small oval device that was hanging from the strap of her bag and pressed a button at its center. Instantly, the corridor filled with a deafeningly high-pitched screaming siren, so loud that my knees buckled. Giant Hogweed let me go and fled, and I wrapped my arms around my head, screwed my eyes tight shut, and dropped to the ground. Straight away, she turned it off, but the sound continued to ricochet around my skull.

"Sorry to do that without warning, Professor," she said. "But the whole point of personal attack alarms is the element of surprise."

I opened my eyes and looked up at her. She was smiling down at me, her hand held out for me to take. I ignored it, picked up my phone, and stood up, my ears ringing.

"That was horrendous," I said, pushing up my glasses.

"But effective. Did you see how fast he ran? Ugh." She shuddered. "I despise that creep. He makes my skin crawl."

"You know him?"

"We're on the same PhD botany program. I can't stand him. Nobody can. He's just so *rude*, you know? Always picking a fight. He's one of these people who thinks the whole world is against him. I hate people like that."

I was reassured to know that others found him as irritating as I did. No. *Reassured* was the wrong word. I was disappointed.

"It's worse since he started doing MDMA," Carla added. "He was wired before he started doing drugs. He's off the chart now. I'd stay well clear of him if I was you."

"Easier said than done," I muttered, wiping my face with my handkerchief.

"Are you okay? You look a bit dazed."

"I'm fine."

"You know you have to report him? He was attacking you. He should be expelled."

"You're right—I probably should," I said doubtfully. "If you're leaving, do you mind if we walk out together?"

"Sure. You need anything from the lab?"

"Not right now."

She flicked off the lights and pulled the door shut. "I'll stand with you till your bus arrives, if you like," she added, taking hold of my elbow as if I were very old and frail.

"That's kind of you," I said, pulling my arm free.

"No problem. Although Aaron's probably long gone by now."

That was his name. Aaron. I would have known that once. Maybe if I'd used it, he'd have shown me some respect. But then again, probably not.

2

IT WAS PAST MIDNIGHT BY THE TIME I GOT OFF THE BUS AT THE bottom of Hampstead High Street and turned for home. Once inside my flat building, I climbed the three flights of stairs in silence. I had a difficult relationship with my neighbors. It was best I didn't disturb them. Actually, I had a difficult relationship with most people, which wasn't ideal for a university lecturer. Even though I'd been back at work for nine months, I still found social interaction, eye contact, and humor challenging. I can't deny that my isolation during the previous year had compounded my difficulties. For much of that time I was, for all intents and purposes, a recluse, my collection of poisonous plants my only company.

The light on my answering machine was flashing. I paid it no attention and walked along the hall toward the kitchen, stopping in front of a framed photograph of Father on the way. He was sitting at the long table in our family home in Oxford, reading a battered copy of Dostoevsky's *The Idiot*. On the table before him was an encyclopedia of plants and flowers; a battered basket full of freshly collected eggs; a pair of pruning shears; three rooting avocado stones balanced atop jars of water; a discarded, moldy sandwich; an ancient, negatives-strewn light box and eye glass; and a whittling knife. His spectacles rested upon the bridge of his large nose. His lips were pursed in thought.

I rapped the glass above his face with a knuckle. "Hello, Father. I'm home."

I should have gone to bed. I had an early start. Instead, I climbed the ladder and went through a hatch in my kitchen ceiling that opened onto the roof garden. Before I returned to the university, I used to visit the garden daily to tend to my poisonous-plants collection. To look after each plant with meticulous care, to make sure their every requirement was catered for. But these days there was no longer any need for protective overalls or gloves, or shoe covers, because the most dangerous plant I now owned was a *Euphorbia characias* subsp. *wulfenii*, which, if its irritating sap was accidently rubbed into an eye, caused redness and blurred vision.

I opened a folding canvas chair that had belonged to Father, sat, and exhaled out the stresses of the day. In this orange-hued city night, all around the ghosts of my collection manifested eerily, reminding me of what I'd lost.

There, against the south boundary railing, now occupied by a lollypop fuchsia, once stood my magnificent *Ricinus communis*.

Over there, where several pots of chrysanthemums were grouped together, used to be the home of my *Datura stramonium*. Beside it, my collection of *Digitalis purpurea* had been exchanged for various culinary herbs, and beside them, replacing my beautiful specimen of *Veratrum viride*, was the euphorbia. And dotted throughout, in different-colored plastic pots were annuals: geraniums, petunias, pansies.

I exhaled a sad breath at the memory of my fifty or so precious poisonous plants, some so incredibly rare they could never be replaced, and reflected on the accomplishment of nurturing so many tiny cuttings to maturity and treating them with such care that it was as if I'd given birth to them and raised them as my own children. I'm certainly very proud of the fact that during the twenty years I had my collection, I'd lost only two plants. And that was during an unprecedented and particularly vicious cold snap that had taken even Kew Gardens by surprise.

With a long, sweeping glance across the rooftop, I acknowledged that this was far from the garden I would have wanted for myself. I would not have chosen the brightly colored plastic pots, the unnecessary accessories, the frivolous and nonfunctional sculptures, and these were not the plants I would have selected. There was nothing about them to excite me. Apart from mildly irritating sap, there was nothing dangerous, nothing exotic, nothing toxic, but I'd agreed to everything to make my Portuguese colleague Matilde—who I'd nicknamed Sweet Alyssum (*Lobularia maritima,* a beautiful little plant with a huge impact)—happy. And I'd agreed to the repurposing of the space from a sterile, precisely controlled field laboratory into a place to have breakfast with her, to read the papers, to sit with her in the evenings while she drank wine, because these were the domestic activities Matilde told me couples did together. Also because, to be honest, in the past I haven't been very lucky in love, and it's time for that to change. It wasn't all bad. My garden might no longer be even a shadow of what it once was, but I still had a place to come each night to reflect on my day. To watch the stars and the planets and the occasional meteor shower through my telescope...or the comings and goings of my neighbors through the windows of the terraced houses behind my block of flats.

It was a clear night. I could see many stars through the veil of light pollution. But I wasn't in the mood for stargazing. I went to my telescope, angled it down to the terraced houses, and panned across the windows. There they all were. My neighbors. Not so long ago, I'd viewed them merely as subjects for an observational study. I'd even jotted down their comings and goings in notebooks and had planned to publish my findings, but that was before I discovered they were real people, with real stories, simply living their lives.

There'd been a few changes in their activities since I'd started back at work. The woman with blue hair and crutches who'd shared biscuits with her dog no longer had a dog. The bickering couple who were forever practicing the same four dance moves had graduated to the next set of four dance moves. The young boy sunken into a beanbag, playing computer games and glugging energy drinks, had moved into an office chair and was hunched over a keyboard. The silent teenage girl with the long braided hair, who was always alone scrolling on her phone, now had a friend to scroll with, lie on her bed with, and share laughter with. But the tall, stooping man who never smiled and stood stock-still for hours looking at a photograph of a mother and baby on his wall was still staring at the photograph, more stooped, thinner.

I looked into the garden of the house opposite and saw my eighty-five-year-old friend, Susan, shuffling around her garden, her white hair shining brightly in the moonlight, a flashlight in her hand as she collected snails to throw over the wall. When I first met her, I'd given her the nickname Black-eyed Susan, after *Rudbeckia hirta*, a perennial prairie plant with yellow petals, its leaves covered with small hairs that were mildly irritating but harmless. I didn't find her irritating anymore. In fact, I could confidently call her my friend. My best friend. I smiled at the sight of her. One day I'd tell her what she did every night was pointless because snails have a homing instinct and always return.

I moved the telescope upward to the windows of the flat above Susan's garden and felt a shiver of emotion as I thought of the mysterious young woman, with her astonishing beauty and tantalizing secrets, who'd lived there the year before. The young woman whom I'd nicknamed Psycho after my *Psychotria elata* plant because of the uncanny resemblance of her full lips to the plant's glossy red bracts. I admit, I may have been a little obsessed with her last year, but I now regularly reminded myself to banish all thoughts of her from my mind. I was very strict about this. Yet here I was, looking through the window of her empty bedroom. I let out a nostalgic sigh.

"That you, dear?"

Susan was looking up at my garden, a genial expression on her face. She couldn't see me. I was sure of that. The *Mandevilla sanderi* vine covering the boundary railings of my garden was too thick, but her face was definitely tilted in my direction.

"Yes," I called down.

"Fancy a cuppa?"

"It's the middle of the night, Susan."

"I know that. I ain't senile."

After the short walk to her house, I found Susan's door unlocked, which made me question her disregard for security, especially at this time of night. With a shaking head, I closed the door securely behind me and walked along the dark hall to the kitchen just as she shuffled in from the garden, the flashlight in her hand.

"Give me a sec. I'll just wash off the snail slime, and then I'll put the kettle on," she said, going to the sink. "How are you?"

I sat at the kitchen table with a groan. "Fine," I said, taking off my glasses and rubbing my eyes with two knuckles.

"Don't sound like it." She turned to face me. "Don't look like it neither. Everything alright at work?"

"Everything's fine. I'm enjoying the teaching. Keeping on top of the grading. It's just… I'm just…"

"Just what, dear?"

"I'm having a bit of trouble with a student."

"Oh? Something-you-can-deal-with trouble? Or call-the-police trouble?"

"Something I can deal with. I think."

"Well, as my dearly departed Stanley used to say, *a trouble shared is a trouble halved*." She fetched the teapot and cups, sat, and looked at me expectantly, her large breasts resting on the tabletop.

It was difficult to know where to begin. Giant Hogweed had been a problem for so long that I'd forgotten when the beginning began. I opened my mouth to speak, and, at the same time, my mobile vibrated in my pocket, making me leap in surprise. I cursed, pulled it out, and dropped it on the table. Despite owning the phone for almost a year, I still hadn't worked out how to turn off this irritating feature.

"Answer it, dear. It could be important."

I didn't want to answer—it was the middle of the night. But I picked it up, prodded the green circle on the screen, and held it to my ear.

"Professor. Listen, I've just been sent an interesting message."

"Who is this?"

I knew who it was. I recognized his voice immediately, but we hadn't spoken for nine months, and I resented his assumption that there was some sort of familiarity between us.

There was a long pause. "It's DCI Roberts. You didn't save me as a contact?"

"I didn't what?"

"You didn't save me— Never mind."

Another pause, so long that I thought he'd hung up. I looked at the screen to check.

"I suppose it has been a while," he said.

"What do you want?"

"How're you doing, Professor?"

Pleasantries were pointless with me. I thought he knew this. I tutted loudly and repeated the question. "What do you want?"

"The message. I thought of you as soon as I saw it. Are you busy right now?"

I checked my watch. "It's well past midnight."

"I know. I'll be with you in twenty minutes. Meet me on your corner."

The phone went silent.

I looked at the screen. "He hung up on me," I cried.

"Was that your policeman friend?" Susan asked, passing me a rattling teacup.

"He's not my friend."

"What did he want?"

I pursed my lips. "I suspect he wants my help with another case."

She took a very slow sip of tea. "That's exciting."

"No it isn't. I'm too busy. It's coming to the end of term. I'll have a mountain of grading to do in the next few weeks. I won't have time to run around for DCI Roberts."

"I could help. You know how much I love a good puzzle."

"I don't have time, even with your help."

"Go on. Let me help you. I ain't got nothing better to do. It'll be fun."

I looked at her dark eyes shining with enthusiasm—Black-eyed Susan, mildly irritating—and shook my head. "Sorry, but you're not going to persuade me." I put my phone on the table. "If I knew how to fix this thing so he couldn't call me anymore, I'd do it in a heartbeat."

Susan held out her hand. "Give it 'ere. I don't think you should block his number, but I'll fix it so you can choose not to answer." She prodded and scrolled the screen with an arthritic finger then handed the phone back. "There—I've saved your friends' numbers as contacts."

"Which friends?"

"Me, Matilde, and your policeman friend."

I frowned at the screen. "Who's Cabbage?"

She smiled. "Me. It's what my Stanley used to call me."

My ears pricked up. "Your husband gave you a plant nickname?"

"He did, bless his soul. I would've preferred something more fragrant, but I couldn't complain 'cause it's from *mon petit chou,* you know?"

I didn't, but I didn't say so.

"Who's Sweetie?"

"Matilde. What do you call her? Sweet something?"

"Sweet Alyssum."

"So cute…"

"And Dickie?"

"Your policeman friend, Dickie. So now, next time he calls, you can ignore 'im."

I screwed up my face. "*Dickie?*"

3

Fifteen minutes later, DCI Richard Roberts and I arrived at the corner of my road at the same time.

He pulled his car to a stop and wound down the window.

"Good evening, Professor. I'm so glad you decided to join me."

I hadn't decided to join him. In fact, that was the opposite of what I'd decided to do. I was about to say so when he added, "We have another poisoning, and your expertise is required at the crime scene."

I paused, suddenly unsure of my footing. "Required by law?"

There was a hesitation before he answered. "Yes."

"Does that mean I'm not allowed to say no?"

Another hesitation. "Yes."

I took a deep, slow breath and exhaled heavily as all the work I'd planned to do the following day passed through my mind and out the other side. "Well…if it's required by law…" At least Susan would be pleased.

I was dismayed to see that he was driving the same battered car he'd had the year before, and the feeling only intensified when I opened the passenger door to be hit with the same stench of wet dog I'd had to endure the year before. Quickly, he scooped up the detritus from the passenger seat and threw it into the back, and, flaring my nostrils, I got in beside him.

"It's good to see you again. You haven't changed a bit," he said.

I gave him a quick side glance as he started the engine. He hadn't either. He was still wearing that tatty blue suit, his shirt buttons straining across his large belly, and the dark rings under his eyes were as pronounced as ever. Even so, I was surprised to admit that it was good to see him as well.

"I see you're still wearing your father's suit," he said as we turned onto Haverstock Hill.

I didn't comment on the blatantly obvious observation, but he kept glancing at me, as if he was expecting a reply.

"Was that a question?"

"It wasn't, but I'll turn it into one—why are you still wearing your father's suit?"

I thought about this. "Because it's a remnant."

"A remnant? I thought your father had his suits tailored in Savile Row?"

"It's a remnant of a memory. A memory of him."

He inhaled. "Ah…"

I fixed my gaze on the road ahead, but in my peripheral vision, he was still glancing at me, so I changed the subject.

"Tell me about the poisoning."

A side lean and a protracted pocket fumble later, he pulled out his phone, touched the screen, and let me read the message.

"All this says is *possible* poisoning in Soho."

"That's right."

"So possibly *not* a poisoning?"

"We won't know till we get there."

I tutted loudly. This might be a false errand.

"Let's just concentrate on the word *poisoning*," he said. "That's enough to pique your interest, isn't it?"

I tutted again and added, "It's the middle of the night."

"And yet here you are sitting in my car, wide awake, when I distinctly remember you telling me last year that you were an early to bed, early to rise person."

I had told him that. It was while he'd been questioning me about a murder. It had been my alibi in fact. But now I chose to keep my mouth shut because it hadn't strictly been true.

The entrance to Berwick Street was clogged with response vehicles, so DCI Roberts parked behind a police van on Wardour Street and we cut down a side road. We arrived in time to see a stretcher being loaded into the back of an ambulance. It didn't move off immediately but stayed where it was in the middle of the road, which meant whoever was inside was in a very perilous condition.

Up ahead, an officer was fixing a perimeter tape around the front of a bookshop, the window of which had been smashed, and a woman was having a heated conversation with a man who was gesticulating angrily toward the shop.

DCI Roberts showed his badge to an officer who was stopping people entering the street, and we walked toward the ambulance.

"D'you see DS Hannah?" he asked, scanning the street. "He's done a good job of securing the scene. He even has forensics waiting, and it's unheard of for them to arrive so quickly."

I looked at the woman having the heated conversation. I couldn't hear the words, but whatever she was saying was gradually calming the man down. Sentence by sentence, the anger subsided until his shoulders dropped. She took hold of his elbow, led him to a police car, and helped him into the back seat; then she turned to speak to an officer. There was something official about her manner. It wasn't the dark trouser suit or the sensible black ankle boots. It was the way she held her body—the straight-backed, square-shouldered stance of a confident person.

"I don't think DS Hannah's in charge," I said.

"He must be around here somewhere. I'll give him a ring." DCI Roberts prodded his phone screen then put it to his ear. "Strange. He's not picking up. I was sure he was on duty."

I turned back to the woman. She was still talking to the officer. "Who's that then?"

He looked at her. "No idea. A journalist? A pushy one if she's sniffing for a story in the middle of the night."

As if she'd heard him, she turned and walked toward us with the authority of the person in charge.

"DCI Roberts?" she called as she approached.

"The same," he said. "And you are?"

"DS Chambers."

"Who?"

"Detective Sergeant Chambers."

He scanned the street again. "Are you from the Westminster precinct? Where's your detective inspector? Credit where credit's due. He's done a good job of securing the scene so quickly."

At this, she stopped walking. "*He?*" She folded her arms. "Oh…you're from *that* generation."

DCI Roberts furrowed his brow. "I'm sorry?"

"*That* generation," she repeated. "The old misogynist copper generation. Well, you'll be surprised and no doubt disappointed to learn that women police officers can also secure crime scenes *quickly.*"

DCI Roberts opened his mouth then closed it again. I gave her a quick look and was instantly distracted by the flower print on her blouse. What were they? *Oxalis acetosella f. rosea? Anemone nemorosa?* It was hard to tell from this distance.

"I'm sorry?" DCI Roberts repeated, and straight away, she replied, "As you should be. As all your generation should be."

There followed a silence that even I understood was awkward. I glanced at DCI Roberts. His eyebrows were bunched together, the corners of his mouth turned down. He looked bewildered.

"Did you secure this crime scene?" he asked at last.

"I did. And I made the urgent request for the forensics team. Time is of the essence in cases like this. And as you were taking so long to arrive, I thought it best to move things along."

"You were waiting for me?"

"Yes, sir."

"Why?"

"Because I'm your new DS. I transferred in from Cardiff yesterday."

"I already have a DS."

"DS Hannah requested a transfer out, and I think I understand why now. He's gone to Manchester. I'm his replacement. Did no one tell you?"

DCI Roberts looked so confused, I almost felt sorry for him. There followed another silence as they regarded each other, DCI Roberts bewildered, DS Chambers assured, and I stood alongside them, turning from one to the other, wondering how long this was going to take. Eventually, I interrupted by clearing my throat theatrically, which woke DCI Roberts up. He turned and looked at me as if I'd just rescued him from a burning building.

"This is Professor Rose. She's a botanical toxicology expert." I sniffed.

"I know who Professor Rose is," DS Chambers said, raising an eyebrow. "So it's true. You really do dress like an old man."

I looked at her and was once again diverted by the flowers on her purple shirt. They were definitely *Oxalis acetosella f. rosea,* wood sorrel. I glanced up at her face. She didn't present as someone who'd wear a flower print. She seemed far too serious.

She looked down at her chest then back to me and added, "I won't shake your hand, Professor. I know you don't like attention drawn to it."

She was right. My hand was still heavily scarred and disfigured from my accident the previous year. I should have grown used to it by now. Grown used to people's reactions to it, but for me, time wasn't the great healer and never would be because my damaged hand was a constant reminder of my own reckless stupidity. I slid it into my pocket.

"The message said the victim was poisoned. Do you have any more information?" I asked.

"Not yet," she said, looking toward the ambulance. "All we know is that he was found slumped in a shop doorway with a syringe in his neck. I assumed the syringe was full of poison."

"Assumed?" I asked.

She turned back to me. "Assumed, deduced, reasoned. Choose whichever word you want. What I'm sure of is that it wasn't saline, not from the way he was thrashing about."

"When did the attack take place?" DCI Roberts asked.

"We don't know. The owner was called to his shop by the alarm company about forty minutes ago because of the broken window. He found the victim when he arrived and called 999."

"The shop owner's the man you put in the back of that police car?"

We all looked at the car.

"He's a bit upset," she said. "He wants to sweep up the glass and cover the window so no one loots his shop. I had to explain he couldn't do that until forensics had finished. I thought he'd be more comfortable waiting in the car."

He didn't look comfortable. He looked in shock, but that was understandable. He'd probably never found a man with a syringe hanging out of his neck before.

"Well…" DCI Roberts said, "I appreciate what you've done so far, but I'll take it from here. It's late. You can go home."

"I'll stay."

"Go home."

"I'll stay…sir."

Anticipating another stand-off, I stepped away and headed for the ambulance. There was no one up front in the cab, which meant they were all in the back. Which meant whatever was going on was most certainly critical. I have to admit, I hesitated before knocking.

They were too busy to answer, of course, so I opened the door and peered inside. What I saw was utter chaos. The crew had their backs to me. They were bending over, restraining a man who was having a violent fit on the stretcher. One was holding an oxygen mask on the man's face with one hand and trying to keep the syringe in his neck still with the other. The other paramedic was using his body weight to hold the man down, while trying to avoid the kicking and punching. And all the while, the man was making an unearthly growling sound, as if he were desperately trying to claw his way out of hell.

"He's in delirium," I said.

I was ignored.

"He's having a violent and no doubt terrifying hallucination," I said, louder. "Probably triggered by whatever's in that syringe."

One of them turned to look at me then immediately turned back.

"He needs an antipsychotic and a sedative. Do you have haloperidol? Or risperidone?" I shouted.

The paramedic glanced back at me. "Are you a doctor?"

"I'm a professor of toxicology."

"You sure he's hallucinating? He's not having a seizure?"

I made a quick calculation. "I'm eighty-two percent sure he's hallucinating. I can't be one hundred percent sure until I know what's in that syringe."

The paramedic looked at me then down at his thrashing patient. "Eighty-two percent will do. The drugs are in that cabinet. You'll have to give it to him yourself. If I let go, the syringe will fall out of his jugular, and we'll have a massive arterial spurt in here."

I climbed up into the ambulance. "Well, we don't want that, do we?"

Moments later, the paramedic pulled up the man's sleeve and held down his arm so I could inject the medication. The other paramedic was still leaning over him, holding the oxygen mask and syringe. I couldn't see the patient's face. I had no idea whom I was treating. All I saw was a body convulsing and writhing, and all I could hear was the furious growling of someone in torment. It was several minutes before his body relaxed and the growls subsided to a guttural moan. And a few minutes more before the paramedics felt it safe enough to let him go.

When at last they were able to stand up, I could finally see who was lying on the stretcher. He looked to be in his early thirties, a muscular frame, a flop of blond hair, blond eyebrows, blond stubble, a deep tan. His clothes were casual but obviously good quality. His pale linen shirt was open to the mid chest. His trousers were rolled at the hems, and he was wearing soft leather loafers, a leather belt, and a very expensive watch. He didn't look like a Londoner. He was far too well kempt, too tanned, too perfect. He looked like I imagined someone would look stepping off a yacht somewhere in the south of France. Certainly not like someone on a night out in Soho.

"Who do we have here then?"

I turned to find DCI Roberts and DS Chambers standing at the ambulance doors.

"I don't know, sir. He wasn't carrying ID," DS Chambers replied.

"Did someone pinch it?"

"If they did, why didn't they take the watch?"

DCI Roberts let out a long hum, which, from experience, I knew meant he wasn't satisfied with an answer. "Why indeed?"

He climbed up into the ambulance and bent over the patient. "Good-looking chap. And probably loaded judging by the watch."

DS Chambers squeezed in as well and jostled for a place next to him. "There's something familiar about this, isn't there, sir?"

DCI Roberts glanced at her. "How so?"

"I looked at your previous cases to help me decide whether or not I wanted to be your new DS, and this reminds me of something."

"You looked at my previous cases?"

"I did."

His thick eyebrows came together.

"You don't have a great track record, do you...sir?" she added.

"*Whether or not,*" DCI Roberts repeated, ignoring her last remark. "Interesting that I was given no say in the matter."

"Something to raise with the super?"

The power play was becoming tedious.

"Okay, out we go. Let's allow these gentlemen to do their job, shall we?" I said, ushering them through the doors.

Outside, DCI Roberts turned to DS Chambers. "Go to the hospital with them. Call me if there's any change." And as the ambulance pulled away, he added, "Alright, enough distraction. Let's get on with the detective work."

I wasn't good at reading moods, but not only could I tell he was angry, I also knew he was trying to hide it.

"How likely is it this young man collapsed the instant the poison entered his jugular?" he asked.

"It depends on the poison. In this case, I'm eighty-two percent certain he was injected with a hallucinogen—he was demonstrating all the symptoms of psychotic delirium in the ambulance, so the poison could have been in his system for a while."

"Then it's likely he staggered here before he collapsed," he said. "But from which direction? We'll know when we do a CCTV trawl." He looked toward Walker's Court at the bottom of Berwick Street. "There's a camera on that wall. We'll start with that one."

He turned around, looking for an officer, but there was only one left, guarding the end of the street while forensics did their work. "Looks like I'll be working this one on my own."

"You have a DS."

"Do I? I'm not so sure."

I was impatient to go home. I had an early start, but DCI Roberts seemed reluctant to leave. He lingered on the corner of Peter Street, his hands in his trouser pockets, making that humming sound.

"What are we waiting for?" I asked.

"Shall we have a cup of tea?"

I made a point of looking at my watch. "You do realize the time?"

The café smelled of frying bacon; a "love it or loathe it" odor that I found revolting. Even more so at two o'clock in the morning. It was full of young people wearing extraordinary clothes and make-up, eating cereal. The only empty chairs were at the end of a sharing table. I eyed them dubiously, but DCI Roberts went straight to them and sat down. He looked at me as I hovered by the door and tipped his head for me to join him. I hesitated. There were too many people and there was too much noise, but I took a breath and made myself cross the crowded café.

"Why are they eating breakfast in the middle of the night?" I asked as I sat.

"They've just woken up."

"Are they night-shift workers?"

This made him laugh, although it wasn't clear why. "No, they're clubbers. They're going clubbing."

"I see," I said, not really seeing.

He ordered two teas and, much to my dismay, a bacon butty.

"You know, you shouldn't be so blatant," he said when the waiter had gone.

"Blatant?"

"With DS Chambers. You were being too obvious. I doubt she minded. It's clear she's in awe of you, but you should be more subtle."

I had absolutely no idea what he was talking about.

"I have absolutely no idea what you're talking about."

"You were staring at her chest."

I let out a shocked cry of protest. "I was not! I was identifying the flowers on her shirt!"

"Sure you were," he said, chuckling. "As I said, I doubt she minded. She obviously likes you a lot more than me. That misogyny quip was grating. Especially from a lower-ranking officer. I mean, I'm not a misogynist."

The waiter delivered our order, and I sipped my tea angrily.

"I said I'm not a misogynist."

I wiped my mouth with a paper napkin brusquely.

"Alright," he continued, "sometimes we can all be a bit unconscious with the *isms*. But when we occasionally slip up, others should be generous and give us a pass, shouldn't they?"

I brushed down the front of my jacket roughly.

"Well anyway, I know I'm not a misogynist. If I said anything even remotely sexist, my daughters would call me out in a nanosecond."

He picked up his bacon butty with both hands and took an enormous bite.

"I was *not* staring at her chest."

"If you say so," he said, chewing. "You know, I've noticed young officers making these kinds of assumptions about me more and more these days. It isn't just that they think me an old-fashioned copper, out of touch with modern attitudes. It's also that since that case last year, I'm being treated differently. Even though no one dares say it to my face, I know my reputation's taken a hit."

He took a huge gulp of tea, another enormous bite, and I watched him, disgusted but also impressed by the way he was devouring the food.

"What about this *DS Chambers* then? Why's she suddenly popped up out of nowhere? And where's DS Hannah? He would've told me if he was transferring to Manchester. Something's going on. I can feel it in my *gut*."

"Perhaps you shouldn't eat so fast."

He looked at me, his untidy eyebrows raised. "Was that a joke?"

"No. You should chew your food thoroughly, not swallow it whole. Thirty-two times is preferable, but twenty-five will do. The more you chew, the slower you eat. The slower you eat, the less you eat."

DCI Roberts patted his large belly. "Are you saying I've gained a few pounds, Professor?"

I took a sip of tea.

"I wouldn't be surprised if she read my old case files to trip me up," he continued. "To prove she's better, smarter. Has a younger brain, sharper wits. Sharper claws."

I thought about this and had to admit there was something prickly about DS Chambers. Not obviously. Not out in the open but under the surface, where you wouldn't see it unless you looked. Like the *Berberis thunbergii* f. *atropurpurea*. An attractive plant on the outside with its pretty purple leaves but covered with hidden thorns. Painful but not toxic.

"Barberry," I said, using the plant's common name.

"Eh?"

"She's a barberry."

"Barbara? Is that her name?"

"I have no idea."

"You just said her name's Barbara."

"No. Bar*berry*. It's a nickname. Father suggested I name people after plants when—"

"Anyway, whatever her name is," he interrupted, popping the last of the butty into his mouth and wiping his chin, "she probably thinks I'm the old-fashioned copper, out of touch and it's time I retired. She probably belongs to that gang of progressives who want to cull all serving police officers over the age of fifty. I guarantee…that young lady wants my job and is playing me to get it."

He waved at the waiter. "That was *amazing*. Who knew a bacon butty at two in the morning could be so delicious? I could eat another one right now."

It was Father who first suggested I name people after plants because when I was a child, I found it difficult to recognize faces and remember names. The first time I met DCI Roberts, I named him Ragweed. Latin name: *Ambrosia artemisiifolia*. A tatty specimen that releases a highly allergenic pollen dust, causing watery eyes, scratchy throat, sinus pain, and swollen, bluish-colored skin beneath the eyes. Irritating to the extreme.

4

A FEW SHORT HOURS LATER, I WAS IN THE LECTURE HALL AT
university. To say I was exhausted would not do justice to what
I was feeling. I could barely keep my eyes open. Not only that,
but also, I'd caught myself swaying twice and had embarrassed
myself by slurring through several particularly tricky Latin plant
names. The students seemed to be enjoying the lecture, however.
Presumably because they thought I was drunk.

The lecture was drawing to a close. I'd overrun by twenty
minutes, but everyone had remained in the lecture hall waiting
for me to finish. There were fewer empty seats than the week
before. In fact, the hall seemed fuller with each lecture I gave. It
was approaching the end of term. The second-year students had
finished the fortnight before. The third-year students had completed their degrees and were waiting for graduation, yet many of
them were sitting in front of me now, listening with the same eager

attention as the first years. It was baffling. Why bother coming when they knew this stuff already?

As I was wrapping up, I spotted a face that shouldn't have been there. High up at the back of the hall, near the rear exit, an older woman with long white hair was staring at me steadily. I had no idea who she was. I'd never seen her before. Around her, students were packing their bags and standing to leave, but she stayed where she was, watching me. I don't know why I felt compelled to do this, but I lifted a hand in greeting, and she did the same. Then someone stood up directly in front of her, blocking her from view, and I adjusted my focus to see DS Chambers standing and waving at me. I dropped my arm and looked around her to the older woman, but she was gone, and DS Chambers was descending the stairs toward me. Quickly, I packed my satchel and headed for the exit. I was too tired to talk to the police. So tired that I was beginning to suspect the woman with long white hair had been an apparition.

Outside in the corridor, a familiar figure was leaning against the wall, nodding to whatever he was listening to through his huge headphones. My heart sank. He hadn't seen me. I was tempted to step back through the lecture-hall doors and wait for him to leave, but that would mean having to talk to DS Chambers. Stuck between two evils, I sighed, stepped out into the corridor, and set off purposefully, hoping he wouldn't notice if I walked fast enough. However, without even looking up, he flipped the headphones down around his neck and blocked my path.

"Prof, got a minute?"

I ducked around him and continued walking. "No. I have a meeting."

"Listen, I'm sorry about last time. I hope I didn't hurt you," he said, keeping pace with me. "I was really anxious, but I'm okay now."

I kept walking.

"Did you hear me? I said I'm okay now."

When I didn't answer, he moved ahead and walked backward in front of me, and my steps faltered because I was suddenly doubtful of the direction I should take. I'd intended to go to my office but didn't want him to know where it was. He stopped, and, at a loss, so did I.

"I've had an idea. I think I've found the answer," he said. "Can I tell you about it?"

I took a deep breath and stepped forward. He didn't move.

"Not right now. I'm very busy."

"When then?"

"I wouldn't like to say. I'm very busy."

"There you go again," he shouted, making me jump. "You're always *busy* or *late*. You never *listen* to me."

He grabbed my arm. The same one as last time, and instinctively, my body folded and shrank away from him, but towering over me, he grabbed my other arm and dragged me up again.

"Why won't you ever listen?"

He was hurting me. I should have resisted. I'd been so angry at my weakness last time, but I was too tired to defend myself. Too tired even to reason with him.

"All I'm asking for is five minutes of your time," he said, shaking me like a rag doll. "Five minutes."

Suddenly, we were startled by a very powerful, assertive voice. "Get your hands off her."

DS Chambers was behind us, her hands on her hips, her expression furious. His grip automatically tightened.

"Are you deaf?" she shouted, pulling back her jacket to reveal the badge on her belt. "I said let her go."

He looked at the badge and dropped his arms. "We were just talking."

"And now you're done."

"No, actually, we're not," he shot back.

"Yes, *actually*, you are. Off you go. The professor and I have a meeting."

He looked down at me with what I assumed was a plea. I have no idea why. I certainly wasn't going to speak up in his defense.

Eventually, he huffed out a breath and said, "Okay, we can talk later." Then he flipped up his headphones and stalked away, and we watched until he turned a corner and was gone. I have to admit to feeling a little bit grateful. My intention had been to avoid her, but at that moment, it was a relief to have her standing next to me.

"What's he on then?" she asked. "Meth? MDMA? He's obviously on some kind of Class A."

"You think he's an addict?" I wanted to add "as well?" because this had also been Carla's observation.

"Of course he is. He's totally strung out. Didn't you see the gurning? Or his eyes?"

I rubbed my arms where his huge hands had been. "I rarely look at people's eyes."

"Well, I do. And I can tell you, they were dilated. He seems a very volatile young man. I'd be wary of him if I were you."

"You're not the first person to say that."

There was a silence, which was a relief because I needed a moment to reset. This was the second time in as many days Giant Hogweed had intimidated me with force. It made me uncomfortably aware of my vulnerability and also frustrated by my inability to defend myself.

"Shall we go to your office?" she asked, breaking the silence.

I glanced at her. I didn't invite anyone to my office and certainly not the police. It was my private space. My sanctuary when the demands of the day threatened to overwhelm me.

"Why?"

"I have something to show you."

"Show me here."

"I'd rather not. It's sensitive information."

I paused. "Does DCI Roberts know you're here?"

"DCI Roberts is busy." She looked ahead and behind then pointed along the corridor. "Is it this way?"

She'd just saved me from Giant Hogweed. What could I do but comply? I sighed and set off in the direction of my office, absentmindedly rubbing my arms as I walked.

"Did he hurt you?" she asked.

"Not too much. It's more that I hate how helpless he makes me feel when he grabs me like that. It makes me angry. With myself as much as with him."

She was silent a moment. "Would you like me to teach you some self-defense moves? There's a very simple way to get out of an arm grab that doesn't require strength. It's all about balance—or rather knocking your opponent off balance."

I glanced at her. "I'm sure you're far too busy catching criminals to make time for that."

In response, she lightly placed her hand on my shoulder and pulled me to a stop. "I've always got time when it comes to another woman's safety. We have to help and support each other. We have to fight for our place in this world, don't we?"

I frowned, not knowing how to respond, never having considered the possibility of helping or supporting or fighting for anyone or anything other than my students. I dropped my eyes, and they came to rest on her blouse, which on closer inspection was covered with a pale flower pattern. I peered closer and squinted. *Bellis perennis* if I wasn't mistaken.

"Hello, *stranger.*"

The astonishingly loud voice made me leap. I turned sharply and came face to face with Matilde, my Sweet Alyssum, and my body jolted as if I'd been caught red-handed doing something I shouldn't be doing. She was looking from me to DS Chambers's hand on my shoulder, to DS Chambers's face, and back to me.

"Where've you been?" she asked. "You haven't been answering my calls or messages."

I frowned at her, wondering why on earth she'd called me a stranger, when I quite patently was not.

"Professor Rose is very busy," DS Chambers said, showing her badge. "She's assisting with a case."

I have no idea why DS Chambers felt it necessary to speak on my behalf. I was quite capable of speaking for myself.

"I've been very busy. I'm assisting the police with a case," I said.

For some reason, Matilde rolled her eyes.

"This is Detective Sergeant Chambers. She's working on the case with me. A man has been poisoned with a hallucinogen. He was stuck with a syringe in Soho—"

"I doubt you're allowed to tell me those details, Eustacia," Matilde said, cutting me off. "That's probably classified information, no?"

I had no idea. I glanced at DS Chambers then back to Matilde, who appeared to be using her eyes to tell me something, but for the life of me, I didn't know what that thing was.

"Anyway," she said, shaking her head. "I won't keep you, as you're so busy. It would just be nice if you answered my messages once in a while, you know? As you're my..." She looked at DS Chambers pointedly. "As you're my special friend?"

I turned back to DS Chambers and noticed some kind of non-verbal communication going on between the two of them, which, again, I could not grasp. But one thing was loud and clear—Matilde was not happy.

"Well," DS Chambers said, drawing out the word, "we must get on. I would say it was a pleasure to meet you, but the professor didn't introduce you."

Matilde turned to me. "No, she didn't."

Then she stepped forward, rose onto her toes, wrapped me in a tight embrace, and kissed my cheek. "I'll see you soon, my darling. Don't be late."

Smiling tightly, she stepped past me, and I stared after her, wiping the wet smear of the kiss from my cheek, wondering what I shouldn't be late for.

"Girlfriend trouble?" DS Chambers asked when Matilde was out of sight.

I turned to her. "I beg your pardon?"

"Never mind. None of my business. Shall we go?"

She followed wordlessly as I led her down a rarely used staircase, along a forgotten corridor, through two sets of fire doors to a passage that on first sight looked like a dead end. I could have taken her to the canteen, or one of the seminar rooms, but I felt indebted to her for making Giant Hogweed leave me alone, so here we were.

When I took the keys out of my pocket, she asked, "Why does your office door look like a broom cupboard. Do you work for the secret service?"

I ignored her, unlocked the door and crossed to my desk.

She stayed on the threshold, peering inside. "It's so dark in here. Why don't you open the curtains?"

I looked at the softly lit room. My quiet space, my personal place to recharge, to calm. To prepare at the beginning of the day and unwind at the end. "I prefer it like this."

"It's a bit gloomy," she said, coming in and stopping before the photograph on the wall. "Is this your father? You look like him. I mean, exactly like him. I heard he was very austere."

I looked up. "How did you hear that?"

"Oh, I don't know. I probably read it somewhere. He was a celebrity after all. Austere, unforgiving…strict. That's what I heard."

It was strange hearing her talk about Father as if she knew him. I didn't like it. She turned around, and I had time to see her small smile before I looked away. It was a closed-mouth, sad-eyed smile, as if she felt sorry for me.

Something hanging from a shelf caught her eye. She crossed the room to it and took it in her hand.

"Is this the famous leather pouch you wore around your neck every day? The one you kept phials of antidotes in when you still had your poisonous plant collection? I read a forensics report about it in one of DCI Roberts's old case files. Your antidotes were described as genius." She moved toward me. "You must be very clever."

So far, she'd expressed an unnecessary opinion about Father, knew about my antidote pouch, and had even read a forensics report about its contents...and she'd been in my office less than two minutes. I shifted back in my chair, regretting my decision to bring her here.

"What did you want to show me?"

"The poison victim's medical report." She took a slim folder out of her bag and handed it to me. "The hospital's identified the poison."

I scanned the page and started. *Datura stramonium.* A powerful hallucinogen—and one of the plants I used to own. I shook my head.

"It says the toxin's a plant-derived scopolamine with other *tropane alkaloids*," she added. "I can't pretend to know what that means."

"It means he's been poisoned with a toxin that causes visual and auditory hallucinations and, if the dose is high enough, death."

"Hallucinations?"

"Yes. Not good ones. *Datura* was used by shamans from

Venezuela to Chile and also parts of Brazil to induce a trance-like state in their ceremonies. The hallucinations were said to be terrifying with a complete loss of awareness that one was hallucinating."

"A bit like psychosis?" she asked.

"Exactly like psychosis."

She paused. "Is that what was happening to him in the ambulance? Was he having a psychotic episode?"

"I believe so."

"Could he still be hallucinating in intensive care and no one would know because he's sedated?"

"Yes."

"How long is he likely to suffer?"

"I suspect he was given a very high dose, so it could be many days, if he survives that long."

She shuddered. "Is this poison readily available?"

"No. It's the exact opposite."

"So how did the perpetrator get hold of it?" she asked.

I assumed this was a rhetorical question so didn't reply, but she surprised me by adding, "Do you have it here?"

"Here?" I asked, looking around my office.

"In the university."

"No. We don't have a specimen of the plant it was extracted from."

"Do you know any other universities or facilities that do?"

"No."

"Can it be found on the dark web?"

"The what?"

"The dark web."

"What's that?"

She narrowed her eyes. "Come on, Professor. You deal with illegal substances all day every day. Don't tell me you've never heard of the dark web."

My expression must have said otherwise because she added, "Well, I can guarantee your students know about it and are most likely using it."

I frowned and made a mental note to ask Carla about this the next time I saw her.

DS Chambers looked around the room and asked, "Do you have another chair?"

"This isn't a room for entertaining."

"Students don't come in here? Staff?"

"No."

"Why? What're you hiding?"

My frown deepened and I folded my arms, but for some reason, she smiled as if she'd made a joke and took an envelope out of her bag.

"I want to show you something."

She put the envelope on my desk. "It's so dark in here. Why don't you open the curtains?"

"I don't like the view."

"Why, what's it of?"

So many irrelevant questions that I was just too tired to answer. I sighed heavily. "A filthy, damp light well full of air-conditioning units. It depresses me."

"Working in the dark would depress *me*," she countered.

I switched on my desk lamp, and she took a photograph out of the envelope and put it into the pool of light. "Look at this."

I glanced at it. "What am I looking at?"

"A syringe."

"I know that. It's the syringe used in the Soho poisoning. Why are you showing it to me?"

"You don't notice anything unusual about it?"

"No."

"Take a closer look."

I pulled the photograph further into the lamp light and lowered my face to it. "I still don't—"

"The plunger," she said. "The color of the plunger. That syringe isn't manufactured in this country. You can't even get them here. I've checked. They're only made in small batches in Colombia."

She paused, I assumed for dramatic effect, then added, "And there's something else." She took out her phone, opened a photograph, and showed it to me. "This is Pascal Martineaux."

I squinted at the screen. "Who?"

"The famous American artist."

I'd never heard of him.

She swiped the screen to another photograph. It was a painting of a syringe with the same-colored plunger. "This is his trademark. If you know Pascal Martineaux, you'll immediately think of this syringe. It's like his signature. And you know what else I've just found out?"

"What?"

She smiled widely. "He recently moved to London. How about that for a coincidence?"

5

I DIDN'T KNOW THIS PART OF TOWN. I WAS A CREATURE OF habit, sticking to my own territories. London Fields was another world. The people, the places, totally different. I left the train station and did something completely out of character: I deliberately walked in the wrong direction and found myself at the entrance of the long, thin park that gave the area its name. In front of me was a cycle path. I stepped forward to cross it and immediately jumped back as a stream of expensive bicycles—some pushing wooden trollies containing children, some with dogs in baskets, some with bags full of flowers and house plants hanging precariously from the handlebars—shot past. I shook my head at the sight of a particularly poisonous tropical plant in one of the bags and, during a lull in the traffic, dashed across and entered the park.

I heard a shout of "*Howzat!*" followed by a cheer and began an absent-minded stroll toward the sound. On the grass, at the north end of the park, a cricket match was underway, the players in their whites, their jumpers hanging around the shoulders of the umpire, their hats on their heads and afternoon tea set up on a long table behind the pitch. It was an incongruous sight in such an urban park, and so was the crowd of young Londoners sitting on the grass around the white-painted pitch perimeter line.

As I watched, a new memory grew of me sitting on grass while Father played cricket. It must have been in Oxford. He was in his whites. He was batting. A woman in a yellow dress handed me a bowl of strawberries, and I looked up at her smiling down at me just as the opposite team shouted "*Howzat!*" I turned back to see that Father had been caught out and was walking off the pitch, listlessly swinging his bat. I must have been very young to have looked upward at the face of the woman sitting beside me.

I spent a little while longer watching the match then turned toward Martello Street. It hadn't been difficult to find Pascal Martineaux's address. All I had to do was ask DCI Roberts to trace it for me. I suppose I could have tracked him down myself, but I was in a hurry. I wanted to speak to him before DS Chambers charged in with her own agenda.

As I approached the park exit, I saw a man up ahead walking with a long, loping gait. His hair was tied into a topknot and he was wearing muted, loose-fitting clothes, and even though I was behind him, I recognized Pascal Martineaux from the photograph DS Chambers had shown me. Walking beside him with the same loping gait was an enormous Great Dane. They seemed in no hurry as they passed underneath the railway tracks and turned on to Martello Street.

He went through a gate to what I assumed was a former factory and didn't close it behind him, and I followed to the building's entrance, where he removed the dog's lead and held the door open for it. But instead of going inside, he turned around to face me. For a moment we looked at each other, neither speaking.

"Pascal Martineaux? My name's Professor Rose. Do you have a moment? I'd like to ask you a few questions about your, um, art."

He kept his eyes on me, taking me in from head to toe, obviously trying to decide whether or not to engage with this strange woman dressed in an old man's tweed suit, her Brylcreemed hair cut short and precisely parted in the style of a 1920s dandy.

"What are you a professor of?"

I wasn't expecting to be asked questions but thought it best to answer if he wasn't going to send me on my way.

"Botanical toxicology."

"A professor of poison?"

"Plant poisons, yes. I wonder if I could ask you a few questions?"

He gave me the once-over one more time then smiled, revealing a row of straight white teeth. "Sure. Why not? Let's go inside."

I followed him along a corridor and up a long flight of stairs to an enormous door, where the Great Dane was waiting. He slipped off his gray suede sandals, placed them neatly next to an identical pair several sizes smaller, and opened the door for the dog to trot through. "After you, Professor."

His flat was a vast open space with one wall comprising entirely of metal-framed windows that overlooked the treetops of London Fields: a sea of green contrasting with the austere polished concrete interior. He crossed to a huge kitchen island on one side of the space, moving like someone who'd achieved serenity—or someone who was heavily medicated.

"Your flat's very…empty," I said, gazing around.

"The word's *minimal*," he replied. "Would you like tea?"

He pushed the wall with the tips of his fingers, and a cupboard door gently opened. "We have rooibos, hibiscus, lemon balm, jasmine, chamomile, butterfly pea flower, ginger and ginseng, ginger and lemongrass—"

"No, thank you," I said to make him stop.

He took a small black pot from a shelf, and I worried I'd have to sit through an entire Japanese tea ceremony before we could talk.

"What do you want to ask me?" he asked, rinsing the pot.

I'd practiced the question. It wasn't the one I wanted to ask, but it was my opener. I took a deep breath.

"This is very kind of you. Thank you. I'm a huge fan. I'm really just so curious about your trademark. I've always wanted to know the significance of it. What does it mean?"

He stared at me a moment then let out a huff. "Really? That's your question? I didn't think you'd be so prosaic."

It wasn't the reaction I was expecting, but I soldiered on. "You always paint the same type of syringe. Is there a reason for that?"

He turned his back on me to make his tea. "Look it up on the internet. It's all there. There's even a Wikipedia page about it. If you don't have anything interesting to ask, and you don't want tea, you may as well leave."

"It's just that the syringe you paint is very unusual," I rushed on. "It's not readily available. In fact, only one factory manufactures it in the whole world."

I was being too specific. He was becoming suspicious—I could see it in his head tilt.

Slowly, he turned around. "Who are you?"

"A huge fan. I love your art." I'd never seen his art. "But what I love the most is your detail. I mean, who else would choose such a specific syringe as their trademark? Even I—a professor of toxicology—have seen less than a handful of them in my whole career. Your level of detail is incredible. Remarkable." I smiled, genuinely pleased with my performance.

"Oh…I get it now. You're an art nerd."

I paused, not sure how to reply, but before I could assemble an answer, a small, noticeably pregnant woman wearing a loose-fitting putty-colored tunic came through an opening I hadn't seen, sat on a stool beside the island, looked at me pointedly, and asked in the same soft American accent as Pascal's, "Who are you?"

"Serena, this is Professor Rose. She's an art nerd. I found her hanging around outside. Professor Rose, this is my wife."

She looked at me a moment longer then put her hands together in the Buddhist prayer gesture, touched her chin with her thumbs, and bowed her head, her long blond hair falling forward. She had a ring on every finger and both thumbs, several in each ear, and one through her septum. She had tattoos on the inside of her wrists and along the outside edge of her little fingers. She had a harsh yet soft quality that I supposed some might find attractive. Pascal Martineaux for example.

"Namaste, Professor. Welcome to our home. Are you a fan of my husband's work?"

"Oh, yes," I said, nodding vigorously. "I'm a superfan."

"A superfan?"

"Yes, indeed."

She looked at her husband with an expression I couldn't read. "Well now, how lovely of Pascal to invite you into our home."

I cleared my throat. I wasn't good at reading atmospheres, but there was definitely something strange about the one in this room.

"Will you have tea?' she asked. "We can't offer anything stronger because we don't allow alcohol in the house. We don't allow any poisons." She rubbed her belly gently. "Especially as we have a new little human joining us soon."

"No, thank you," I quickly said, before she could begin the long list of choices.

I glanced at the enormous front door. There was little point staying any longer. It was obvious he wasn't going to tell me why his trademark symbol happened to be the weapon used in a poisoning that had put a man into intensive care. Besides, I couldn't shake the feeling DS Chambers had sent me on a wild goose chase. She had piqued my interest with a red herring. I couldn't help thinking that all I'd managed to do was raise the suspicions of two people who no doubt had nothing to do with the Soho poisoning, and I'd made a fool of myself in the process.

"I really must be going…"

But then my eyes widened at the sight of a ten-foot-tall tropical plant in the corner of the vast space. "Good God! You have a *Monstera obliqua*?" I cried, louder than I'd intended.

They both turned in its direction.

"Is that what it's called?" Serena asked. "I thought it was a Swiss cheese plant."

I went to it and held out a hand, wanting but hardly daring to touch it. "They're both split-leaf philodendrons, but this variety's incredibly rare. Incredibly expensive as well, especially one this size. I've never seen such a tall specimen."

"Oh, it wasn't that expensive. Was it, darling?" she asked, turning to Pascal.

"It was fifteen thousand pounds," he replied.

My eyes widened and my mouth dropped open. I gritted my teeth to close it again. I'd paid a lot of money for some extremely rare poisonous plant cuttings but never, ever that much.

"Is that expensive?" Serena asked. "I always get confused with the currency exchange."

"And that's plant number three," he added flatly. "You killed the other two."

She let out a short, ghastly laugh. "It's true! I'm terrible with plants. So arrest me! I'm a plant murderer!"

I wasn't absolutely confident with sarcasm, but I did know a plant killer when I saw one, and this small, pregnant woman was definitely it.

She shrugged and added, "Honestly. Who cares? They're only plants."

I could have bitten my tongue, turned around, and left. Instead I said, "That *Monstera*," then paused to steady my voice. "That *Monstera* is older than you. It's received decades of dedicated care. There are very few of them in the world. It should be in a botanical garden, being cared for by specialists. Not here in this dry, over-heated environment."

There followed a silence during which I assumed she was deeply considering my words. Then she said in a small, wavering voice, "I see… Oh, now I feel terrible. Just awful. Oh… I could cry. I really could." And she wiped an eye delicately.

"It's already showing signs of stress," I continued. "I strongly recommend it be moved to a facility where it will get the attention it desperately needs. If you're in agreement, I can organize a collection straight away and have it taken to the University College London glasshouses."

Another silence, then in a completely different voice she said: "Why would I give something that cost fifteen thousand pounds to a complete stranger? Why do complete strangers think they deserve my stuff just because I have the money to replace it? I'm so sick of blood-sucking leeches. Everywhere I go, I'm plagued by them. You're just another parasite, aren't you?"

I blinked at her in astonishment. "I assure you, I have absolutely no interest in your money. My concern is purely for the welfare of this *Monstera obliqua*."

"Jesus," she shouted, making me jump. "It's. Only. A. Plant. Get a life!"

I must admit, this exchange was making me quite angry. I couldn't understand why she was being so unreasonable, but I inhaled deeply and continued in my calmest and most measured lecturer's voice, "I already have a life, thank you very much. What I'm trying to do now is save *this* one."

Serena narrowed her eyes and flared her nostrils, and I could see that she was just as, if not marginally more, angry than I was. But rather than direct her fury at me, she rounded on Pascal and hissed, "You let a *superfan* into our home? What the actual *fuck*?"

And with a sigh, he stepped out from behind the kitchen island, tapped me on the shoulder, and said, "Let's go to my studio."

He led me to the opening Serena had come through, along a corridor with bedrooms and bathrooms on each side then on to another enormous door that took us to what was ostensibly the very large, next-door flat. His studio was the antithesis of his living space. It was chaotic, crowded, and filthy, which in some ways was a relief. It was crammed with completed canvases stacked up against the walls, resting on the many easels, lying on the framing table. He was obviously prolific.

"She's an heiress," he said unexpectedly. He was sitting on a stool, one leg crossed over the other, watching me.

"I beg your pardon?"

"Serena. Her father's Jarvis Carmichael. The billionaire. She's very, very clever, but she has no concept of the value of money. We eat at fine dining restaurants most nights. We have a car and a driver. He hangs out at a café nearby until we need him. We have a housekeeper. She hides in her room all day and creeps out to clean when we're not home. We send our bed linen out to be laundered. We have organic fruit and vegetable deliveries. Artisan bread deliveries. Exorbitantly priced, compassionately reared meat deliveries. And that's for the dog. We're pescatarian. We have a personal yoga teacher, Pilates teacher, masseuse. We even have an old shaman woman who casts affirmation spells using herbs and stuff. I think she's actually a witch."

He picked up a bag of tobacco and papers and rolled a cigarette. "She gives me the creeps actually. I usually hide in here when she comes." He lit the cigarette, exhaled smoke, and picked a piece of tobacco off his tongue. "Serena's been researching solar panels, air source heat pumps, green roofs, indoor composting, wool bale insulation. She thinks a lot about sustainability. We don't use plastic or chemicals. We eat a lot of seaweed. She considered activism, but *Daddy* said no."

I don't know why he felt it necessary to justify his wife and his life to a complete stranger. I have no idea why he thought I'd care.

"Why are you telling me this?"

"To let you know Serena always gets her way. If she sees something she wants, she gets it. If she sees some*one* she wants, she gets them. If she wants something done, it's done."

I had the distinct feeling he was telling me something other than what he was telling me, although I had no idea what that was. Father described this as "reading between the lines." I admit, I'd struggled with the concept when I was a child, and I was struggling now. How one read between the lines in a conversation was a complete mystery.

"I still don't know why you're telling me this."

"We've only been in London six months," he went on, "and she's already bought two apartments and three houses in London Fields and Homerton. She flew her interior designer over from the States to work with local architects on the redevelopment. They'll look amazing when they're done. They'll have the Japanese aesthetic. She loves that."

And then I caught a glimpse of what he was actually saying. He wasn't singing his wife's praises at all.

"It must be very difficult for you," I said.

He let out a single *ha* and said, "Funny," then looked at my face and added, "Oh, you're not joking. You think I'm emasculated."

He paused to relight his cigarette.

"Sorry," he said, waving his hand. "I'm only allowed to smoke in here. It's forbidden next door."

Watching him waving away the smoke brought on an unfamiliar feeling. Possibly sympathy, although I wasn't absolutely sure. I wanted to ask what happened when Serena didn't get her way. What level of vitriol was in her punishments. Instead, I said, "If you live with someone with a big personality, you can't really have a personality of your own. Some people put up a fight. Some people accept the situation. And some people are absorbed by the other so completely that nothing of themselves remains."

I'm not sure where this observation came from. Probably from Father. Most of my observations came from him. Pascal's eyes were fixed on me; I could feel them, so I made a sweeping gesture with an arm, taking in the whole of his studio, and added, "Thankfully, it appears you're not one of those people. You seem to have a very fulfilling life of your own."

He inhaled deeply. "I'm preparing for an exhibition. The

opening's on the twelfth. Come if you want." He tapped the cig-arette above an overflowing ashtray and added, "I'll ping you the location. What's your number?"

I had no idea what this meant.

"Give me your mobile," he said, holding out his hand, and without knowing why, I complied.

"So, Professor…what do you *really* want?" he asked as he tapped the screen.

I paused. "I told you. I'm a huge fan."

He handed back my phone, uncrossed and recrossed his legs. "You're not a fan or an art nerd. You have no clue who I am."

"I do. You're Pascal Martineaux, the famous American artist," I replied with confidence.

He let out a snort. "You're not even pronouncing my name right." He took a sharp drag of the cigarette. "I let you into my home because I like your look. I like the way you speak. So English. So proper. It's like you've stepped out of another time and found yourself here." He took another drag. "But now I'm wondering if I made a mistake."

"I assure you—" I began then closed my mouth because the charade had collapsed, and I had no idea how to stand it up again.

I opened my mouth again. "I just want to know about the syringe."

"Why?"

"Because…" Should I tell him? How much should I tell him?

"Because two nights ago, a man was jabbed in the neck with a syringe full of a powerful hallucinogen, and now he's fighting for his life in an ICU. The syringe was the same as the one you use as your trademark. And I'm wondering…" Should I have told him so much? Too late now. "I'm wondering—"

"Are you the police?"

"No. But I am assisting the police as a toxicology expert."

He stubbed out the cigarette, stood, and turned his back, and I watched his shoulders rise and fall as he took several deep breaths.

Eventually, he turned around and gave me the white-teeth smile. "You'll have to excuse me. I have a lot to do before the exhibition. There's one more painting I want to include, and I haven't even started it yet. That door leads to the stairs that'll take you to the exit. You don't mind seeing yourself out?"

"It's just that the syringe used in the attack is only manufactured in one small town in Colombia, and I'm wondering how on earth it found its way to Soho."

He crossed the studio and opened the door. "Goodbye, Professor."

And all I could do was walk through it.

As he closed it firmly behind me, I heard Serena screaming words that could only have been about me: "He let a superfan into the apartment! A fucking *superfan!*"—and I looked down the corridor in time to see another woman going through the enormous front door into their flat. It was really only a fleeting glimpse of a shoulder, a flash of white hair, before the door closed and the screaming cut off. And after a moment of staring at the empty corridor, I turned for the exit, trying but failing to remember where I'd seen her before.

6

THE FOLLOWING MORNING, I WAS IN THE LAB PREPPING SAM-
ples for a tutorial. It wasn't an arduous task, just tedious, and
when it was done, I sat back on the stool and let my eyes roam
over the microscopes, centrifuges, and spectrophotometers until
they came to rest on the sample fridges next to the kitchen area.
Everything was in its place, all the equipment spotlessly clean,
and I smiled with the satisfaction of knowing I'd made the right
choice with Carla. Because not only had she rescued me by scaring Giant Hogweed away with her alarm, but she was also a very
diligent assistant.

My eyes moved from the fridges to the kitchen counter, and
instantly, all the kind thoughts for Carla vanished. It was a mess. I
let out a huff of annoyance and went to take a closer look.

A French press and two unwashed coffee cups were beside
the sink, biscuit crumbs and sugar scattered over the counter. The

dirty cups and sugar were bad enough, but the biscuit crumbs? Carla knew the rules; there was absolutely no eating in the lab. Under no circumstances whatsoever. And why two cups for heaven's sake? Surely it's not so arduous a task to rinse one's cup rather than take out a clean one?

I picked up the bin and swept the crumbs and sugar into it, tutting as I did so. This behavior needed to be nipped in the bud. The sooner the better. In fact, I was about to fetch my mobile to call her when the lab telephone rang. It rang so rarely I'd forgotten the lab even had a telephone. I glanced at it, waiting for it to stop, then, with a sigh, went to answer it.

"Professor? It's the secretaries' office. A DS Chambers is on her way to see you, and she's not happy."

Moments later, DS Chambers flung open the door, stormed into the lab, and shouted, "What the hell did you think you were doing?"

"I beg your pardon?"

"Don't pretend you don't know what I'm talking about."

I went to my workstation and sat down. "I don't know what you're talking about."

"That stunt you pulled with Pascal Martineaux. I've just come from his flat, and do you know what happened?"

I could tell she wasn't expecting a reply.

"He laughed in my face when I asked him why his trademark was a syringe." She was blinking hard, breathing hard. She crossed the lab and leaned toward me over the counter, her weight on her arms, all the hidden thorns on show. "Do you know what he said?"

Again, I didn't reply.

"He said you're better at pretending to be a fan than I am. I mean! I wasn't even pretending. I actually am a fan!"

I couldn't help myself. I let out a guffaw, and for some reason, this instantly extinguished her anger.

"Eustacia..." she said, dropping her head.

"Professor," I corrected.

"I know you're helping with the case, but you can't just waltz in and take over my investigation."

I let a moment pass. "Why did you bring it to me then?"

She looked up. "What?"

"Why did you insist on coming to my office to show me what you had on the syringe if you weren't expecting me to investigate it?"

"I came to show you the victim's medical report and to ask about the hallucinogen."

"So why mention the syringe?"

I knew why. She was doing what Father called *showboating.* He also said that one should be circumspect with show boaters.

Her shoulders slumped and she sank onto a stool. "I'm not really sure now."

"If it makes you feel any better, Pascal Martineaux didn't tell me a thing."

"That makes me feel worse," she said, her voice rising. "He

might've given me something if you hadn't blundered in before me. Thanks to you, that door's definitely closed."

Blundered in? It crossed my mind to tell her about his exhibition opening.

"By the way," she added, "you're pronouncing his name wrong. It's *Mar-ta-no*. The X is silent."

And I would have done, if she weren't so insulting.

Suddenly, she slapped her thighs, stood up straight, and said brightly, "Oh well. Can't be helped. We move on."

Then she turned a full circle, gazing around as if she'd only just realized where she was. I recognized her expression. I'd seen it a hundred times on the fresh faces of the first-year students. That mixture of excitement and wonder.

"This place is amazing. It's so clean and white. It's like sci-fi. Should I put on a lab coat?"

"That's not necessary."

She looked at them hanging on the pegs. "But should I?"

"Aren't you leaving?"

"No. I'm thinking…if I'm not going to be disadvantaged on this case, you need to give me a quick botany lesson."

I let out a snort. "There's no such thing."

"Be inventive," she said, looking at her watch. "I have twenty minutes. But remember, I know nothing. Talk to me as if I'm a child."

I paused to think. I'd never given a botany lesson to a child. "How old?"

"Let's say ten."

I, too, looked at my watch. The tutorial students weren't due for another hour. I'd planned to fill that time with grading, but giving a botany lesson to a ten-year-old seemed much more appealing. "Alright. But only for twenty minutes."

"So I should put on a lab coat?"

I sighed. "Go on then."

She took her time choosing then put one on, fastened a button, and pushed up the sleeves. Oh, but this was such a bugbear of mine. I'd lost count of the number of times I'd had to admonish a student for such a sloppy attitude to safety.

"No, no, no," I said sternly as I marched over to her. "If you insist on wearing a lab coat, you must wear it properly. It's provided for your safety; it's not a fashion item."

I straightened the lapels, did up all the buttons, and tugged down the sleeves, but rather than show remorse for her mistake, she seemed pleased, happy even. Which was puzzling.

I went back to my station. "Shall we begin?"

She nodded enthusiastically.

"There are three hundred ninety-one thousand species of plants. Ninety-four percent are flowering. These are called *angiosperms*. The other six percent are *gymnosperms*, which don't produce flowers or fruits because they don't have ovaries. Would a ten-year-old know about ovaries?"

"Of course."

"The word *gymnosperm* comes from a composite of a Greek word that means 'naked seed.' Their seeds aren't protected by flowers or fruit as most other seeds are. An example would be a conifer, which produces cones." I glanced at her. "Okay so far?"

She nodded, slightly less enthusiastically.

"Plants are divided into different groups: woody, herbaceous, annual, biannual, perennial, bulbs, corms, and tubers, but I won't go into each of their properties and behaviors right now."

I paused to check in again, and she smiled.

"Taxonomy is how plants are named, described, and classified. And often how they're identified. A hierarchical system containing seven categories is used to name each and every plant. When I was a child, my father taught me the mnemonic *kids prefer candy over fried green spinach* to help me remember the different categories. Kingdom, phylum, class, order, family, genus, and species. Kingdom means all living organisms, so plants belong to the Plantae kingdom. Phylum—"

"Whoa, hold up," she interrupted. "I think a ten-year-old would be struggling right now."

"Are you struggling?"

"Well…yeah."

"Okay, let's take a shortcut. Generally, we only refer to plants by the last three categories, the family, genus, and species. So, for example, this pretty plant"—I pulled up a picture of her nickname on the smart board—"is *Berberis thunbergii* f. *atropurpurea.* Its family is Berberidaceae, its genus is *thunbergii,* and its species is *atropurpurea.* When plants have *atropurpurea* at the end of their names it generally means it's the purple-leafed variety."

"Purpurea sounds like purple," she said, sounding as pleased as a ten-year-old. "I'll remember that one."

"Good, because I'm going to test you later."

Straight away, she shot back, "Over a drink?"

I glanced at her. She was grinning, although I didn't know why.

"I beg your pardon?"

"Shall we go for a drink so you can test me later?"

I shook my head. "I don't drink. Besides, I never socialize with colleagues when I'm on a case."

Why I said this, I had no idea. This was the first case I'd worked on—officially.

"Apart from DCI Roberts," she said.

I frowned. "I beg your pardon?"

"You went out for breakfast together. In Soho. The night the poison victim was found."

"How do you know that?"

"Roberts told me. He just came out with it. I think he was trying to make a point. You know, trying to tell me he had women friends. That he didn't just hang out with the old geezer coppers." She was watching me closely. "So why's it okay to socialize with him but not with me?"

I wouldn't have called sitting in an overcrowded café in the middle of the night while having to endure the sight of DCI Roberts devouring a bacon butty socializing, but then, I wasn't the best judge. Other than my students, I only wanted to be with two people—Susan and Matilde—and I had neither the time nor the inclination for anyone else.

"I suppose some people deserve more attention in one's life, so why waste time with the ones that don't?"

She fell silent. I could feel her watching me, so I busied myself with straightening the students' worksheets on the countertop.

Eventually, she broke the silence by saying, "You're so...confusing, Eustacia."

"Professor," I corrected.

"One minute you're friendly; the next you're mean. Your mixed messages are bewildering. But also, incredibly...enticing."

I had no idea what she was talking about, and I strongly objected to being called mean. After all, hadn't I just made the time to give her a botany lesson? I looked at my watch pointedly and said in my lecturer's voice, "Your twenty minutes are up. Now, if you wouldn't mind being on your way? I'm very busy."

7

I was finishing a light meal in my kitchen when my phone vibrated in the highly irritating way that it did. I looked at the screen expecting to see the word *Dickie* or *Sweetie* or *Cabbage*. Instead, there was a calendar alert. *Pascal Martineaux exhibition opening 7 p.m.* I had no idea how my phone could possibly know about Pascal Martineaux's opening, especially as I'd forgotten all about it.

I looked at my watch. It was seven p.m. I would be late. I abhorred lateness, but I imagined artists weren't concerned with such things, so I didn't rush as I picked up Father's *A–Z London Street Atlas* and left the flat.

The high street was busy, the tables outside the many restaurants full. People were sitting on benches underneath the London plane trees, chatting and enjoying the warm evening. I kept my eyes on the pavement and walked purposefully through the crowds toward the bus stop, distracted by thoughts of DS Chambers and her invitation to go for a drink. So distracted that it was a while before I became aware of a feeling of unease that I now realized had been with me since I first stepped out of my flat building. I ran a hand across the back of my neck, glanced behind me, and scanned the faces of the many people, but no one was looking at me, so I lifted my shoulders high and dropped them again, trying to shrug off this feeling, and continued on my way.

No one was waiting at the bus stop, and this part of the high street was deserted. I perched on the edge of a bench and turned to see if a bus was coming.

There was no bus. There was, however, a figure quickly ducking through a shop doorway. They could have simply been going into the shop, but there was something strange about the movement, as if they were hiding from someone.

I shrugged again, stood, and paced the length of the bus stop, glancing up the hill every now and again, hoping for the bus. Hoping not to see the figure again. But the next time I turned, there they were, sidestepping into a driveway a hundred meters away, and before they disappeared, I saw it was a man.

I glanced up the hill. Still no bus. I looked back to the man. He'd moved closer. What was he doing? Why did he not just walk along the pavement? Why did he keep ducking out of sight?

The feeling of unease began to build into anxiety, increasing my heart rate, my breathing. I spun back to the high street, willing with all my strength for a bus to approach, but there was none. There was, however, a black cab with its light on. Then, just as the man stepped out from his hiding place and began to sprint toward me, I did something I'd never done before. I threw out an arm, flagged down the taxi, jumped in, and shouted, "Drive. Just drive!"

And as we pulled away from the curb, I turned to look through the rear window and saw Giant Hogweed slowing to a stop, staring after me, panting.

Half an hour later, the taxi turned off Mare Street and dropped me on a side road that the driver told me led to the railway arches. The road was so dark and deserted, it was menacing. Not at all where I wanted to be after my encounter with Giant Hogweed. Why he'd felt it necessary to frighten me like that, I had no idea. Nor did I know why he thought I'd be willing to talk to him after he'd scared me half to death. His behavior always had been peculiar. There were times as an undergraduate when he'd left me totally baffled. And it wasn't only me. It was the same with most people he came into contact with. The difference between then and now, though, was that he'd grown physically stronger. Much, much stronger.

Father's A–Z was so ancient, none of these roads had existed when it was published, so I wandered aimlessly, up one street, down another, feeling like I was on a road to nowhere. Eventually, I stumbled upon the arches, but the gallery entrance was so unassuming that I walked past it three times before I found it, and that was only because someone else had found it before me. As I followed them through the metal door and along the dark entrance passage, my attention was drawn by a small street-art stencil of a syringe on the brick wall. I was in the right place.

Emerging from the passage into the huge space beyond was like stepping back two hundred years, and gazing up, I stopped to appreciate the Victorian engineering, the rudimentary scaffold, the hand tools, the manpower, the injuries and most probably deaths involved in the construction of such intricately arched ceilings. Then I lowered my eyes to the gallery space beneath, crowded with modern-day people, and blinked several times to bring myself back to the present.

The gallery was cavernous. In its center, a man was sitting on a stool playing an accordion, and the sound that echoed around the space and bounced through the arches was almost ominous. The gallery walls were dotted with many unframed canvases of different sizes.

I walked to the first one. It was a painting of young Pascal with a woman standing in a garden with grass too green and lush to have grown in this country. I recognized bougainvillea, cacti, a Mandevilla vine, the same as the one covering the railings around my roof garden. Pascal looked to be about five. He was leaning against the woman, an arm wrapped around her leg. The woman's arms were folded across her chest, and she was standing with one foot resting on top of the other, a pair of huge sunglasses covering half her face. I looked again at Pascal. He was staring out of the canvas with a blank expression, and it would have been a dull composition were it not for his piercing, unnaturally green eyes.

The next painting was of two children on a beach, one of them Pascal. They were hunkered down around a hole they were digging in the sand. Pascal was again looking outward with those unnerving eyes. He was older than in the previous painting, maybe nine or ten. The other child was a girl, possibly in her early teens, her folded limbs too long for her body, giving her a cranelike appearance, gangly and awkward. Her hair hung in a long braid over one shoulder. The white sand beach was deserted. The sea and sky merged into smudges.

I looked at the children cooperating intently on their pointless task and remembered the solitary games I used to play in the garden in Oxford. Mostly of sitting on the swing under the mighty oak, leaning back and staring up into the canopy, swinging back and forth for hours on end.

Next was a portrait of the woman from the first painting, older, her skin weathered and stretched by the sun, streaks of gray in her hair. She was looking directly at me with the same intense green eyes, and there was no mistaking the family resemblance. Pascal's mother. She had to be. And the girl on the beach was his sister.

I turned to look for him and found him in the middle of the gallery, standing taller than the people who had gathered around him in a tight knot. He was wearing a white suit. His hair was loose and long. I let out a cynical huff at the blatant messiah trope, and as if he'd heard me, he slowly turned his head, looked at me, and made a single deliberate nod.

I took a step toward the next painting but was immediately stopped by a voice.

"Hello. I'm *so* happy you came. Would you like a catalogue?"

A young woman was standing beside me, smiling as if she knew me. She was holding a single sheet of paper.

"It has the prices and a short description for each painting."

I looked down and saw £30,000, £50,000, £75,000.

"No, thank you."

"Would you like me to tell you about the artist?"

"No." But then an idea occurred to me. "Tell me about his trademark."

She smiled. "So you've noticed the small syringes in all his paintings? They're a symbol of his emancipation. A representation of when his shackles fell away, and he was finally free."

"Free from what?" I asked.

"I'm sorry?"

"You said the syringe gave him his freedom. Freedom from what?"

"Oh… I…"

A wave of panic passed across her face and she looked around the gallery for Pascal as if expecting him to come to her rescue. "To be honest… I was just given a script. I don't really know much…else."

She had the look of a student who'd only revised for half the exam paper, and I immediately felt sorry for her.

"Did you say there's a syringe in *all* of his paintings?"

"In every single one," she said with relief.

I went back to the children on the beach and scanned it from top to bottom.

"Do you see it?" she asked.

"No."

"Do you want a clue?"

It felt like a game. One I was losing.

"No, thank you." And I moved on.

The next painting was of the teenage girl from the beach, now a young woman. She was sitting on a wooden crate, wearing denim shorts and a crop top. One leg was stretched out in front of her, the other slightly to one side. She had an elbow on her bent knee, and her head was tilting sideways, resting on her fist. She had the same blank expression, the same eerily green eyes, so unsettling that the hairs on my arms stood up.

The next few paintings were of young men and women, all with piercings and tattoos and striking good looks, and all with the same vacant expression in their green eyes. I made a vague attempt to search for the syringe in each, but my heart wasn't in it. The eyes were too unnerving. I couldn't understand why Pascal would want to destroy each portrait with such a disturbing act of vandalism.

I glanced around the gallery, at every canvas, but I no longer saw the paintings. All I could see were the luminous eyes staring back at me. I shuddered, ran a finger along the inside of my collar, and forced myself to move on, because although I didn't want to be there anymore, I couldn't bring myself to leave.

This one was of a man sitting sideways in front of a window, the light behind throwing him into silhouette. None of his features were discernible apart from the green eyes. However, there was something about the shape of the cheekbone, the slope of a shoulder, that seemed familiar. I took a step forward for a closer look just as an unexpected voice made me start.

"I love this painting. It's one of my favorites."

Pascal was close beside me, speaking quietly. I turned and forced myself to look at his eyes. They were blue.

"Do you like it?" he asked.

"I don't think I do."

He made his single nod and asked, "Why not?"

"The eyes are making me uncomfortable."

"Art is meant to be challenging."

I considered this. "Do they represent jealousy? Are all these people jealous of you?"

He let out a low huff. "There you go again with your prosaic questions. I thought professors were meant to be clever."

"Intelligence comes in many forms," I said churlishly. "I've been told there's a syringe hidden in every painting. Where is it in this one?"

"If you look with an open mind, you'll see it. You should go take a look at the last painting." He pointed across the gallery. "It's another one of my favorites."

I looked to where he was pointing then walked to the final painting in the exhibition, and my eyes widened as I stared at myself. There I was, the corners of my mouth turned down, the slight crease on my forehead. I was wearing Father's suit. My short hair was slicked back and precisely parted. My lips were pursed. The detail was astonishing. Right down to the scarring on the back of my hand. The only obvious inaccuracy was the disturbingly green eyes behind my steel-rimmed glasses. No wonder the young woman greeted me as if she knew me. I was part of the exhibition.

I focused on the delicate pattern of *Monstera* leaves in the background, looking like devouring insects had reduced them to skeletons, and realized this was the painting Pascal had been referring to when he'd asked me to leave his studio. He wanted to include me in his exhibition.

I suppose I should have been flattered. I wasn't. I felt decidedly uneasy.

So absorbed was I in these thoughts that it was a while before I realized someone was standing beside me. I glanced sideways at an older woman with long white hair who was staring at the painting as intensely as I was. Slowly, she turned her face, and I found myself looking directly into her eyes—her deep brown, searching eyes—and I was flooded with an unexpected surge of emotion that left me breathless.

"*A thing of beauty is a joy forever.*"

I blinked. Her voice was as soft as a dandelion clock.

"*Its loveliness increases; it will never / Pass into nothingness; but still will keep / A bower quiet for us, and a sleep / Full of sweet dreams, and health, and quiet breathing.* Did he ever read Keats to you?"

"Did who ever read Keats to me?"

"The old man. Did you study *Endymion*? It was one of his favorites."

I had no idea what she was talking about, but I wanted her to keep talking.

"The old man?" I asked.

We were interrupted by a booming voice behind us. "Fancy meeting you here, Professor."

I swung round to see DCI Roberts walking toward me then immediately turned back to the woman to hear her say, "I need to talk to you, Eustacia. It's important."

I turned back to DCI Roberts—he was almost by my side—then spun again to the woman, only then noticing her cane. She reached out, touched my arm, and said, "Find me." Then she was gone. I scanned the crowded gallery and caught a flash of white hair before it disappeared into the passage leading to the exit.

"Are you alright? You look a bit flushed," DCI Roberts said.

"I'm okay. I think," I replied. "What are you doing here?"

"DS Chambers has her eye on the artist. She thinks he might have something to do with the Soho poisoning. Thought I'd come along and take a look for myself. I was expecting to find her here. Instead I find you. And not only you but also a portrait of you." He paused to put his hands in his pockets and shifted his weight back to appreciate the painting. "Uncanny likeness, isn't it? Apart from the creepy eyes. Do you know the artist?"

The likelihood that DS Chambers had told him I'd been to Pascal's flat was probably high. In fact, she may even have made a complaint about me, so I couldn't tell a lie.

"We talked briefly."

"You're full of surprises, Professor."

"He could have painted it from a photograph. It looks a lot like my staff profile picture on the university website."

There was the humming sound, but he didn't push for more. Instead, he turned his head to take in the gallery.

"My God, I've never seen so many hipsters in one place. Look at the mustache on that guy. He could be a turn-of-the-century pugilist."

I followed his gaze, trying to spot the hipsters, but I admit, I had no idea what I was looking for.

"What do you think of the art?" he asked, turning back to me.

"I'm sure it's very good, but it's not really for me. It's too... disturbing."

"*Disturbing*'s the right word. And the accordion music's giving me chills." He shivered dramatically. "A nice young lady told me there's a syringe hidden in every painting, but you probably knew that already as you're chums with the artist."

I gave him a side glance. "I haven't found one yet."

"No? I thought they were pretty obvious."

"Did you find it in the painting of the children on the beach?"

"Sure. That was an easy one. It was in the girl's hair. I'm having trouble finding it in your portrait though. Wait, there it is." He lifted a finger. "Ah…"

I looked to where he was pointing and saw it hidden in the background pattern of *Monstera* leaves, the needle right next to my neck.

DCI Roberts covered his mouth with a hand and spoke through his fingers, "Well, well, well… What do we have here, then?"

8

THE FOLLOWING MORNING, MY MOBILE VIBRATED WITH A MES-
sage from *Dickie,* asking me to meet him at his office. Kentish
Town police station was not my favorite place. It contained far
too many bad memories, and even though I was assisting with a
case, I couldn't shake the feeling of shame as I entered the building. It'd been almost ten months since I was last there, but not
much had changed. The reception was still crowded with angry,
demanding people, and the same long-suffering duty officer was
trying to maintain order. The corridors were just as badly in need
of redecoration, and DCI Roberts's office, when I stepped through
the door, still smelled as awful as his car.

He was eating his lunch, which in my opinion looked decidedly unhealthy. He half stood when I entered, mumbled a greeting
through a mouthful of crisps, and indicated that I sit by waving a
hand at the office chair on the other side of his desk. He washed

down the crisps with a gulp of vending-machine tea and wiped his mouth with the back of his hand.

"Are you alright?"

"Of course. Why wouldn't I be?" I asked as I sat.

"The syringe in the painting last night…the syringe next to your neck."

"Och," I said dismissively. "I'm not worried about that."

"You're not?"

"I said I'm not."

"But, Eustacia…it was a death threat."

I looked at him, not quite sure what he wanted me to say. "Why did you want to see me?"

"I strongly recommend you get self-defense lessons."

"You wanted to see me to tell me that?"

"No, but I strongly recommend you have them."

"Your detective sergeant has already offered them to me."

His large eyebrows lifted. "She has? I was going to offer you a few lessons myself, but if she got there before me, I suggest you take her up on them."

He cleared his throat, shuffled some papers. He seemed put out.

"Why did you want to see me?" I asked again.

"To watch the CCTV footage of the Soho poisoning."

I leaned forward eagerly. Had he found Pascal?

He turned his computer monitor to face me and pressed a

button on his keyboard—the south end of Berwick Street filled the screen. It was dark, but it seemed relatively busy with people coming into camera from Peter Street, walking toward the camera down Berwick Street, or emerging with their backs to the camera from Walker's Court. I checked the time on the bottom of the screen—10:19 p.m.

"It's busy," I said.

"Soho's always busy this time of night. It's amazing we have no witnesses."

The footage continued a while longer with people coming and going; then DCI Roberts pressed *Pause*.

"Why are you stopping?"

He pointed to the screen. "Because there's our victim in the shop doorway."

"Wait, go back, go back," I gasped, not understanding how I'd missed him.

DCI Roberts skipped back to where the footage started, and I leaned closer to the monitor. I'd expected to see a man staggering along the pavement, other people jumping out of his way, pointing and shouting, but there was nothing like that. Just the empty doorway, people passing, then our man sitting on the ground in front of it.

"How on earth?" I asked.

He pressed *Pause*. "Indeed. It's dark but there are a few streetlights. We can see it's busy. There are bars and a couple of pubs further up the street. Lots of people walking up and down, but we're pretty sure our man's not part of the crowd. We've gone through it frame by frame, and we haven't found him. So now, the doorway's empty. People are walking past. The doorway's empty. People walking. Then suddenly he appears, like magic. And absolutely no sign of a perpetrator."

"You didn't find Pascal?"

"We didn't."

I stared at the screen. Something didn't look right from my memory of the night. Then I saw it.

"Why isn't the shop window smashed?"

"Well spotted. That happens later." He skipped the footage forward. "It's a bit of a farce actually. Quite funny if you're a Laurel and Hardy fan."

He pressed *Play* and straight away I saw that the effects of the toxin had taken hold of the victim's body. He was writhing on the ground in front of the doorway. His arms were covering his head as if to protect himself, and his legs were pumping as he scrambled back against the shop door. There were fewer people on the street now. Most didn't see him, and those who did looked at him then avoided him.

"Nobody's helping," I said, feeling unexpectedly upset.

"They probably think he's drunk—or high. They can't see the syringe sticking out of his neck because his arms are covering his head."

Then a group of young men came out of a pub next to the shop. They'd quite obviously had a lot to drink. One of them tripped over the victim's legs, fell to the ground, jumped up, and punched the man walking behind him. That man looked stunned then threw a punch back, and like a match thrown into a box of fireworks, the whole group started fighting.

DCI Roberts let out a snort of laughter, but I didn't see the humor. While they were fighting above him, our victim had been fighting for his life, and they hadn't even seen him. Then came the charge that broke the shop window. Two men against one, rushing at him at full speed, shoving him hard against the glass, making it shatter, and the shock of the window breaking rendered them immobile. But only for a moment because within seconds, they'd all scarpered.

"Nobody helped him," I said again sadly.

"Yes, they did."

I glanced at him. "Who?"

"The alarm company who called the shop owner and the shop owner who called the police."

"That's not the same."

"Don't feel bad for him. Even if someone had tried to help, they probably would've pulled out the syringe, and then he would've bled out. He might be in an ICU right now, but at least he's still alive."

"Have you found out who he is?"

He nodded. "His name's Charlie Simmonds. He's a financier from New York. He was reported missing when he didn't turn up for a meeting in Canary Wharf and hadn't been back to his hotel. His family has been informed. I believe his brother's flying over now."

"He's American?"

"He is. As is Martineaux. We have a coincidence. Although, I have to say, I don't much like coincidences. In my experience, they almost always turn out to be false leads."

I thought of Pascal. The needle he'd painted next to my neck wasn't a death threat—I was sure of it. I couldn't believe he'd be so blatant. But why had he chosen to paint it there? Did he know Charlie Simmonds? Was he trying to tell me something? I glanced at DCI Roberts to find his narrowed eyes fixed on me.

"What're you thinking?" he asked.

I wasn't ready to tell him because I didn't yet know myself. "I was just wondering if you saw the woman standing next to me at the exhibition last night."

"Which woman?"

"The one with long white hair. She was talking to me when you joined me at my portrait."

He shook his head. "Long white hair? That's a distinctive look. I think I would've remembered. Why? Should I know her?"

"Probably not. I just wanted confirmation," I said aloud, then to myself—*that she wasn't a figment of my imagination.*

"One more thing," I added. "What does the color green mean to you?"

"Envy?"

"That's what I thought."

9

LATER AT THE UNIVERSITY, I WAS DISMAYED TO FIND GIANT Hogweed leaning against the wall outside the lab, his huge headphones over his mustard-colored woolen hat. He was chewing gum and nodding with a rapid, urgent energy. I considered retreating around the corner, but he'd already seen me, so, exhaling heavily, I continued toward him. I had to. There would be half a dozen students arriving for a practical soon. He straightened as I approached and took off his headphones but offered no greeting.

"What on earth were you thinking last night?" I asked sternly.

"What?" He looked genuinely confused.

"What were you thinking when you tried to creep up on me and"—I hadn't wanted to dwell on what he might have done if I hadn't hailed that taxi—"scare me when I was waiting for my bus."

"Oh, that," he said flippantly. "I wanted to show you I've found something, but I knew if you saw me coming, you'd run off like you always do."

"You do know threatening behavior is unacceptable, don't you? And it's not the first time. I could report you."

He looked at me then repeated slowly, "I wanted to show you something, but I knew you'd try to avoid me. You're always trying to avoid me." He pulled his laptop out of his backpack, and I was momentarily distracted by the childish cartoon cover. "So I'm going to show you now."

"No. I have to prepare for a practical."

I made a move for the door. He stepped in front of it and held up one giant hand, revealing a red, eczema-inflamed wrist.

"Just listen for one second. I've found an alternative source of toxins for my research, so I won't be bothering you about your collection anymore."

I stood still. "Go on?"

"I've found a website selling synthetic scopolamine, hyoscyamine, and tropane alkaloids. It says they're exact replicas of plant *Solanaceae* poisons."

"Selling?"

"Yeah. It seems legit. It says the toxins are being produced with university-grade equipment."

"Which university?"

"It didn't say."

I could think of two universities that might be doing this work,

Imperial and Kings, but I doubted they intended for the results of their experiments to be sold on the internet.

He stepped away from the lab door and said, "Let's go in and I'll show you."

I didn't want him in the lab, but I recognized the bouncing urgency in his manner that could tip into unpredictable behavior at any moment, so I unlocked the door and flicked on the lights. He walked straight to the counter, took a small notebook out of his backpack, flipped to a page of letter and number combinations, placed it beside him, and opened his laptop. Reluctantly, I followed, standing as far away as I could while still being able to see the screen.

"Look at this," he said.

His fingers were flying across the keyboard so fast I had no hope of keeping up. I glanced at him as he typed. Even on the stool, his head was higher than mine, and every now and then, he absentmindedly scratched the eczema on his neck, causing a cloud of dead skin to rise then settle on his shoulder. He tapped the return key with a final flourish and said, "See?"

I looked at a pulsating red skull on a black screen. "What am I looking at?"

"A site on the dark web."

"The what?" Then I remembered DS Chambers mentioning the dark web and that my students were probably using it. I also remembered I'd meant to ask Carla to explain what it was.

"Ah yes," I said confidently. "The dark web."

He clicked the skull, and a list of toxins appeared with prices next to them.

"It's a British site, see? The prices are in pounds. Someone's making synthetic toxins in this country. You can buy whatever you want, and you won't have to worry about getting it through customs. You won't even need documentation. You can just order from here, and it'll be delivered straight to your door. Amazing, huh?"

"These are all synthetic?" I asked.

"Yeah."

He scrolled through the list. It was short and the toxins were commonplace but still tricky to duplicate. Whoever was manufacturing them had to have a lab. Or access to one.

"Look, they have *Cicuta maculata, Atropa belladonna, Ageratina altissima, Ricinus communis.* Everything I need for my research." He clicked to the next page. "They even have hallucinogens."

I gave him a sharp look. "You don't need hallucinogens for your research."

"I know, but it's cool, right?"

I didn't like the excited enthusiasm in his voice. It sounded dangerous.

He clicked back to the previous page. "I'll go ahead and buy these three for now."

I shook my head vigorously. "No. I don't think you should."

He turned to face me. I kept my eyes on the screen.

"Give me access to your collection then."

I tutted loudly. How many more times?

"Look, it's simple—either you give me the cuttings, or I buy what I need from here."

I continued shaking my head.

"I buy these three toxins now," he said, his volume rising, "or I carry on hounding you every day until you give me the cuttings."

He was breathing hard. I could sense his building anger. I glanced at the door; he'd closed it behind him.

"Well?"

"I..." I began, my voice wavering. I cleared my throat. "I want to make it clear that I strongly advise against this, but..."

"But you can't stop me," he finished for me. "What are your card details?"

I shot him a look. "I beg your pardon?"

He was clicking so fast he was already halfway through the purchase process.

"Your card details," he said again.

I couldn't believe what I was hearing. "You don't expect me to pay?" I gasped.

"Well, I can't, can I? I haven't got any money."

At my silence, he turned to face me and said, "It's the university's responsibility as part of the botany PhD program to provide the materials necessary for a student to complete their research.

It's in the prospectus. You're refusing me access to your collection, so you must provide me with an alternative. This is the alternative."

I blinked rapidly. "The university would never agree to you purchasing synthetic toxins from the dark web."

"I know. Which is why you have to buy them."

"I most certainly do not."

"You're the head of Department of Botanical Toxicology. If not you, who?"

"No one!" I cried, my patience lost. "No one in their right mind would do something as dangerous as this." I pointed at the laptop. "Those are just Latin words on a screen. How on earth would you know what you're buying?"

He made an ugly smile. "How did you know what you were buying when you ordered your cuttings from God knows where?"

Because I had a trusted network of buyers and couriers that I'd built up over decades, I thought. Out loud, I said, "That's totally different. I followed proper procedure."

He made a strange sound that could have been laughter. "We all take risks, don't we? If we didn't, we wouldn't be alive. What's the worst that can happen?"

Scenario after scenario of the worst that could happen raced through my mind.

"We buy it, we test it," he continued. "If it's not what we expected, we dispose of it and start again."

We? I could have reminded him—yet again—that I wasn't

his supervisor. Instead, I said, "I'm sorry to disappoint you, but I assure you I will not be purchasing anything from an untrusted and most probably uncertified organization, and I strongly recommend you don't either. These toxins could be highly dangerous, and you'd have no idea what you were unleashing on the world if something went wrong. Now, I suggest you put this terrible idea out of your head and concentrate on rewriting your PhD proposal."

He was silent, the long fingers of his huge hands resting on the keypad.

I went to the door and opened it. "You need to leave now because I have a lot of work to do."

He didn't move. "I'm not going anywhere until you agree to pay for the toxins."

"That's not going to happen. Please leave before I call security." I had no idea how to call security.

Outside in the corridor the students were gathering, curious as to why I was threatening to call security. Giant Hogweed was wearing an expression that Father had often likened to thunder, but he looked more like a dragon to me, about to roar fire.

After several tense seconds, he stood, collected his belongings, and marched to the door, but before he went through it, he stopped—I assumed to make some final cutting remark. I flicked him a quick glance and immediately wished I hadn't. The look in his eyes, the expression, was something I never wanted to see again. It made me shudder, and, maybe in response to the shudder, he kicked the door back toward me with all his strength, and the edge hit me on the side of the head.

The pain. The white searing pain made me screw my eyes shut, crumple to my knees, and wrap my arms around my head. All I could do was rock and moan and squeeze my head with my forearms. I couldn't even breathe. The students were instantly beside me, shouting and gasping, their arms around my shoulders, and after a while, I became aware of a voice.

That's enough now, Eyebright—pull yourself together. Come on—up you get.

And it was a while more before I realized it was Father's voice. I could hear the students. How could I not, they were shouting so loudly, but Father's voice was just for me.

That's enough now. Up you get. We don't have time for tears.

I took a breath and, very tentatively, opened my eyes. The lab was a blur, and my first thought was that I'd sustained a brain injury. Then I saw my glasses, flung across the floor, lying beside the counter. I lightly touched my head, winced and inspected my fingers. They were covered with blood. I heard a familiar voice. It was Carla barking instructions at the students; then she was on her knees beside me, peering into my face.

"Are you okay? Professor? They're saying it was Aaron. You have to report him this time. You have to."

"My glasses," I said.

She stood up. "Who saw what happened?"

I heard several affirmatives, and then Carla was pressing a wad of paper towels against my head, lifting me up by my elbows, and we were walking.

How I arrived at the dean's office, I have absolutely no idea. Possibly because my eyes were screwed shut against the pain. The dean took one look at me, and very soon after, I was climbing into the back of an ambulance for the short drive to University College Hospital's accident and emergency department. And not long after that, I was lying on a hospital bed in a curtained-off cubicle. I was exhausted. I wanted to go to sleep, but a very insistent nurse kept popping in to shake me awake while we waited for the doctor.

I've no idea how long I endured this ordeal before the doctor finally arrived, closely followed by DS Chambers, because I'd lost all sense of time.

The first thing the doctor made me do was sit upright. I didn't want to sit upright. I was very happy lying down. The second was to run through the obligatory checks for concussion—asking what day it was, telling me to count backward from one hundred, flicking a beam across my eyes to check for pupil reaction. Asking if I felt nauseous, disorientated; whether I had a headache. Of course I had a headache. I tutted loudly and lay back down, but straight away, DS Chambers was on the bed behind me, pushing me up again.

"Come on, babe. Listen to the doctor," she said, taking hold of my waist, which I thought a highly inappropriate restraint.

Babe?

I shifted forward, but her grip was surprisingly firm.

Babe?

I despised hospitals. I was extremely uncomfortable, exhausted, and in pain, and all these things were threatening to push my anxiety past manageable. But even worse, I didn't have my glasses. I closed my eyes, inhaled deeply through my nose, opened my eyes, and saw the blurred outline of DCI Roberts standing at the entrance of the cubicle, which, I have to admit, was a huge relief.

"Are you alright, Professor?"

"I don't see why I have to be restrained," I said. "I'm not a criminal."

He looked at DS Chambers. "I don't see why either. You can let her go, Sergeant."

She released me and went to stand next to DCI Roberts. I would have lain down again, but that suddenly seemed inappropriate with two police officers, a doctor, and a nurse all standing around me in the small cubicle; an unnecessarily large number of people for such a trivial injury. Didn't they have more important demands on their time?

It was after this uncharitable thought that I spied Carla standing behind DCI Roberts, peering over his shoulder. She'd taken me to the dean's office, and now she'd come to the hospital. That was quite a responsibility to take on for someone so young. She stepped forward and handed me my glasses, and when I'd put them on, I met her eyes and nodded to send her my thanks, and she nodded back to acknowledge it. Were those tears in her eyes?

"Let's take a look at that wound, shall we?" the doctor asked, and I turned sideways and hung my legs over the side of the bed.

She leaned in and parted my hair, peering closely at my head. "Well, you'll be pleased to hear it's not as bad as it looks. Heads always bleed a lot. You just need a few Steri-Strips but no stitches." She turned to the nurse. "Can you bring the razor?"

"Razor?" I asked, alarmed.

"It's okay—I won't go wild. I'll just shave around the wound. It's lucky you keep your hair short. By the time the strips peel away, your hair will've grown back."

While the doctor worked, DCI Roberts and DS Chambers watched with rapt attention, expressions of fascinated disgust on their faces.

"Why are you here?" I asked brusquely, resenting the way they were staring at me as if I were some kind of grizzly circus act. "If it's to ask what happened, my recollection is hazy."

DCI Roberts tore his eyes away from my wound and looked at my face. "We know what happened. There were many witnesses all very keen to tell me, and we have the young man in custody."

"Already?" I asked, surprised by how quickly he'd acted, but perhaps it hadn't been quick at all because I had no idea how long I'd been at the hospital.

"We can hold him for twenty-four hours, but first we need to know if you're going to press charges."

I frowned, not at all sure I wanted to press charges. A criminal record could jeopardize his education, and although I and many others found him difficult, I couldn't do that to a student.

"What about his PhD?" I asked.

"There's no PhD. He's been expelled," DS Chambers said.

I turned to her. "I beg your pardon?"

"We've just been with the dean. He told us you aren't the first staff member he's attacked. He did the same last year to his previous supervisor," DCI Roberts said.

"I wasn't his supervisor."

"No? The young man thinks you are."

"That was the problem."

"Well, anyway, the dean said he should've been expelled then, but his father is a very influential alumnus. Very generous. Apparently, he paid for your lab."

I frowned, and then a thought struck me. If his family was so wealthy, why couldn't he afford the synthetic toxins? Why demand I pay? But then, perhaps, buying illegal substances from the dark web was not something a student could ask a parent to help with.

"Are you going to press charges?" DCI Roberts asked.

I'm not sure why I paused. It wouldn't damage his education because he'd already been expelled, but even so, what was stopping me? Perhaps it was something behind the temper and the anxious, unpredictable behavior. Father once described one of his students as a "troubled soul." When I'd asked what that meant, he'd said the student's values and conscience had been corrupted by some darkness within themselves that wasn't necessarily of their own making. I didn't know what this meant then, but perhaps now, with Giant Hogweed, I might be having an inkling of an understanding.

"I need to think about it," I said hesitantly.

"What's there to think about?" DS Chambers asked with impatience. "I witnessed him grab your arm and twist it till you cried out in pain. Your assistant told us she stopped him attacking you outside your lab. And today he kicked a door into your head. He's a violent man who needs to be stopped. Press charges and we'll arrest him for assault. We'll put him away so he can't hurt any more women."

"I'll think about it," I said again.

Anger was an easy emotion to read. DS Chambers's face was displaying all the typical signs, but she didn't seem to be angry with Giant Hogweed. She was angry with me.

"*You* of all people should be the first to charge a violent man," she cried. "This isn't the first time you've been a victim, is it? I read in one of DCI Roberts's case files that someone strangled you last year. You could have died. For God's sake, Eustacia—"

DCI Roberts coughed against his fist. "Alright, Sergeant, that'll do."

"But, sir, she's—"

"I said *that'll do*."

There followed a silence that was quite possibly awkward for everyone in the cubicle. Not for me though. I was too busy fighting the waves of pain radiating from the side of my head.

The doctor cleared her throat. "You say you can hold the man in custody for twenty-four hours, and I'd like to keep the patient in hospital overnight for observation, so let's give her until tomorrow morning to decide what she wants to do. I suggest you go away now and come back in the morning."

DCI Roberts turned to her. "It would be more convenient all round if she made the decision now."

The doctor shook her head. "I'm not yet satisfied the patient isn't concussed. I need to carry out observations overnight and see how she is in the morning. When a person's concussed, it's recommended they don't make important decisions. This sounds like a very important decision, so I suggest you go away and come back in the morning."

I glanced at DCI Roberts. His thick eyebrows were pulled so low I couldn't see his eyes.

Just then, Matilde burst through the curtains, sprang across the cubicle, leaped onto the bed, and wrapped me in her arms.

"Oh, my darling, my darling," she shouted. "Carla rang to tell me you were in A&E. Are you okay? Oh, my darling…your head! You're going to have such a bruise. Your poor, poor head."

As a child, when someone came to the front door of the Oxford house—the postman, say, or Girl Guides asking for money—Father would complain, "It's like Piccadilly Circus in here." It wasn't until I was an adult and went to Piccadilly Circus for the first time that I understood what he meant.

"It's like Piccadilly Circus in here," I said, which, oddly, made Matilde draw away from me.

"It is," the doctor agreed. "I believe everyone was just leaving?"

I took hold of Matilde's hand. "I'd like this one to stay."

"Alright, she can stay, but the rest of you…" She turned to DCI Roberts, who exhaled heavily but nodded.

"I'll see you in the morning, Professor. I trust you'll be feeling better by then."

DS Chambers was still scowling but no longer at me. Her face of fury was now very firmly fixed on Matilde, which was puzzling.

"We'll go," she said. "If the professor agrees to take me up on my offer of self-defense lessons."

DCI Roberts threw her a warning glare. "DS Chambers…"

"Sir, she needs to be able to defend herself against violent men like Aaron Bennett. She's getting away with Steri-Strips this time. Next time, she might not be so lucky. She needs to at least know basic self-defense, and I have several moves I can show her."

"You can talk to her about it in the morning."

"No. I'm not leaving until she agrees."

She turned to me. Her expression hadn't changed. "You feel sorry for him, don't you? That's why you're not agreeing to press charges. Do you know what sympathy is? It's a false emotion. It's just something we do to feel better about ourselves when really, we don't give a shit about the other person."

At this, the doctor raised her eyebrows and exchanged a glance with the nurse, and DCI Roberts said, "Sergeant, time to go."

But she ignored him and slowly walked toward me, as if she was measuring every step, put a hand either side of my legs, and moved her face close to mine.

"Do you agree to self-defense lessons?"

Matilde was squeezing my hand very, very hard, I assumed to signal that I should agree. So I nodded.

⁂

"What happens now?" Matilde asked when everyone had left. "Is she going up to a ward?"

"We don't have any beds at the moment," the doctor said. "You can both stay here until one comes free." She turned to me. "Are you okay? Do you need anything?"

"Pain relief," I said.

"Do you have a headache? How's your vision. Are you feeling nauseous?"

"You've already asked me those questions."

"And I'll ask several more times. Why do you want pain relief? Do you have a headache?"

"No. Head *pain*." I pointed to the side of my head. "Right here."

"Okay, a nurse will bring paracetamol." She scribbled something on a chart then put her pen in her breast pocket. "He'll come back periodically for observations, and I'll stop by to see if you can be discharged before I go off duty."

"When will that be?"

"Eight o'clock tomorrow morning." She fitted a blood-pressure cuff to my upper arm and pressed a button to inflate it.

"And what am I supposed to do until then?"

"It should be okay to go to sleep, if you want to."

I sniffed. "It's far too early to go to sleep. Besides, I do not sleep anywhere except my own bed."

"It's midnight, my darling," Matilde said gently.

"Midnight?" I cried.

The practical Giant Hogweed had so abruptly put an end to was timetabled for noon. How could twelve hours have passed since then?

"I apologize for your long wait. We're short-staffed tonight. Short-staffed every night. Anyway, if you do feel sleepy, I suggest you don't fight it." She removed the cuff and jotted numbers on the chart.

"I absolutely refuse to sleep in a bed that is not my own," I said more forcefully. "I would rather be at home."

"Me too," the doctor said and made the smile that wasn't a smile. "If you feel the need to close your eyes, I would grab the opportunity—if I was you."

"Well, you're not me," I said with impatience. "And I'm telling you that I cannot sleep anywhere other than—"

"Eustacia," Matilde shouted, making me jump. "You don't have to sleep. I'm sure we can find ways to entertain ourselves."

Two hours later, we were sitting cross-legged on the bed, Matilde's laptop between us, a half-played game of *Scrabble* on the screen. I typed in my word and turned the laptop to face her. Hands down, I was winning. She stifled a yawn.

"Seven letters? And an X?" she cried, squinting at the screen. "Wait. What's a digoxin?"

"It's the toxin derived from *Digitalis purpurea* that's been developed into a medication for heart disease. It's one of the many plant poisons that can kill as well as cure. Taxine from yew tree berries is another. It can kill, but it's also used as a treatment for breast cancer. Salicylic acid is nature's version of aspirin and is found in meadowsweet and willow. Just enough acts as a pain relief. Too much can cause internal bleeding."

"This is unfair," she interrupted loudly. "You keep using scientific words I've never heard of. I don't stand a chance. Remind me never to play this game with you again."

She was pouting. Her arms were folded. She wouldn't look at me, and for some reason, these displays of displeasure made me smile. I squeezed her knee, and she let out a soft puff of air.

"Now you know what it's like for me," I said. "Most of the time, I have no clue what we're doing, but I do it anyway because it makes you happy."

She uncrossed her arms and looked at me. "You do it to make me happy?"

"Everything I do is to make you happy."

I wasn't absolutely convinced this was correct, but it seemed the right thing to say in this moment.

Matilde smiled. "If that's so, my darling, what will make me happy is you getting self-defense lessons. What would make me *happiest* is knowing that disturbed young man is behind bars and you are safe."

I paused. "I don't think I'm going to press charges."

"Why ever not?"

I paused again. "Because I'm curious."

"About what?"

"I want to know what he's going to do next."

It was three a.m. Outside, the world had slowed, Tottenham Court Road and Euston Road almost silent, Warren Street Underground station closed until morning. The rubbish trucks would be arriving soon, sweeping away the previous day. The local residents would be tucked up in bed, enjoying a good night's sleep. All was calm and quiet.

Not in here though. Not in a Central London A&E

department. How the doctor expected me to sleep in this din was beyond me. In the cubicle to my left, someone had been vomiting violently for over an hour. To my right, a man was screaming about spiders and babies with knives, and outside, in the corridor, I think a nurse was crying. Machines were beeping. Alarms were sounding. The florescent light in my cubicle was flickering, and I was still waiting for the painkillers to kick in.

Time passed. By 4:15 a.m., no one had been to see me for hours, which probably meant they were no longer worried about me. Which probably meant I could go home. Didn't it?

From my place perched on the edge of the bed, I looked down at Matilde sleeping peacefully beside me, her dark curls spread out over the pillow, her breathing slow and steady. I lifted the thin blue blanket over her shoulder and thought how lucky I was to have someone like her like someone like me. Perhaps she would even love me one day. No. That sort of thing didn't happen to me.

I sniffed and stood up. If I had to be stuck in this hellhole for another four hours, I might as well go for a walk.

University College Hospital was vast, and at first, I had no idea where I would find what I was looking for, until I stopped someone to ask.

Many floors and corridors later, I arrived at the entrance to the ward, pressed the entry bell and looked into the camera. I have no idea why they released the door to let me in. Maybe it was my lab coat, and they hadn't seen the blood over one shoulder and sleeve.

There was no one at the nurses' station, no one in any of the side rooms, so I wandered around the ward unchallenged. It didn't take long to find him because there was a policeman asleep on a chair outside his room. Very quietly, I pushed the door, expecting it to be locked, but it opened without a sound.

The room was dim with only the light from the heart monitor illuminating Charlie Simmonds's face. Once my eyes had adjusted, I took a step forward but immediately stopped at the sight of a man sleeping on a chair in the corner of the room, a cabin bag on the floor beside the chair, Charlie's watch on his wrist. The brother, I presumed.

Silently, I went to the bed and looked down at him. There was a cannula in the back of his hand hooked up to a saline drip, a blood-pressure cuff around his arm, an oxygen tube in his nose, electrocardiogram wires stuck to his chest. He was in a deep, heavily sedated sleep, his eyes flicking back and forth underneath the closed lids, completely defenseless and so, so vulnerable.

I bent down until my face was level with his and whispered, "Did you see who did it? Did you look into their eyes before they stuck you with the needle?"

10

I MANAGED TO AVOID SEEING DCI ROBERTS THE FOLLOWING morning because I discharged myself at five a.m. and went home. Matilde was still asleep in the cubicle when I left. I didn't want to disturb her—she looked so peaceful. I was now standing in front of my bathroom mirror, turning my head from side to side, assessing the damage. One side of my face was definitely more swollen than the other, although I couldn't see the full extent because of the large white dressing covering half my head. I could, however, see the beginnings of the bruising spreading across my forehead and cheekbone. I sighed at the thought of the solicitous comments and sympathetic looks I'd get from the students when I went back to work, but for now, it was the weekend. Two whole days for the excitement and the swelling to die down.

When I'd got home, I'd bathed and changed into Father's pajamas. Luckily, the lab coat had protected my suit from the blood.

It was now soaking in a water-and-vinegar solution in the kitchen sink. I could have thrown it away—there were plenty more in the lab—but I was my father's daughter: waste not, want not.

My hair was a mess, and there was nothing I could do about it because of the dressing. I couldn't slick it back. I couldn't part it. I would just have to endure the disorder until the wound healed.

Tutting, I leaned closer to the mirror and was shocked to see a white hair. My first one. I gripped it between finger and thumb, yanked it out, and inspected it closely. Apart from my hairstyle and the suit, nothing about me had changed for decades. I was the same height and weight, had the same bra size and glasses prescription I'd had when I was twenty. This surprising white hair was the first indication of time passing. I sniffed and dropped it into the toilet, and, unexpectedly, the woman with long white hair who'd approached me at Pascal's exhibition popped into my head.

She knew my name. How? I had no idea who she was. She knew Father. She hadn't referred to him by name, but she knew he'd home-schooled me. How? I couldn't explain the rush of emotion I'd felt when I first saw her at the exhibition. Why would that happen with a complete stranger? I'd planned to spend the day sleeping and recuperating. But I was suddenly gripped by a burning determination to find out who this woman was. Our only connection was Pascal, and if he was the connection, he must also be the answer. There must be a reason to speak to him again, if only I could think of it.

I left the bathroom to pace the hall, glancing every now and again at Father's photograph. Then I had an idea.

𝕶𝕶

This time I didn't stray into London Fields for the chance of conjuring another nostalgic memory but made my way straight to Pascal Martineaux's building. I hadn't forewarned him of my visit. How could I? I didn't have his telephone number, but he didn't slam the door in my face. Quite the opposite. After seeing the dressing on my head, he invited me in, sat me down, and offered me a cup of tea, which I quickly declined.

"What happened to your head?" he asked.

"I was hit by a door. A student opened it with a bit too much force, and it caught the side of my head."

"On purpose?" Serena was sitting cross-legged on the floor, drinking from a stone cup.

I'd been wary about seeing her after the *Monstera* incident. I'd prepared myself for hostility, but although her tone wasn't exactly friendly, it wasn't antagonistic either.

"It was an accident," I lied, to bring an end to the subject.

"That's alright then," she said, as if she'd been instructed to be civil if ever she saw me again.

Wolfsbane, I thought. Latin name, *Aconitum napellus*, a plant appearing so innocuous, it's grown all over the country by hapless gardeners. That's what she was, a wolf in sheep's clothing. But beware, because one dose, and death is almost instantaneous.

"What can we do for you, Professor?" Pascal asked.

"I'm thinking of buying a painting," I said with a confidence I wasn't feeling because I'd never bought a painting in my life.

"You would?" he asked, surprised.

"Well, that's just wonderful," Serena cried. "Which one? Wait, let me guess. It has to be your portrait. Yes. It just has to be that one."

I balked at the suggestion. Why she thought I'd want a painting of myself with sinister eyes and a needle next to my neck was beyond me. But was this sarcasm again? I glanced at Pascal. He was frowning at her, shaking his head, and I decided from then on, I'd take my cues from him.

I frowned and shook my head. "I'd like to buy the painting of the young woman sitting on the wooden crate."

Pascal's expression slammed shut. "It's not for sale."

Serena stood up, went to him, and laid a gentle hand on his chest. "Honey...we agreed, remember? Everything's for sale."

Then she turned to me and said in a whisper loud enough for him to hear, "Don't worry. I'll talk to him. You shall have your painting."

I was about to mutter some token words of thanks but was interrupted by the overly loud, ugly buzz of the door intercom.

"Good. She's here," Serena said.

Moments later, the front door opened, and I was astonished to see the woman with long white hair standing before me, wearing the same expression of astonishment to find me standing before her. It had been my intention to quiz Pascal about her away from Serena, perhaps in his studio while pretending I was thinking of buying a painting, but here she was, right in front of me, weighed down by an enormous bag and leaning heavily on a cane.

"Professor, meet Pandita-vaggo. My shaman," Serena said.

The woman's eyes opened wide as she took in the dressing.

"What happened to your head?" she asked, putting the bag down.

"A student opened a door too hard and it hit her," Serena answered for me.

"Are you alright?"

"She's fine," Serena said. "Now, Professor. You'll be interested in this. Pandita will be conducting a crystal sound bath meditation shortly. Would you like to join us?"

"A what?" I asked, half listening.

"A crystal sound bath meditation," she repeated. "It's a powerful, ancient sound-healing therapy. Every part of our body—in fact every atom in the universe—creates a vibration that resonates in a certain way. When our bodies and minds are sick, the illness stops us vibrating at our healthy frequency. Sound healing sends sound waves through our body to bring harmony through oscillation and resonance. It helps restore our body's natural balance and allows us to heal."

My eyes were still locked with the woman's, Serena's words background noise. I didn't want to look away because I was experiencing the same rush of emotion I'd had at the exhibition. It was almost unbearable, but also, I didn't want it to stop. It had to, though, because Pascal broke the spell by walking between us to collect the heavy bag and carry it to the huge windows.

My phone beeped a text. I pulled it out and looked at the screen. It was from *Sweetie*. *Where are you?*

"Do you like the new color scheme?" Serena asked.

I glanced at her, not sure if she was talking to me. "I beg your pardon?"

"We've just had the space redecorated. Do you like it?"

I put my phone away and made a quick, impatient scan of the room. It looked exactly the same...apart from the absence of the *Monstera obliqua*.

"It's much fresher, isn't it?" she said with a smile of satisfaction.

"Where's the plant?" I asked.

She looked to where it had been. "Oh...I gifted it to a good friend. He'll take good care of it."

"You gave it away?" I gasped.

"I did."

"But...if you were going to give it away anyway, why didn't you give it to me? Why didn't you let *me* take good care of it?"

She tossed her hair. "Because you're not a friend. Anyway, I much prefer the space its absence has created. I love the soft minimalism of the room now, don't you?" She looked at me with a small smile and added, "We live a simple life. We don't need many possessions. The Japanese aesthetic is based on simplicity, which historically was born from poverty. We live like the poor, and we are proud to do so."

I ground my teeth and replied, "I suppose it's always wiser to appear poorer than you are. You don't want to attract the attention of burglars."

The woman was arranging a selection of differently sized, pure-white quartz bowls in a semicircle around a rattan mat. When she'd finished, she sat cross-legged on it. She was looking at me pointedly, as if she was expecting me to do something, and as if I was expected to know what that was.

Serena took another sip of her drink and said to the woman, "I've had half. Will that be enough?"

The woman shook her head. "You must finish it, and you must drink a cup every day."

Serena inclined her head deferentially then looked at me. "Pandita-vaggo is a medicine woman as well as a shaman." She held up the stone cup. "The professor's a botanist. Tell her what's in this potion. She'll be interested."

She's giving a pregnant woman a potion? I thought, alarmed.

The woman shook her head. "I wouldn't call it a potion. It's a tea made of medicinal herbs that are beneficial during pregnancy."

"Tell her what they are," Serena said. "Not just the herbal remedy stuff. The other stuff as well."

The woman looked at me. "Shall I?"

I didn't particularly want to know. Besides, I was still biting the inside of my cheek over the *Monstera*, but for some reason, I was nodding.

"It's a mix. There's marshmallow, *Althaea officinalis*—*Althaea* is derived from the Greek word for 'soft'—a light diuretic and anti-inflammatory that helps to mitigate water retention and swelling, which can be problematic during pregnancy. It literally makes the body 'soft.' In the Middle Ages, mallow was used as an antidote to love potions and aphrodisiacs."

Serena laughed and clapped her hands. "I love that. Give it to the men so the pregnant women can take a break from their amorous advances."

"Oat straw," the woman continued, "*Avena sativa*—a mild sedative to help relieve fatigue and stress. It also soothes the nervous and digestive systems. Spearmint, *Mentha spicata*—relieves headaches, nausea, and vomiting. But it shouldn't be taken while breastfeeding because it can suppress the flow of the mother's milk. Rose petals, which promote healthy gut flora. They're also a mild diuretic and antiseptic so can prevent urinary tract infections. The apothecary rose was said to represent the blood of Christian martyrs. Its dried petals were rolled into beads then strung into chains. These chains later became known as rosaries."

As she spoke, I let my gaze move slowly over the crystal bowls, knowing her eyes were fixed on me. Her feather-soft voice was like a hypnotist's, and if I wasn't careful, I would fall into her words. Fall through them.

"Lemon balm," she continued, "*Melissa officinalis*—helps elevate the mood, brings happiness, and eases the spirit. It's also a mild sedative and can lower the blood pressure. When taken in the final months of pregnancy and during the birth, it can gently aid relaxation and ease contractions. Finally, nettle, *Urtica dioica*—an herb rich in vitamins A and C, iron, calcium, silica, magnesium, and potassium. It helps protect the gut lining from infection and enhances the extraction of uric acid. It eases pain in the muscles and joints and does a whole host of other beneficial things. It's an all-round good guy. During the seventeenth century, nettle stings were thought to prevent sorcery, and its presence near or in houses stopped milk being soured by witches."

I wanted to find something wrong with what she was saying, some small mistake, but I couldn't find a single thing. Her medicinal and plant folklore knowledge was flawless and also familiar, as if I'd heard it before…if only I could remember where—and when.

"I insisted on the nettles," Serena said, breaking my train of thought. "Because historically Native North American women took it in pregnancy to prevent hemorrhaging during childbirth. I know there are modern treatments for this, but I wanted that ancient connection, you know?" She tipped back her head, downed the rest of the tea, and gave a small shudder. "I much prefer rooibos, but sometimes you have to do what the doctor orders." She placed her cup down on the island with care. "There. All done. Shall we begin?"

The woman nodded, and Serena turned to me. "Join us. It's a very powerful experience. You might be surprised by your response to it."

Ideally, I would have preferred Serena to leave the room so I could talk to the woman alone, but I could see that wasn't going to happen.

My phone beeped again. I took it out to see another message from Matilde. *For God's sake, Eustacia. Answer my texts!!* I switched the phone to silent and put it back in my pocket.

"No, thank you. Pascal and I have some business to attend to." I looked at him. "Shall we go to your studio?"

⟨⟨

It was a relief to be back in Pascal's studio after the stifling perfection of Serena's domain. Usually, I found mess and chaos upsetting, but being surrounded by the haphazardly squeezed tubes of oil paint, the unwashed brushes and trowels, and the splattered floor and walls was paradoxically calming. I perched on a tall stool and tucked my heels onto the foot rail. Pascal straight away crossed to his desk to roll a cigarette, rapidly tapping the tobacco along a paper as if his life depended on it. He lit the thin cigarette, inhaled deeply, squinted at me through the smoke, and asked, "Did you like your portrait?"

I'd completely forgotten about his warning or death threat… or whatever it was. It just didn't seem important compared to finding out the identity of the woman in the other room. Coughing slightly from the smoke he seemed to be deliberately blowing in my direction, I said, "I'm not an expert when it comes to art. Most things actually, if they're not related to botanical toxicology, but it was certainly lifelike. I recognized myself, at least."

For some reason, this made him laugh.

"I'm glad you recognized yourself *at least*. I'd be a pretty poor artist if you hadn't *at least* managed that."

Was he going to mention the syringe he'd painted next to my neck? Was he going to issue some kind of threat now? Something along the lines of a warning that I should stay away from the investigation into the Soho poisoning?

"The poison victim could wake up," I said then immediately wondered if I shouldn't have.

"Could he?" he asked. "Why d'you think I'd care about that?"

The syringe next to my neck.

"Because you seemed to care the last time I mentioned him."

He took a drag, held his breath then spoke through smoke, "Don't know what gave you that idea."

The syringe next to my neck. I shook my head because I now knew what plant he was—adder's-tongue. Latin name *Ophioglossum vulgatum,* a perennial fern with a spore-bearing stalk resembling a snake's tongue. Also, someone who skirted around the truth.

"I must be mistaken. Never mind. Let's change the subject. Why won't you sell the painting of the woman on the crate?"

"That's not your business. You can buy one of the others."

"I don't want one of the others."

He took another drag. "Okay. Your choice."

I looked around the studio. It should have felt empty with all the paintings that had been stacked up against the walls now hanging in the gallery, but it didn't. It was an artist's cornucopia overflowing with supplies, as if Pascal had a limitless budget to buy whatever he wanted. Which, of course, he did.

He stubbed out his cigarette, stood up, and brushed the loose tobacco and ash from his trousers. "Okay, then. I'm going to take the dog for a walk."

And just in time I remembered why I was there.

"Who's that woman?"

"What woman?"

"The woman in there with the long white hair and the bowls."

"You know who she is. You were introduced. She's Serena's shaman. The one she brought over from California. Why?"

"She spoke to me at your exhibition. She quoted Keats."

"She quoted Keats?" Pascal laughed. "That's so random." His laughter subsided into a chuckle, and he sat down again. "She's so weird."

"So you don't know who she was before she became a shaman? You don't know anything about her past?"

He narrowed his eyes. "Do you think she's a criminal? Should I be worried about leaving my wife and unborn child with her?"

He was smiling as he said these words, but I wasn't sure if he was joking. It didn't seem like a joking matter to me.

"I don't think she's a criminal," I said quickly. "At least, I don't think I do."

Suddenly, an unearthly sound filled the studio, as if a hundred wet fingers were rubbing the rims of a hundred glasses, with the volume turned up to a hundred. Instantly, my hands flew to my ears. I'd never heard such an awful din in all my life.

"What on earth is that?" I cried.

"It's the sound bowls. If you think it's loud in here, imagine what it's like lying right next to them."

"This is the vibrating sound healing?"

"Yep. Bet you're glad you decided not to join. Watch out," he said, picking up a long leather leash. "The dog's going to come crashing in any second. She absolutely hates it. Sends her into a spin."

Sure enough, seconds later, Pascal's huge Great Dane came bounding into the room, jumped up, put her massive front paws on Pascal's shoulders, and began to whimper and shake.

"Alright, baby, alright. Let's get out of here." He lowered the dog's paws back to the floor and clipped on her leash, but before he left, he turned to me and said, "You can hang here if you want to wait to talk to the witch when she's done."

"How long will she be?"

"Half an hour-ish?"

I groaned. "I don't think I can stand this racket for a whole half hour. It already feels like my fillings are about to fall out."

He smiled. "Wait outside then. She parks her car in the yard. It's a white Mini. She never hangs around for long. You can catch her when she leaves."

Forty minutes later, the woman emerged from the building carrying the large bag on her back and leaning on the cane. She smiled when she saw me standing beside her car.

"Thanks for waiting," she said, heaving the bag into the boot. "I was hoping you would."

"You said you wanted to talk to me?"

"Yes, I did." She paused before adding, "I wanted to tell you to stay away from Pascal."

Just then, we heard the creak of the gate, and we turned to see Pascal coming through it with the Great Dane. He leaned down to unclick the dog's leash then straightened and looked at us.

The woman got into her car and wound down the window.

I bent down and pushed up my glasses. "Why?"

"He's listening," she said quietly. "We can't talk now."

"When then?"

The woman smiled. "You found me once. You can find me again."

It occurred to me to tell her I'd had no idea she'd be here and that our meeting was purely fortuitous.

"How can I find you?"

"You're very clever, Eustacia. You have been since you were a tiny child. You'll find a way."

"But I can't even pronounce your name."

She laughed. "Pandita-vaggo is the name Serena gave me to make her spirituality more authentic. It means *the wise* in Pali. She likes to think of me as the wise leader and she the meek follower."

Pascal was now holding the front door of his building open for the dog to trot through, still watching us steadily.

"My name's Jessica. Jessica Parks."

She reached a hand out of the car window and touched my sleeve. "I remember this suit. It fits you very well."

Then she looked up at me and smiled, and from this proximity, I could see the fine wrinkles at the edges of her eyes, the soft downy hair on her cheeks, her clear, lightly tanned skin. And I suddenly saw an image of a peony-pink duvet. Smelled freshly laundered linen. Felt the soft rhythmic thump of a heartbeat against my cheek. Heard a voice singing as softly as a dandelion clock. Tasted...tasted...what was it? Cinnamon?

"Eyebright," she said. "I remember now. The old man used to call you Eyebright because its Latin name sounded like Eustacia."

"*Euphrasia nemorosa.*"

"That's right. *Euphrasia.* Also because your eyes were always bright with curiosity."

She smiled again and nodded. "Well then, goodbye for now, Eyebright. I have great faith we'll see each other very soon."

She pressed the button for the electric gate, started the engine, and drove away, but before the car turned the corner, I pulled out my phone and took a photo of her license plate.

11

THE GYM WAS NOWHERE NEAR THE POLICE STATION BUT AN interminably long bus journey away in North London. I'd had a full day of teaching, and, I don't mind saying, I was quite tired by the time I arrived.

DS Chambers was already there, doing stretches on the mats. She jumped up when I entered and jogged over to me. "Here you are at last. I've been waiting ages."

"The bus was very slow."

"Why didn't you come by tube? It would've taken twenty minutes."

"I never take the tube. I have a phobia of being underground."

She tilted her head. "Okay... Well, why don't you get changed, and we can make a start."

"Get changed?" I asked, surprised.

"You didn't bring a workout kit?"

I frowned. "Was I meant to?"

She tilted her head the other way. "You've never been to a gym before, have you?"

It was true, but it also sounded like a veiled insult.

I sniffed with disapproval. "Why do I need to change out of the clothes I will no doubt be wearing the next time someone grabs my arm? Surely it would be better to work within their limitations?"

She smiled. "Fair point. At least take your jacket off."

I didn't want to take my jacket off.

"Take your shoes off as well. They're not allowed on the mats. You can leave them on the bench over there," she said, pointing.

I sighed but crossed to the other side of the gym, folded my jacket, laid it on the bench, and sat to untie my laces. When I stood again, DS Chambers was lifting weights. The sight of her made me acutely conscious of my feeble frame against her physical prowess. In her skintight leggings and sports bra, she looked like an Olympian. I sighed again, then walked back to her and stood awkwardly beside the mats.

"I'll be with you in a sec. I'll just finish this rep."

Whatever that meant.

"Why don't you warm up while you wait?" she asked.

I swung my arms a bit and jogged on the spot, but this made her laugh, which I didn't appreciate. Then after six more lifts, she put the weight back in its cradle, walked toward me, grabbed my arm, spun me around, and threw me onto my back. I gasped and stared up at her, my eyes wide with indignation, and she put her hands on her hips and looked down at me.

"You okay, babe?"

I clambered to my feet, furious that she'd given me no warning. "Of course not. I've only just come out of hospital."

"You want me to be gentle with you? Well, let me tell you, a violent man wouldn't be gentle. He'd see that dressing on your head and use it to his advantage."

I gave her a look, but as soon as I'd caught my breath, she grabbed my arm again, twisted me round, and I flopped onto my back. This time, the wind whooshed out of me, making me close my eyes tight, wrap my arms around my torso, and roll onto my side.

"This is the move I'm going to teach you," she said, and I opened one eye to find her squatting in front of me.

"It's a very simple countermove if someone grabs your arm. You grab theirs back, twist round, forcing them to let go, then drop your weight while you're twisting, and you'll drag them down with you. Once they're on their back, you run."

She sucked air through her teeth. "That's the official advice anyway. In my opinion, once they're on their back, stamp on their genitals as hard as you can, take a photo of them, then run. Once you're a safe distance away, call the police and send them the photo."

I stared at her. Then I imagined doing this to Giant Hogweed and shook my head vigorously to get rid of the disturbing image of him rolling around on the ground in agony.

She took my hand without asking and pulled me into a sitting position. "Men are taller. Their center of gravity higher. You'll get them down faster if you use one foot to kick their legs out from under them."

She bent her knees, pivoted on one foot, and held the other leg out straight as she turned.

My head shook slowly. "I don't think I can do that."

"It's okay," she said, standing. "We'll start with the basics today; then next time we can move on to the intermediate moves."

"Next time?"

She leaned down and held out a hand to pull me up, but I ignored it and stood awkwardly.

"Right, let's do that again in slow motion; then it'll be your turn to throw me."

She put me through this torture for what seemed like an eternity but which, in reality, was probably only half an hour, and to make matters worse, she looked to be enjoying it. I can categorically confirm that I was not, until the moment I managed to throw her. I was so surprised that I let out a whoop of joy, but before I had a chance to savor the victory, she jumped up, flipped me over, and then I was on my back with her sitting astride me and my wrists pinned above my head.

She should have been congratulating me, shaking my hand; instead, her face was hovering above mine, uncomfortably close, and she said, "*Never* get complacent. Never let down your guard. Men get angry if they think you've won."

She held me like this for a full minute then let go of my wrists, sat back on my belly, and looked down her nose at me. Was she angry? She didn't look it. In fact, I could have sworn she wore a slight smile.

"You know, I really do think we should go for a drink," she said.

I shifted my eyes to the ceiling. "I told you—I don't drink."

"A mocktail then."

"A what?"

She smiled openly this time, showing her teeth. "An alcohol-free cocktail."

I thought about this as I lay there. I didn't want to be lying there, but she was showing no signs of getting off me, and the last thing I wanted was to be thrown again.

"Ah, I see… *mock*tail. That's clever." My words were a little breathy because she was actually quite heavy.

"You've never had one?"

"Never."

"Then you're in for a treat."

She leaned forward again, so close that I could feel her breath on my face.

"You know that purple plant you showed me on the smart

board in your lab? I found out its common name's barberry. I also found out your nickname for me is Barberry."

"Who told you that?"

"DCI Roberts." She leaned even closer. "When you showed me the plant, you said it was 'pretty.'"

Heat crept up my neck. "Did I?"

"Yes…you did."

She moved even closer, and when her eyes dropped to my mouth, I was instantly thrown back to that terrible night when *his* hands were around my neck, squeezing…squeezing…his face close to mine, his hot breath on me, his bloodshot eyes bulging, the vein in his forehead throbbing. Then from some undiscovered core, I found a strength I didn't know I possessed. I jerked up my pelvis and threw her so hard that she rolled away until she hit the gym wall with a loud thud, and when I saw her slumped there, I suddenly had an idea that made me jump to my feet and run across the gym to grab my jacket and shoes. And as I pushed through the exit doors, I heard her shout, "Jesus fu—" before they slammed shut behind me.

꙰꙰

The last time I'd watched the Berwick Street CCTV footage, I'd been expecting to see a staggering man with a syringe hanging out of his neck, not someone miraculously appearing in the shop doorway as if they'd been transported there by some kind of futuristic technology. But he had to have come from somewhere, and seeing DS Chambers roll away and hit the gym wall had given me the idea that I might know where that could have been.

I got off the bus at Wardour Street, cut along Broadwick, walked down Berwick Street, and stood outside the shop where Charlie Simmonds was found. The street was busy. All along the road, the market was in full swing with fruit and vegetable vendors hawking their wares. The shop's front window had been replaced, the pavement swept clear of glass. There was nothing remaining of the night of the attack.

Next to the shop was the pub the group of men who had come out of before the fight. Through the gloomy windows, I could see several customers sitting at the tables drinking pints of beer. I took a sidestep for a better view, felt a movement beneath my foot, and looked down. Then I took a deep breath and did the thing that, ordinarily, I did not like doing. I went into the pub.

It was a long time before anyone appeared behind the bar, but I waited patiently rather than calling out for service because time seemed to be moving at a slower pace in here. When the bartender finally arrived, he wasn't impressed that I didn't want to buy a drink and responded with truculence when I proceeded to ask him questions.

"Do you have a basement?"

"Yes."

"Could I have a look at it?"

"Why?"

"I want to check something."

"What?"

I should have anticipated there might be questions and also should have prepared answers.

"Mold" was all I could come up with.

"Are you an inspector?"

"No, I'm a botanist. I'm, um, interested in mold."

He gave me a look that was quite clearly skeptical and shook his head. "The toilet's in the basement. If you buy a drink, you can use it."

"I'm not interested in using your facilities. I simply want to look at your basement."

"The use of the toilet is for customers only. Company policy."

"I'm not interested..." I sighed. "Alright, I'll have a glass of sparkling water."

He took a small bottle from a fridge, cracked the lid, and handed it to me with a glass. "That'll be five pounds."

"*How* much?"

The toilet was accessed via a steep, narrow staircase that wound round and down into the dark basement. The space was divided by a hallway. On one side was the toilet, on the other a door with a sign saying "Staff Only," which meant I was not permitted to go through it.

I waited in the hallway to see if anyone came out of the toilet or down the stairs, and when I was confident the basement was empty, I opened the "Staff Only" door. Inside was a room with a small kitchen area and, behind that, another door that I assumed led to the storeroom. However, I didn't bother investigating that because after one quick glance around the room, I found what I was looking for.

An hour later, I was back in DCI Roberts's office rewatching the CCTV.

"What time shall we start?" he asked.

"I think our victim was in the pub next door to the shop, so let's start at ten p.m."

"Why do you think he was in the pub?"

"Because he collapsed just after he left it."

DCI Roberts looked up. "He never left the pub. You and I both watched the door very closely, several times."

"He didn't leave by the door."

He was waiting for an explanation, but I was eager to see if I was right. I knocked the table with my knuckles. "Come on—let's get started."

We stared at the sped-up footage for several minutes until I shouted, "There, stop. Go back. There he is."

DCI Roberts rewound, and we watched Charlie Simmonds enter the pub.

"Okay, now, let's see if Pascal follows him in."

We stared at the monitor right up to the point Charlie emerged out of the ground and rolled into the neighboring shop's doorway.

"Wait, where did he just come from?" DCI Roberts cried, pressing the space bar to pause the footage.

"The beer keg delivery hatch," I said. "It's no longer in use, but it can be accessed from a room in the basement. So we can assume Pascal stuck him with the syringe in the basement, and Charlie escaped through the delivery hatch."

DCI Roberts was staring at me with the expression he pulled when he realized I was several steps ahead. I leaned forward, pressed the space bar, and we stared at the monitor.

"Now...let's see if we can find Pascal."

There was no sign of him. I rewound and stared again. And again, but he was nowhere to be seen.

"That's that then," DCI Roberts said. "It wasn't Pascal."

"Perhaps he was already in the pub before Charlie arrived?" I suggested hopefully.

DCI Roberts grunted. "Several officers, including me, have spent a long time on this footage, starting hours before Charlie appeared in the shop doorway. If Pascal was on Berwick Street that night, we would've seen him."

"You're sure?"

He gave me a long look. "Feel free to check for yourself."

I shook my head, but instead of disappointment, I felt relief.

I was glad Pascal wasn't the one who'd pushed the syringe into Charlie Simmonds's neck. But then, how did he know about it?

"Someone else followed him in," I said. "Someone we haven't considered yet."

"About twenty people went in after him."

"And none of them looked like they were intent on a poisoning," I finished for him.

DCI Roberts sighed heavily, and I knew exactly what it meant. This was not going to be as straightforward as we'd hoped.

"How did you know about the delivery hatch?" he asked after a moment.

I shrugged. "I had a feeling I missed something that first night we went to the scene. Then something happened today that made me think I might know what it was, so I went back for a second look."

"A feeling?" he asked, his large eyebrows lifting. Then he began to laugh. A big booming laugh. "Are you telling me you had a *hunch*, Eustacia?"

12

I was in the main hall giving a taxonomy lecture on Carl Linnaeus and his influential system of binominal nomenclature when my phone rang mid-sentence. I had a rule that I expected all students to abide by, and it was that all phones be switched off before entering the hall, and so, when my phone rang at top volume, the cacophony of laughing and scoffing was almost deafening. I pulled it from my pocket, glanced at the screen, saw an unfamiliar number, turned it off, and dropped it into my satchel.

"Alright, settle down," I shouted above the din. "I know, I know—one rule for me, another for the rest of you, but I assure you, this was an oversight. Now, where were we?" I turned back to the smart board. "Ah yes…nested hierarchies, as nicely exemplified in this illustration of Russian matryoshka dolls…"

Fifty minutes later, as the students were trickling out of the hall, I turned on my phone. There were four missed calls from the unfamiliar number and a string of texts from Matilde. I waited for the last student to leave then returned the unknown number's call.

"I know who's making the synthetic toxins," the voice said as soon as he picked up, and I recognized Giant Hogweed. Why the secretaries' office had given him my personal number was beyond me.

"Who?" I asked.

"I can't say over the phone. Someone might hear."

His voice was breathy, as if he was walking quickly.

"Text me then."

"No. I don't want to leave a digital trail. Come and meet me, and I'll tell you in person."

"I can't. I'm very busy."

I heard a sigh.

"Listen, I'm sorry about what I did to you. And I want to thank you. That policewoman, DS something—she was really angry you didn't press charges. *Really* fuming. So, thank you, and I promise I won't hurt you again. I'm trying to change. I'm working on myself. I'm getting help, a therapist, so please...please come and meet me."

I paused. "I can't, because my timetable's full until seven. It'll have to be this evening."

"Okay. This evening. Cool. I'll see you then."

"Wait. Is it a university lab?"

"I can't say. Someone might hear. I'll tell you later."

"But is it in London?"

There was a pause. "Yes."

So not Oxford or Cambridge. "Is it—"

"I have to go," he cut in. "Come to my flat this evening. I live near uni. I'll text you the address."

I stared at the screen, waiting for his text, expecting it to arrive instantly. It didn't. While I waited, I opened a message from Matilde suggesting we meet in the staff canteen for a cup of tea. I had fifteen minutes before a tutorial. Not enough time to walk over to the canteen, order, and drink tea then walk back. I clicked back to the home screen and waited for Giant Hogweed's text then remembered Matilde's complaint that I never replied to her messages. It was true. I didn't because the majority of them were either nonsensical or simply a string of small emoticons that my students informed me had different meanings—which, of course, I didn't know. I clicked back to Matilde's message, typed *no time*, pressed *Send*, and returned to the home screen just as the text arrived.

❦❦

At 7.15 p.m., I turned off Gower Street onto Bedford Avenue to be met by an imposing street-long row of redbrick mansion blocks, six stories high, and let out a whistle—Giant Hogweed definitely came from money. I climbed the entrance steps to the wide front door of the first block and looked for his flat number on the intercom panel. It wasn't there, so I walked along the road to the next set of steps, found his number at the bottom of the panel, and pressed the corresponding button.

There was no reply.

I pressed again. No reply.

I cupped my hands and peered through the front-door glass and saw a wide entrance hall, a staircase and a lift with a metal shutter. I pressed the button. No reply.

With a sigh, I turned to leave, and at the same time, a man opened the front door carrying a tiny dog. He greeted me with a faintly wary look, bent to put his dog down, and I stepped forward to prevent the door closing. When he'd moved a fair distance along the road, I looked over my other shoulder and slipped through the door. Inside, I quickly located Giant Hogweed's flat and found his front door ajar. Had he left the door open for me?

I pushed it open and peered inside. "Hello?"

Silence.

"Hello?"

I took a step back. Something felt decidedly wrong, but the only way to find out what that might be would be to go inside.

I took a step forward. "It's Professor Rose."

No reply.

"Hello?"

A hallway stretched before me with doors along one side and another at the end. I turned to my right to look into the first room, which was a well-equipped kitchen. A few steps along the hall was another door into a room containing a large desk, a leather office chair, and shelves filled with clothbound hardback books. The third door revealed a lounge with an ornate two-seater sofa, deep armchairs, engraved side tables, and a tall glass-fronted rosewood cabinet. I frowned. This wasn't a student flat.

The bedroom was behind the fourth door. Against one wall was an enormous mirrored antique wardrobe. Hanging from the ceiling, an impressive chandelier. And on the floor beside a four-poster bed was…Giant Hogweed.

My hand flew to my mouth. "No!"

He was lying on his side, his face turned away.

"No, no."

The arm furthest from me was stretched out, the sleeve rolled up. A tourniquet was lying untied under his upper arm, and hanging out of a vein was an empty syringe. Beside his arm was a small glass bottle.

"What have you done?"

Slowly, I inched toward him, knelt, and tentatively pressed two trembling fingers against his neck. There was no pulse. With a moan, I pulled out my phone and dialed 999.

While I waited for the emergency services, I tucked my legs beside me, leaned back against a bedpost, and let my eyes rest on Giant Hogweed's face. It was the first time I'd looked at him for longer than a split second. It was also the first time I'd seen his face in repose. Usually, his expressions displayed the exaggerated emotions I found easy to read—anger, frustration. But now he looked completely at peace. Whatever turmoil he must have been feeling before he injected himself wasn't evident in his expression now. Or perhaps there was no turmoil. Perhaps this was simply an accident.

Sitting there in the silent, still room, I gradually became aware of my body. Of the tears stinging my eyes, of my breath catching in my chest, of the tremble creeping through my limbs, so I left him and went to his study, because remaining by his side was becoming increasingly unbearable. It had been a long time since I'd seen a dead body, and seeing another had triggered some deep response that I thought had been long dealt with. I sat at his desk and closed my eyes, tapped my eyebrow, the side of my eye, under my eye, under my nose, my chin and my collarbone, tapping and breathing deeply—one, breathe, two, breathe, three—running through the quietening ritual I'd been taught, until my body calmed and the shaking subsided.

After several minutes, I opened my eyes and inhaled deeply. My body may have finally calmed, but my mind was racing. Had Giant Hogweed succumbed to temptation and bought a hallucinogen from the website he'd shown me and accidentally overdosed? Or had the substance not been what he thought it was and he'd accidentally poisoned himself? I couldn't be sure either way until I'd analyzed whatever might be left in the small bottle, but DCI Roberts would give forensics priority over that.

I wondered what else he might have purchased from the website and ran my eyes over the desktop. There were no more small bottles. The drawer was open an inch. I used my pen to pry it wider and looked inside. Again, no bottles. It seemed strange that his intention had been to buy toxins for his research, but the only bottle I'd seen was the empty one lying next to his body.

In front of me was a pile of typewritten sheets. I tilted my head. It was his PhD thesis proposal, titled "The Toxicology of Plant-Induced Homicides: Uncovering the Secrets of Lethal Botanical Agents." Without thinking, I picked the pages up and began to read the introduction. He'd opened with the sixteenth-century toxicologist Paracelsus and his tenet "the dose makes the poison," meaning everything can be toxic if the dose is right, even oxygen, even water. He talked about toxins that had therapeutic properties with one dose but were deadly with another. He moved onto toxins that could take years to kill and others that were so dangerous, it would take only one drop for instant death.

I flicked the page and read *Atropa belladonna*—a plant with two common names: the first, belladonna, meaning "beautiful woman," because in the Middle Ages, the juice of the berry was used as a blush for the lips and cheeks; then if diluted with water and used as eyedrops, it dilated the pupils, making the woman look more attractive. And the second, deadly nightshade because of the toxic chemicals solanine and atropine contained within its berries and leaves. Here he cited evidence of the contract killing of the Roman emperor Claudius by the serial killer Locusta, ordered by Agrippina the Younger.

He then mentioned *Conium maculatum*, hemlock—a plant that contained toxic alkaloids in all of its parts, causing paralysis and death. Here he wrote about the ancient Greek philosopher Socrates, who, after being found guilty of heresy, was sentenced to drink hemlock by his own hand. A slow and gruesome death. I turned to the next page, which had a long list of more poison murders, faceless names going back in time with short notes on the toxin that killed them and how it had been administered. I let out a dismissive huff. This was rudimentary undergraduate-level research. Where was he going with it? Certainly not a PhD. But then I sighed when I remembered he wasn't going anywhere ever again.

"Professor Rose!"

My body jerked at the bellow of my name, and the pages flew out of my hands and scattered onto the floor.

"What the hell do you think you're doing? This is a crime scene!"

I spun around to find DCI Roberts standing at the study door.

"I'm not doing anything. I was just waiting for you."

His eyes narrowed almost to slits. "Did you touch anything else, besides those pieces of paper?"

"No."

He muttered something I didn't catch, tossed me a pair of gloves and shoes protectors, and asked, "Where is he?"

"Last door on the right. It's open."

Several officers followed him down the hall, but before I joined them, I quickly scanned the desk for Giant Hogweed's laptop. It wasn't there. His open backpack was on the floor beside the desk, so I used my pen to open it wider, but the laptop wasn't inside either. I made a quick visual sweep of the room—it was nowhere to be seen. I sighed. Even if I found it, I couldn't very well take it away with me. The police would stop me in an instant.

I was about to follow to the bedroom when something sticking out of the backpack's front pocket caught my eye. I bent down and straight away recognized the small book that had been open on the desk beside Giant Hogweed when he'd shown me the website in my office—the book with the page of number and letter combinations. I pulled it out and flicked through the pages; then I checked the empty doorway and quickly slipped it into my jacket pocket.

13

Giant Hogweed's notebook was open on the desk in front of me, and I was slowly rereading the page, but for the life of me, I couldn't fathom what the random letters and numbers could possibly mean. He'd referred to the book several times when he'd shown me the website on his laptop, so it must be a code of some sort for accessing the dark web. I tapped my pen against my teeth. The year before, I'd broken a code to unlock some text messages on a mobile phone. I took a breath and pulled a fresh sheet from my ream of paper. If I could break one code, I could break another.

Several hours and many wasted sheets of paper later, I'd got precisely nowhere. I stood up, stretched, slipped the notebook into my jacket pocket, and wandered through to the kitchen. On the way, I paused at the photograph of Father.

"This is a tricky one," I said, rapping a knuckle on the glass above his face. "I don't suppose you could give me a clue?"

I waited for an answer to come through the ether.

"No? Okay, then. No harm in asking."

In the kitchen, I glanced at the hatch in the ceiling. The roof had always been my thinking place. Maybe, if I sat quietly, I'd have a eureka moment and the key to break the code would come to me effortlessly.

Father's canvas chair was leaning against the wall. I opened it, sat, looked up at the sky, and thought about the code. Giant Hogweed had obviously been an intelligent student to invent such an unfathomable combination of letters and numbers. Maybe I'd underestimated him. Maybe if I'd looked past his difficult personality, I could have agreed to be his supervisor. Maybe then, he would have listened to me and not bought a deadly concoction from an illegal website. I sighed and looked over the railings at the terraced houses behind my block, thinking that as far as Giant Hogweed was concerned, there was no longer any point in maybes.

There were few windows lit up in the houses, and those that were glowed only dimly. Not surprising. It was well past midnight. I stood and went to the railings and looked down into the gardens, wondering if I might see the family of foxes who lived in the old World War II bunker at the end of the communal gardens, but after scanning the whole length of the garden, I saw no foxes. There was, however, Susan shuffling around her garden with her flashlight. Smiling, I called down to her, "Fancy a cuppa?"

She was standing with her back to me at the kitchen sink when I arrived, the teapot and teacups on the table.

"Kettle's almost boiled. Sit yourself down," she said.

I did as instructed, then let out a light sigh.

"You sound tired, dear," she said, turning around, but when she saw me, she gasped. "Oh my God! What happened to your head?"

I touched the dressing. "I was hit by a door."

She scowled and folded her plump arms. "The expression is 'I walked into a door,' and we both know what that really means, don't we? Come on then. Out with it. Who battered you?"

"He didn't strictly batter—"

"Stop making excuses for 'im."

I pulled in my lips. "A student."

"The one who was giving you trouble?"

I nodded.

"Well, I hope *he* got into trouble for it."

"He was expelled." *And then he died.*

"Good. Serves him right. Now then." She poured boiling water into the pot and sat down opposite me. "I've been meaning to have a talk with you about something."

"Oh?"

"Matilde visits me every Friday. Did you know that?"

"No."

"She's a good friend," she added, which I assumed was her way of telling me that I was not. "Anyway, I need to tell you she's very upset with you."

"Is she?" My brow knitted. She hadn't seemed upset at the hospital.

"She arranged a lovely birthday for me. Cake, flowers, champagne. Took me to Queen Mary's Rose Garden in Regent's Park. Oh, it was like heaven with the gates shut. She even gave me a beautiful Portuguese shawl. But—you didn't turn up."

I inhaled sharply. "Ah…"

That's what Matilde meant when she'd told me not to be late that day I was talking with DS Chambers at the university.

"Don't make no odds to me. Once you're old, you stop counting the years. But she went to so much trouble." She passed me a teacup. "She tried not to show it, but I could see she was upset. I think it wasn't just about you missing the party, though."

I looked up.

"She kept going on about a pretty woman police officer. I think she thinks your head's been turned."

The image of DS Chambers sitting astride me in the gym. Her face above mine, the heat of her breath on me.

I cleared my throat. "I don't know what gave her that idea."

"Don't you?"

I cleared it again, suddenly uncomfortable. "No."

Susan was watching me; I could feel her eyes. I lifted mine to the ceiling.

After a while she asked, "Do you mind an old woman giving you a bit of advice?"

"Not at all," I answered, thinking the opposite.

"If you want to keep your sweet Matilde, I suggest you surprise her, make a fuss of her, show her you appreciate her, ask about her life, her hopes, her dreams, and it wouldn't hurt to smile at her every now and again. She told me you never smile."

I considered this for one minute then said, "I'm not really like that."

"I know, dear. But you've got to make an effort."

Still decidedly uncomfortable, I put my hand in my pocket, felt Giant Hogweed's notebook, and grabbed at the chance to change the subject.

"Do you remember the last time I was here I got a call from DCI Roberts?"

"Your friend Dickie?"

"He's not my friend, but yes. I decided to assist him with the case, and I remember you saying you'd help." I took the notebook out of my pocket, opened it, and put it on the table in front of her. "I've been trying to break a code, but it's proving very difficult. You said you loved puzzles. Does this mean anything to you?"

She didn't even look at it. "You'll make an effort with Matilde from now on?"

"I will," I said, nodding and pushing the notebook closer.

I waited for her to pick it up, and then, when she didn't, I nudged it a little closer.

"Promise?"

I gave her a quick look. "I promise."

"Alright. Give it 'ere then."

It was already right in front of her, but I nudged it again, and she picked it up, glanced at the page, and handed it back to me.

"It's not a code. The first line's a VPN address."

"A what?"

"A VPN. It's an address you log into so your internet browsing history can't be traced back to your computer."

I stared at her. "How do you know?"

"How do you not?"

I blinked once, twice, and she tipped her head to one side, leaned across the table, and patted my hand. "Look at your poor bruised face. You look all beat up. You should go 'ome. Get some shut-eye."

"So, I just type this into a computer, and I'll be taken to a website?"

"The first line's the VPN. The second line's the URL."

I shook my head slowly because I had absolutely no idea what she was talking about.

"I mean it, dear. You look done in. Finish your tea. Go home, and go to bed."

⟨⟨

As I was leaving the flat the following morning, I was waylaid by a call from DCI Roberts asking me to pop into the station to read Giant Hogweed's toxicity report. I was keen to get to work early to type the letters and numbers from the notebook into the office computer before my morning lecture, but I was just as keen to read the report. The tox report won.

"Thanks for coming in," he said, handing me a file. "I thought you'd be keen to know the toxin that killed Aaron Bennett is the same one that put Charlie Simmonds into intensive care."

"A coincidence?"

"Or there's a connection," he replied.

"How could there possibly be a connection between these two men? They couldn't have known each other…could they?"

"Are you asking me?"

"Yes."

DCI Roberts hummed softly. "Charlie Simmonds is a thirty-five-year-old financier from New York who is in London for business. Aaron Bennett was a twenty-three-year-old PhD student from Bourne End. I can't think of any reason why they would know each other; however, perhaps they both knew the person behind the toxin."

I considered this. "Were they a drug dealer? No. Simmonds was attacked. Dealers don't attack their clients."

We fell silent as we turned over the possibilities.

"Are you sure it was the same toxin?" I asked.

He pulled out Simmonds's toxicity report and put it with Giant Hogweed's. *Datura stramonium* was named on both, but there was no mention of the *Datura* that killed Giant Hogweed being synthetic. I frowned. I was sure he'd purchased the substance that had killed him from the website he'd shown me, so why weren't the chemicals needed to manufacture it listed in the report?

"I wonder," I said, falling silent.

After a minute, DCI Roberts asked, "You wonder what?"

I looked up from the page. "Could I have a go at testing their blood? I may reach a different result."

"The blood's been tested twice already. It says so on the report."

"I know. But your lab may not have considered a certain combination of chemicals. They were probably just looking for the core components. I'd like to have a go in my lab. Or we could ask them to test again?"

He shook his head. "They won't test again. We don't have the budget. Besides, I've given them another job."

"What's that?"

He pulled an evidence bag out of the file, containing a sheet of once tightly folded lined paper, covered in small handwriting that looked as if it had been roughly torn from a notebook.

"The pathologist found a list of plants in the front pocket of Aaron's jeans during the postmortem. It looked like ingredients. Judging by the subject matter of his PhD, I'm wondering if he was planning on mixing some poisonous potion or other. The lab technicians are busy cooking now, and we're all waiting to see what comes out of the oven."

Judging by what I'd read of Giant Hogweed's thesis, he wasn't looking at poison combinations. He was more interested in pure toxins.

I craned my neck to look at the list. "What are the plants?"

"I can't remember off the top of my head, but sage was one of them."

I frowned. "Can I see it?"

After a hesitation, he passed me the bag, and I scanned the list then turned the bag over. There was a single word written on the other side of the paper—"Prof."

"This is for me," I said, looking up in surprise. "He wrote this for me. Can I keep it?"

"No."

⁂

There was a message waiting for me when I finished the morning lecture saying a package had been delivered to the lab. I was impatient to go to my office to type the VPN and URL into my computer but just as keen to open the package. Inside were two evidence bags, each containing a test tube of blood labeled with Giant Hogweed's and Charlie Simmonds's names. There was also a photocopy of the plant list.

Cat's claw
Snowbush rose
Globe thistle
Mayflower
Scarlet sage
King's spear
Blue sage
Knife-leaf wattle

I read it again, thinking it odd that a postgraduate botany student would use common plant names, but didn't dwell on this, because I was distracted by how unsystematic the list was. It made no sense. There was nothing to link them together, no common properties, apart from the two sages. And anyway, the plants weren't toxic enough to be of any interest to his research. So what was he thinking?

I dropped the photocopy on the counter and turned my attention to the test tubes.

Four hours later, I had the results. It was as I'd expected for Giant Hogweed. His blood did indeed contain the chemical combination to prove the *Datura* was synthetic. What I was not expecting was that Charlie Simmonds's blood contained exactly the same combination. So exact that there was no doubt the *Datura* had been manufactured in the same lab and even came from the same batch. There could be a connection between the two men after all, because if Giant Hogweed had managed to find some money, he and the person who'd attacked Charlie Simmonds had bought the same synthetic toxin from the same website. The connection was the website. Now I just needed to find my way back into it, track down an illegal laboratory, and ask whoever was running it to tell me who bought the toxin that put one man into intensive care and killed another. I exhaled heavily. How difficult could that be?

14

IT WAS LATE. I WAS ON MY ROOF, MULLING OVER THE LIST OF plants, wondering about the arbitrary nature of Giant Hogweed's choices. Why put culinary herbs and inedible wildflowers together? Why include ornamental alongside medicinal plants, and why were their origins scattered all over the world? It made no sense.

I closed my eyes and visualized each plant's life cycle, from germination, through flowering, seeding, and dying back. I thought about their historical and cultural uses—cat's claw, a climbing vine with a small yellow flower. Used in Central and South America as an antidote to snake bites and as a treatment for venereal disease, rheumatism, malaria. Mayflower, a slow-growing prostrate shrub with fragrant pale-pink-and-white flowers, used by the Cherokee people to induce vomiting and to treat diarrhea. But still, I could find no connection.

As I sat with my eyes closed, a memory slowly materialized of a walk through the Oxford countryside when I was a child. Father and I often went for long, rambling walks when I was feeling anxious, or angry, or sad. He suggested we do this to "restore equilibrium." I used to think the walks were to restore *my* equilibrium, but perhaps they were as much for his benefit as mine. In this memory, we were crouching beside a clump of mayflower, and he was telling me about its medicinal properties. But no. It wasn't Father. It was a woman's voice. It was a woman crouching beside me. I screwed my eyes tighter, trying to enhance the memory, and I saw a gentle smile, black hair held in a messy bun with a pencil. Was this the same woman I'd remembered while I was watching the cricket in London Fields? The woman who'd given me strawberries?

Straight away, all thoughts of the plant list flew from my mind. I hurried down the ladder and went to my bedroom, took a box from the top of the wardrobe, and sat with it on the bed. Inside were Father's documents, letters, and what I was looking for—old photographs. I dug through the box until I'd found them all and spread them out on the bed. They weren't new to me. I'd looked at them countless times because they were photographs of my mother.

There were my parents in Magdalen College Hall surrounded by dignitaries. My tall, slim mother wearing a long red gown, her blond curls tamed with golden pins. Beside her, Father in the suit I was wearing. There was Mother in our Oxford garden, pruning shears in hand, a trug full of roses in the crook of her arm, wearing men's corduroy trousers, a pretty vest, a straw hat. There was Mother in a flower-print summer dress, reading newspapers and drinking coffee at the long table in the Oxford kitchen. And on and on, more and more, mostly of Mother but sometimes of them both, photographs I was so familiar with.

I remembered the time, around the age of six, when I'd asked Father where she'd gone, and he'd seemed thrown by the question, as if he didn't think I'd ever ask it. Then after a very long pause, he'd said, "False hope is still hope. Unrequited love is still love," which I'd found immensely puzzling. He'd never spoken about her again. But at least I had these photographs.

For the first time, something struck me. Where was I? These were obviously taken before I was born, but where were the photographs of Mother pregnant? Where were the mother and baby/toddler/small-child pictures? I let out a soft hum, not because of the sad realization that I owned no photographs of myself under the age of three but because the woman I'd remembered giving me strawberries and teaching me about mayflower did not have blond curly hair.

The intercom buzzed, making me leap and drop the photograph I was holding. Who on earth could be calling on me at this time of night? I shook my head, having no idea, and decided that if I ignored it, they'd go away.

Less than a minute later, the intercom buzzed again. I ignored it. However, when it buzzed a third time, whoever it was kept their finger on the button, filling the flat with a sustained blast of the horrible noise, forcing me to answer it.

"Professor? It's DCI Roberts. I have some information about Aaron Bennett."

I looked at my watch. What on earth could be so important that it couldn't wait until the morning? *Plenty*, I thought, pressing the door-release button.

I went out onto the landing and looked down the stairwell as the main door to my block slammed shut, and at the sound, a flashback of the first time DCI Roberts came here passed through my mind. It had been on that horrendous day, the worst day, but he'd only seemed interested in my telescope. That and the fact that I didn't have a poisonous-substances license. I inhaled deeply as the awful memories flooded back then shook my head vigorously to get rid of them.

"Hello, there. It's been a while since I've been here," he said when he finally arrived at the half landing. He was smiling, as if he was having fond memories.

"It's very late," I sniffed.

He began his slow ascent up the final flight. "Yes, it is. I was working and lost track of time, but I thought I'd stop by on my way home."

"You could've just called."

He reached my landing and inhaled deeply—I assumed to disguise the fact that he was out of breath.

"As I said, I was passing and thought I'd drop by to see if you were home."

I fixed my gaze on the wall above his head. "Well? What is it?"

"I'd prefer to talk inside." He peered warily down the stairwell as if one of my neighbors could be listening. "Shall we go in?"

It was the middle of the night. It was obvious none of my neighbors would be listening, but I stepped to one side and allowed him to pass.

"What's the information?" I asked again, closing the door behind him.

He didn't answer but walked along the hall and into the kitchen, which I thought highly presumptuous. When I caught up, he was standing at the bottom of the ladder, looking up at the hatch.

"Come on, man," I said. "I haven't got all night. What did you want to tell me?"

Then he took me by surprise by replying, "The sky's clear—we should have a good view of a planet or two."

I blinked at him. "Are you asking if you can use my telescope?"

He smiled. "I am."

I blinked again.

"I thought you came here to tell me something important."

"And to use your telescope. I was driving home, and I looked up at the sky and saw all those stars, and I thought of your telescope. I've always wanted to try it, and now your roof's no longer a poison deathtrap, this seemed like a good opportunity. So I turned the car around and here I am."

"You said you were passing."

"I passed, then I turned back." He put a foot on the bottom rung of the ladder. "Shall we go up?"

He was a big man. The bulk of him in my kitchen was making me anxious, but I didn't want him in my living room, either. If he was going to be anywhere, I supposed the roof, with the vast open sky above us, would be the best place.

"Alright. But not for long. I have an early lecture tomorrow."

"Excellent," he boomed, making me jump. "I would've brought a bottle if I'd thought you'd actually say yes." There was that smile again. "I don't suppose you have anything?"

I looked at the kettle.

"Alcoholic?" he added.

I didn't, of course, because I didn't drink, but then I remembered Father's bottle of whisky that I kept at the back of the condiments cupboard.

I took it out and showed it to him. "Will this do?"

"It'll do nicely," he said with a nod. "Very nicely indeed."

He sat on the wooden kitchen chair Matilde and I had managed to maneuver through the hatch, his eye at the telescope. I sat on Father's canvas chair because I wasn't confident it would support his weight. He had one hand on the focus, the other around a large glass of whisky. I sat with my hands resting on my lap. He was right. It was a clear night. Even with the hazy amber light pollution, the sky was covered with stars. I glanced at him. The smile was still on his lips. Not the thin-lipped cynical smile I knew so well. If I were to hazard a guess, I would say he looked happy.

"Are you going to tell me about Giant Hogweed now?"

He kept his eye against the telescope. "Who?"

"Giant—Aaron Bennett."

"Oh, his case has been closed."

I frowned. "I beg your pardon?"

"The coroner's finding was that he died from misadventure. Not suicide. Not anything else. He injected himself with a hallucinogen and accidentally overdosed. Forensics only found his prints on the bottle, and no evidence of foul play on his body."

"What about the syringe?"

"Eh?"

"Were his prints on the syringe?"

He looked at me. "If someone else's prints were on the syringe, the case wouldn't be closed. The coroner knows what he's doing."

"But do you agree with him?"

"Not my place to agree or disagree. If the super agrees with him, that's all I need to know. Besides, we have thirty unexpected deaths in London every day. Day after day. Aaron Bennett was just another one." He paused. "Anyway, you're right, I could have just called, but I thought you'd want to know straight away."

"Why?"

He glanced at me. "Because he was one of your students."

"He wasn't one of my students."

"He wasn't? But the two of you seemed so...involved."

I shook my head. "I didn't want us to be involved. He was a nuisance. That doesn't mean I'm relieved he's no longer a nuisance," I added quickly. "But, then again, maybe I am."

"You're glad he's dead?"

"Of course not."

A moment passed.

"Did you find his laptop?"

"Should we have?"

"Yes, you should have," I cried. "Didn't you do *any* forensics?"

His face grim, he asked, "Are you suggesting I didn't do my job correctly?"

"Yes, I am. You knew he was a student. Students have laptops. Laptops contain evidence that could be vital to the case."

"The case is closed."

I growled with frustration because I needed that laptop. "Maybe it would still be open if you'd found it."

"You sound like DS Chambers, and I'd rather not be reminded of her right now."

"DCI Roberts, that laptop—"

"Professor Rose, will you stop going on about the laptop. The case is closed. The subject's closed."

I slumped back in my chair and folded my arms, seething. He

put his eye back to the telescope, and we sank into an uneasy silence.

"We reach an age, don't we?" he said, after a while. "When it's reasonable to start thinking about retirement. But I've heard so many stories of people dropping dead the day after they retire that it scares the living daylights out of me. Does it scare you?"

It hadn't once crossed my mind. "Can't say I've given it any thought."

"No? Is it not something you think about?"

"Not really. I'm forty-five. I still have twenty-one years before I can retire."

His large eyebrows shot up, and many expressions played across his face while he cautioned himself about what to say next, but in the end, he said nothing. Just turned the telescope to look at a different part of the sky.

"You know something? Maybe it's fate DS Chambers came along. She's arrogant and pushy. She walks into the station like she owns the place. She talks to me like I'm senile. She's rude to the staff, her colleagues, the public. You know what her favorite saying is? *So last century.* The station technology is *so last century.* My investigative processes are *so last century.* I know I'm old enough to be her father, but I'm not that out of touch. Maybe her turning up is fate telling me it's time to retire."

Father used to say fate was just a lazy justification for the bad choices people made. I disagreed. It was a lazy justification for all of their choices.

"My girls will disappear off to university next year," he continued. "It might be nice to spend some time with them before they go. Get to know them. Make up for all that lost time while I was at work. All the growing-up years I missed."

If he was so concerned about the time he'd missed with his daughters, why on earth was he sitting on my roof in the middle of the night when he could be at home with them?

"What d'you think?" he prodded.

"Are you asking if I think you should retire?"

He turned to face me. "Yes."

I lifted my gaze to the sky, picking out Orion, Pegasus, and Cassiopeia, and finally said, "I have absolutely no opinion on the matter."

I shifted my chair forty-five degrees. There was Jupiter, clearly visible with the naked eye but probably spectacular through the telescope.

"Of course you don't," he said after a moment. "Silly of me to ask."

Then he drained the whisky glass and stood up.

"It's late. I suppose it's time I went home. Thank you for your hospitality, Professor. It was kind of you to invite me in."

"It wasn't a kindness," I said, standing as well. "I let you in because I want you to do something for me." I pulled out my mobile phone. "I want you to trace a license plate."

15

MY MIND WAS FOGGY THE FOLLOWING DAY, MAKING MY LEC-
ture a struggle, and I vowed never to answer the door or the phone
to DCI Roberts in the middle of the night ever again. It was a relief
that I had an hour of respite to spend alone in the lab before the
afternoon tutorials. However, when I arrived and found the door
open, that sense of relief scattered. Carla leaped at my entrance
and quickly pushed what I assumed to be the remains of a sandwich into her bag. I glared at her. Here she was flouting the no-
food rule again.

"What are you doing?" I asked.

"Cleaning," she replied, picking up a cloth. "How's your head?"

Immediately, I was reminded of how she'd taken control when
Giant Hogweed attacked me. How she'd got me to the dean's
office, how she'd even brought my glasses to the hospital, and all
thoughts of sandwiches vanished.

"It's getting better, thank you. It doesn't hurt as much."

"That's good news. By the way, you just missed the dean. He said he's been looking for you all morning."

"Did he say why?"

"No, but you have to go to his office. He said he emailed you because you weren't answering his calls. I told him you don't read emails—or answer your phone."

I looked at my watch. I had less than an hour before the tutorials started. The dean's office was on the top floor of the administration building. I should go.

I put my satchel on the counter and cast a scrutinizing eye over the lab, checking every surface and cabinet front, and conceded that the place was spotless. Carla had done a good job… apart from the kitchen area, again, where she'd left out the French press and two unwashed coffee cups. Again. I tutted loudly.

"You know the rules about hot drinks in here, Carla. I'll allow you to make coffee on the condition you wash and put everything away afterwards. There are two cups here, which means twice today you didn't wash up."

Color rose in her cheeks.

"This isn't the first time," I added pointedly.

"I'm sorry, Professor. It slipped my mind. I'll wash them now."

"An ordered environment makes for an ordered mind, and in a toxicology laboratory, order is vital."

She ducked her head. "Yes, Professor. It won't happen again."

꒰꒱

The dean seemed annoyed. With me or just generally, I couldn't tell. There was a man and a woman in his office, sitting on the opposite side of the dean's desk. I glanced at them then crossed to the only vacant chair. The man was enormous and only just fitted on his chair. In contrast, the woman was small, like a bird. They were staring at me. Taking in the dressing on my head, the bruising on my face.

"This is Mr. and Mrs. Bennett," the dean said as I sat. "They're Aaron's parents."

Ah... I thought and shifted uncomfortably, hoping they wouldn't ask what happened to my head, because what could I say? Their son had just died.

At least I thought I'd thought it. Turns out I'd spoken the thought aloud.

"Ah?" Mr. Bennett thundered. "Is that all you can say?"

"I'm sorry for your loss," I added quickly, fixing my eyes on the dean's ugly carpet tiles.

"This is your fault," he growled.

I looked up. "I beg your pardon?"

"Aaron sent us an email. He said if anything went wrong with his research, it would be your fault."

I shook my head vigorously. "I strongly refute—"

"You were his supervisor," he cut in. "You were responsible for him."

"I wasn't his supervisor."

"He told us you were."

I sighed heavily. "And I told him time and time again that I was not his supervisor. I was never his supervisor, and I never would be."

There was a pause. "Why would you never be his supervisor?"

How could I answer this? Because he was an unpredictable, violent young man whose intimidating behavior was well known throughout the university? I glanced at the dean. He was shaking his head while not shaking his head. Which was puzzling.

"Because—"

"Because," the dean immediately cut in, "the professor had too many demands on her time this year to take on this additional role. We were in the process of allocating him a new supervisor."

Mr. Bennett turned to the dean. "He said he wrote to you as well. Did you get his email?"

I looked at the dean. His eyebrows had pulled together, causing a vertical crease to form in his forehead. He was fiddling with objects on his desk.

"I—yes, I did receive an email."

"And what did you do about it?"

The dean inhaled deeply and put his hands on his lap. "Mr. Bennett. Aaron was—how can I put this—well known to me. He often wrote emails complaining about various members of staff and other students for things that he found to be unfair or unprofessional. I pursued the early complaints, but when each one turned out to be unfounded, I became more, er, circumspect when the next email arrived."

Mr. Bennett was silent while he absorbed these words.

"Are you telling me," he said in a low voice, "that when you received his last email, you ignored it?"

"I'd received so many, Mr. Bennett."

"But you ignored it?"

The dean inhaled deeply. "I'm afraid on this occasion I didn't treat it with the seriousness I now realize it deserved. Especially as it was the first time he'd complained about Professor Rose. He was a huge fan of the professor. In fact, I'd go so far as to say he revered her."

I frowned.

Mr. Bennett straightened in his chair. Even sitting down, he was close to my standing height. He was certainly intimidating. Much like his son.

"Then, because you chose to do nothing, my son's death is as much your fault as hers."

The dean lifted a hand in protest. "Mr. Bennett, it's only natural you're looking for someone to blame."

"Damn right, I'm looking for someone to blame," he shouted. "Nobody's telling us anything. We don't even know what actually killed him. All we've been told is he was found dead with a syringe in his arm."

Mrs. Bennett began to cry quietly, and the room fell silent to acknowledge her tears, but after a suitably respectful pause, I stood up and cleared my throat because, as the toxicologist in the room, it was time I shed light on the matter.

"Mr. Bennett, Aaron overdosed. He took a very high concentration of a substance extracted from a toxic plant. The plant contained tropane alkaloids, which bring on frightening and disturbing hallucinations. He also suffered a fever high enough to kill brain cells and cause the autonomic nervous system to fail. As the heart and lungs are regulated by the autonomic nervous system, Aaron most probably either suffocated to death when his lungs stopped working, or he died of heart failure."

"Shut up! Shut up!" Mrs. Bennett screamed, making me leap then sit down and shrink back in my chair, close my mouth, and drop my gaze to avoid meeting eyes with the dean, whom I could feel glowering at me.

"I'm so sorry this terrible, *terrible* accident happened," the dean said quickly to bring things back under control.

"This was no accident," Mr. Bennett shouted. "My boy was *murdered.*"

I looked up. "Murdered?"

"Yes. Murdered. My son would never deliberately inject himself with a poison that would give him terrifying hallucinations. He didn't take drugs."

I remembered what Carla and DS Chambers had said about

Giant Hogweed and Class A drugs. And I remembered his dilated pupils, the gurning, the agitated and unpredictable movements, and I wondered at the naivety of parents whose children can do no wrong.

I could hold my tongue no longer. "Aaron died from an overdose of *Datura* toxin. A highly hallucinogenic illegal drug."

"We aren't denying he died from an overdose," Mr. Bennett countered. "That much is blindingly obvious. What we can't accept, what we will never accept, is the part in the report that says he died from 'misadventure.' He did not accidentally do this to himself. Someone did it to him. Deliberately. And it would not have happened if you hadn't sent him down the 'synthetic toxins' rabbit hole in the first place."

"The what?" the dean asked.

"I didn't," I said weakly.

"If you'd allowed him access to your poisonous plant collection, his research would have been conducted in a controlled environment. He would have had you overseeing his work. He would have—"

"Mr. Bennett, Professor Rose no longer has a poisonous plant collection," the dean interrupted.

"Aaron didn't believe that. He said she was hiding the collection because it was illegal." He turned to me. "If you'd given him access, he wouldn't have got himself tangled up in the dark web."

"The dark web?" the dean gasped. "Professor Rose would never—"

"Stop defending her," he shouted. "You obviously have no idea what she's been up to."

The dean fell silent; then all eyes were on me. I cleared my throat again.

"He did show me a website he'd found that sold synthetic toxins," I said hesitantly. "But I strenuously dissuaded him from purchasing anything from it. I emphasized the uncertainty of the provenance, the danger, the illegality. I said everything I could to discourage him from buying anything. I thought I'd succeeded. I thought he'd given up on the idea, but he went ahead anyway."

"I don't believe you," Mr. Bennett said.

"I beg your pardon?"

"You might have said a few platitudes, but then you stepped back and let him do what he wanted because you wanted him to stop bothering you."

It was true I wanted him to stop bothering me, but I certainly didn't intentionally allow him to walk toward his death.

"I assure you, that's not what happened."

"You let him get involved with bad people, and maybe the deal went wrong and maybe he threatened to expose them. And maybe that's why they killed him."

I glanced at the dean. His jaw had dropped. His eyes were bulging. I saw a horrible vision of him giving me my marching orders. I'd lost my job once before. I certainly didn't want to lose it again.

"Conjecture," I said before I could stop myself.

"Conjecture?" Mr. Bennett roared, thumping the arm of his chair and leaping to his feet. "*Conjecture?*"

He was towering over me, and I couldn't help but glance up at his red face, where I saw the outrage in his eyes, I saw his wife cowering away from him, and I saw Giant Hogweed, thirty years from now…if he had lived.

"What the professor means," the dean said, attempting a placatory tone, "is that we don't know what happened. All that is known is Aaron died of an overdose, and there's no evidence to disprove it wasn't self-inflicted. I don't know what more we can say to you, Mr. and Mrs. Bennett, except that we are *truly* sorry for your loss."

Mr. Bennett turned round, and I was presented with his broad back. "We didn't come here for sympathy. What use is sympathy? We want action. The police aren't going to do anything. They've closed the case." He turned back to me. "You have to do something. My son's death was your fault. You have to find his killer."

I considered his words. I was certain Giant Hogweed's death had nothing to do with me. In fact, I'd go so far as to say that if he'd listened to me, he'd still be alive.

"That policeman said you'd help us." Mrs. Bennett's voice was high, fluting, and tremulous with emotion. "What was his name?" she asked her husband.

"Roberts."

"That's right—Mr. Roberts said you'd help us."

"Did he?" I asked, surprised.

"Yes. He said you were ever so clever."

She wasn't trying to flatter me. She was merely repeating DCI Roberts's words. Her shoulders were trembling, and she was staring at me with red, exhausted, pleading eyes.

"Sometimes you can't help wondering what you did wrong. As a parent, I mean."

The room quieted at her words, but the silence was quickly shattered by Mr. Bennett rounding on her and yelling, "Don't be so bloody absurd, Ginny!"

I watched her shrink back in her chair, saw the years of abuse etched in her face, and I heard myself say, "Alright, I'll talk to DCI Roberts. I'll see what I can do."

Why I said that, I have no idea. Talking to DCI Roberts was an empty promise because he didn't have the power to reopen the case. He couldn't help me at all. No. The only way to prove or disprove their son was murdered was to do it myself.

16

WHEN I ARRIVED AT THE TUTORIAL ROOM, THERE WAS A NOTE on the door from the students I was due to see. I can't say I was annoyed they'd canceled, because I had a lot on my mind and spending an hour dissecting essays on forensic botany, albeit fascinating, would have been a distraction. Straight away, I turned on my heel and headed for my office, because now that I'd decided to begin an investigation, it was all I could think about.

At my desk, I took Giant Hogweed's notebook out of my satchel and eyed my computer dubiously. I had no idea why the IT department insisted I have one. I wasn't even confident I knew how to turn it on.

I pressed a button on the keyboard and looked at the screen. Nothing happened. I pressed several buttons at once. Again, nothing. I let out a sigh, stood, and walked around to the other side of my desk, looking for a power button. There it was, and at last, the machine whirred into life. Victorious, I let out a whoop and returned to my chair. But the feeling rapidly dissipated when the screen changed. It was now covered in small icons, the purposes of which I had absolutely no idea.

I picked up the notebook and very slowly and carefully typed out the first line on the keyboard, then looked at the screen. There was no discernible difference as far as I could see. All the icons were exactly the same as they had been.

I sighed and dropped the book onto the desk, acknowledging that this was going to be much more difficult than I'd first thought. Then I remembered Giant Hogweed saying he didn't want to leave a digital trail. I wasn't sure what he'd meant at the time, but now I reconsidered what I was doing. If, somehow, I did manage to access the dark web using my work computer and IT found out, I would be in serious trouble. Quickly, I turned off the computer, hoping against hope that what I'd typed into it would somehow magically disappear.

Momentarily defeated, I sniffed deeply and leaned back in my chair to mull over an ever-growing list of questions. If Giant Hogweed went to all the trouble of buying the hallucinogen from the dark web, surely he would also have bought the other toxins he needed for his research? If he did, where had he hidden them? They weren't on or in his desk. I was sure of it, and if they'd been anywhere else in the flat, the police would have found them. But he didn't have the money to buy anything from the site. I touched the dressing on the side of my head. He'd made that very clear.

I don't know how long I sat there ruminating. I'd completely lost track of time because when I eventually checked my phone, there were three missed calls and a string of texts from Matilde, and when I looked at the time, I was astonished to see it was nine p.m.

"Damn!" I cried, leaping to my feet.

We'd arranged to meet at our favorite bar. I was an hour and a half late. Matilde was sitting at our usual table, reading a magazine, her legs neatly crossed beneath her. Over our many visits to this bar, I'd perfected a route from the front door to our table that avoided any contact with the fronds and tendrils of the various poisonous plants on the shelves and hanging from the ceiling, which the manager had insisted on keeping, despite my many complaints. I set off now, dodging and ducking my way across the floor until I thumped down on the chair opposite her, knocking the table with my knee and spilling her drink. She lifted her glass and placed a napkin underneath to mop up the wine.

"There you are, my darling. Where've you been?"

I was sweating. I'd run all the way from the bus stop. I took out my handkerchief and wiped my face. "I was in a meeting with the dean and the parents of the PhD student who died."

"Ah...that must have been difficult." She poured me a glass

of sparkling water. "But isn't it a bit late for a meeting? Couldn't it have been scheduled for during the day?"

"It was at five o'clock."

"And it went on this long?"

"No. I went to my office afterwards to think. I suppose I lost track of time."

"You did, my darling. You lost track of four hours. I hope all that thinking was productive?"

"It was. I think." I took a huge gulp of water and glanced at her. "Sorry I'm late."

She dropped her copy of *The Economist* into her bag. "It's alright. I'm used to it. I've learned to bring reading matter with me whenever we arrange to meet."

I think she was angry. It was hard to tell with Matilde because her natural speaking volume was so loud, it was difficult to differentiate her normal voice from her raised one. She made the smile that wasn't a smile. I drank more water.

"We need to have a little talk, Eustacia. That's why I wanted to meet this evening."

"Oh?" I said with curiosity.

"I want to ask you a question."

"Oh?" I said with caution.

She linked her fingers and put her small hands on the table. "Who am I?"

I paused to think. She wasn't looking for the literal answer, which was a Portuguese lecturer called Matilde Acosta. No. She was looking for something else. I furrowed my brow, and then the answer came to me. I opened my mouth.

"And don't say 'a strong, independent woman,'" she cut in.

I closed my mouth.

Matilde sighed. "Who am I to *you*, my darling? And don't say 'work colleague.'"

I cast my eyes around the bar, desperately trying to think of the right answer, but I was floundering, and I could tell it showed on my face.

"Eustacia!" she said loudly, making me snap to attention, making heads turn. "I'm talking about our relationship."

"Oh," I said with relief. "You're my…"

Matilde tilted her head, waiting for me to continue. When I didn't, she asked, "Your what?"

I blinked. We hadn't used labels before. I had no idea why she was asking to now, but then I reminded myself that I was determined my luck with love would change. "My…person?"

This appeared to be the correct answer, because Matilde's body relaxed. "That's right. I'm your person, and you're my person. And when people have people, they don't allow other people to barge in and try to steal that person away."

She'd lost me.

"Do you understand what I'm saying?"

I gave her a blank look.

"Okay, let's try this. Just because someone shows an interest in you, it doesn't mean you have to show an interest back. Interest doesn't have to be reciprocal. You can say no. You can say thank you, I'm flattered, but no."

I blinked at her, and she took both my hands.

"I've liked you for a very long time, Eustacia. You are my darling. But I'm getting the feeling you're turning away from me. Promise me… *Promise* me you won't let that pretty young police officer steal you away?"

Was this what Susan had meant about my head being turned? Did Matilde think I was going to run off with DS Chambers? I let out a guffaw. As if that would ever happen!

"Of course not," I said, grinning.

"Good. Because you may be naïve in many ways—and this is what I love about you—but you weren't born yesterday."

Okay. She'd lost me again. I waited for some further explanation. When none came, I asked, "Can I ask a question now?"

"Of course. Ask me anything."

I inhaled. "Do you know how to access the dark web?"

Her eyes flew open. "The *what*?"

"The dark web is a place where you can find companies that sell illegal products and services."

"I know what the dark web is."

"Good, because I want to buy something from it, but I don't know how."

"Eustacia…you are joking?"

I shook my head vigorously. "I'm very serious. I promised the PhD student's parents I'd find out who murdered their son."

"Murdered?" Matilde shouted, making heads turn again. "I thought it was an overdose."

"So did the police. They've closed the case, but his parents believe he uncovered an illegal synthetic toxins operation on the dark web and threatened to expose them, so they murdered him."

Matilde was staring at me. "And you promised his parents you'd find out who's running the operation?"

"I did."

"Are you *crazy*?"

"Obviously I'll be careful. I'll disguise my identity, use a false name. That kind of thing. I just need to know how to get onto the dark web in the first place. The student showed me the website. It has a black screen with a red skull in the middle."

"Eustacia! For God's sake!"

I looked at her. "Are you saying you don't know how to get onto the dark web?"

"Of course I don't!"

I slumped back in my chair, defeated yet again. She knew so much about the world from her newspapers and magazines. I was sure she would know this. I sighed dramatically. All those hours sitting at my desk, figuring out a plan to track down the supplier, purchase a substance, and take it to the police wasted because

I knew nothing. Because I was so *naïve*, I couldn't even work a computer.

"Listen, whatever you're thinking of doing, don't," Matilde said with urgency. "I mean it. This sounds very dangerous. I'm telling you, my darling. Don't do it."

"Can I have a sip of your wine?"

She exhaled. "Eustacia…you don't drink."

I picked up her glass and took a sip. It tasted vile. Then it occurred to me that there might be another way to find the operation. Maybe I didn't have to go searching for them with a computer; maybe I could search for them with my own legs.

I took another sip. It tasted worse than vile. Why people drank this stuff was beyond me.

17

THE LABORATORIES AT IMPERIAL COLLEGE LONDON
University were similar to mine but larger and more plentiful.
As they should be—this was a university of science after all. I'd
called my counterpart, a Professor Hutchins, that morning and
he'd seemed amenable to meeting with me. I was waiting for him
now in the pristine reception of the Life Sciences department,
feeling at once out of place and also as if there was no other place
I should be. When he arrived, I was very surprised to see that he
was wearing a tweed suit and steel-rimmed glasses, which was dis-
concerting. And when I stood to greet him, I noted that we were
the same height and build. In fact, the only difference I could see
between us was that he was completely bald.

"Professor Rose," he said with a pronounced lisp. "It's an absolute pleasure to meet you. I've heard so much about you."

"You have?" I asked. I hadn't heard anything about him.

"Oh, yes! I've been following your work for years. Decades even."

"You have?" I asked again.

"Oh, yes! Would you like to follow me? We can go to my office."

He led the way with short staccato steps, the heels of his shoes sounding loudly in the corridor.

"That paper you wrote on toxicokinetics. Fascinating," he threw over his shoulder, and I couldn't help nodding because I'd found the subject fascinating as well.

Soon we arrived at a door labeled with his name, and he pulled a chain from his trouser pocket, swung a bunch of keys up and into his hand, and unlocked the door. "Here we are," he said, holding the door open for me. "Home sweet home."

He gestured for me to sit and went to his own oversized chair behind his oversized desk. "Now, what can I do for you, Professor?"

I didn't hesitate. "Are you manufacturing synthetic toxins?"

His eyebrows came together. "Synthetic toxins?"

"Yes."

"Do you mean polyfluoroalkyl substances?"

"No."

"Not polychlorinated biphenyls? They've been banned for years…as you know."

"No. I mean synthetic replicas of naturally occurring plant toxins."

He paused. "We don't do that here."

"I know you're not *meant* to. I'm asking if you are?"

Again, he paused then sighed as if I'd disappointed him. "Now, why would we do that?"

"For profit," I replied. "Synthetic toxins are much easier and cheaper to mass manufacture than extracting poison from plants."

"It's also illegal," he added.

"I know."

He held up a hand. "Just to be clear...are you asking if I—or my colleagues or my students—are undertaking illegal experiments in these laboratories for the purpose of profit?"

I nodded vigorously, relieved that he was finally following. "That's exactly what I'm asking."

He covered his eyes with the hand he'd held up. "Professor," he began in a totally different voice, "I have to admit, I was very excited to receive your call this morning. I've admired you and your work for a long time. I was looking forward to discussing ideas with you. Perhaps even suggesting the possibility of a joint research project. But to discover that the only reason you wanted to meet with me was to accuse me of illegality is...how can I put this...crushing."

He exhaled another heavy sigh. "This is Imperial College London. One of the most elite science, engineering, and medical universities in the world. Our professors, lecturers, technicians, and staff are amongst the best in the world. Our academic research is highly acclaimed. Our international funding stream is rock solid. Our students are the brightest and the best in the world. Why on earth do you think we would risk that reputation by illegally manufacturing synthetic plant toxins"—his voice was becoming progressively louder and higher as he spoke, culminating in two high-pitched squeaks—"for profit?"

I gave him a moment to calm down before asking, "So you aren't manufacturing synthetic toxins?"

"No, we most certainly are not!" he shouted, leaping to his feet.

I stood as well. "In that case, I'll try Kings."

"Kings?" he cried. "For the love of God! If you value your reputation, don't go accusing Kings of criminality as well."

I thought of my reputation. In particular, of how it had been the last time I'd lost it. It had been devastating. Soul-destroying. I'd thought I would never recover.

I walked to his office door, but before passing through it, I turned back to him. "Thank you for your advice, Professor, but someone, somewhere is making these toxins and selling them on the dark web to people who most probably have no idea what they're buying." I paused. "And with or without yours or Kings' help, I intend to find out who it is."

On reflection, it probably wasn't a good idea to come straight out with the question. There were probably more subtle ways to find out if anyone was using his labs to make the toxins. But subtlety wasn't one of my strong points. In fact, I can say with confidence, I didn't understand it at all. I was also taken aback by his reaction. As far as I could see, I'd been perfectly reasonable. But then, if I reversed our positions, I suppose I would have been furious if he'd accused me of manufacturing synthetic plant toxins in my lab. And Kings would probably be just as furious. I could see now that searching for the lab with my legs was never going to work. I was back to square one.

I turned despondently to the door.

"Wait."

I turned back.

"If you put it like that, I'll help you. Tell me what you need me to do."

And straight away I replied, "Do you have a laptop? Preferably one that won't leave a digital trail?"

I don't know why he insisted we go to the Serpentine café in Hyde Park. Perhaps because he was worried someone in his department might discover what we were about to do. Or perhaps he just fancied a cup of tea with a view. We sat side by side at an outside table to avoid the café staff overhearing our conversation, and he pulled a laptop out of his bag and placed it on the table. It was covered with protest stickers declaring that "No one is illegal" and "End the hostile environment" and "Advertising shits in your head—it's a form of visual and psychological pollution." And the most prominent one: "Go frack yourself."

"Is that your laptop?" I asked as he logged into the café's Wi-Fi.

"Of course not. It belonged to an old overseas student. Okay, we're up and running. Give me the codes."

I opened the notebook and handed it to him. He was slower than Giant Hogweed with his one-finger typing, but eventually, he arrived at the black screen with the pulsating red skull.

"Frighteningly easy if you have the codes," he said. "But how did you get them in the first place?"

It was a moment before I realized this wasn't a rhetorical question. I glanced at him. I couldn't very well say *from a dead person.*

"I'm afraid that's confidential information. This is still a live investigation."

That was a lie, but he wasn't to know.

"Then why didn't you go to Digital Forensics? They can do all sorts of clever things with computers these days."

I thought quickly. "Because they have a huge caseload, and why would I let this sit at the bottom of it when you've just done in fifteen minutes what would've taken them weeks?"

That seemed to satisfy him because he nodded and moved the cursor over the skull. "Well? Shall we go for it?" he asked, his finger hovering over the keypad.

"Yes. Let's go for it."

He tapped the keypad, and the black screen opened a list of toxins.

"Look at that!" he cried. "*Cicuta maculata, Atropa belladonna,*

Ageratina altissima, Ricinus communis, Datura stramonium, Abrus precatorius, Nerium oleander. There's even *Nicotiana tabacum.* This is so exciting. Let's see what happens when we click on one. Which one would you like?"

"The *Datura.*"

He clicked on it, and the price appeared. One bottle was a thousand pounds. How could Giant Hogweed afford a thousand pounds?

"Shall we buy some?" Professor Hutchins asked.

"Absolutely not," I cried. "That would be highly illegal."

And for some strange reason this made him laugh. "Even if it wasn't, I couldn't begin to afford these prices. Could the police not pay for it? Are we not working undercover on a *sting* operation?"

I glanced at him. He was smiling broadly. I didn't trust myself with things like perception, and I certainly couldn't tell if his smile was genuine excitement or if he didn't for one second believe I was assisting the police, but I thought it best I stick with the story. "No, the police could not pay for it."

"But I thought the whole point was to find the people making these toxins. Surely the way to find them is to buy something?"

I paused as a thought occurred to me. "Even if we could afford these prices, how would we do it so the payment isn't traced back to us?"

"Now...that's a very good question, Professor. I'm certainly not going to let you use my credit card."

I thought of the purchases I'd made in the past, when I'd been building my poisonous plant collection—the clandestine midnight meetings with my courier, the envelopes of cash, the discreet packages slipped into Father's waxed overcoat pocket—and I had an idea.

I picked up Giant Hogweed's notebook and the laptop and stood. "May I borrow this?"

"You may, but you're not leaving already? What about your tea?"

I looked down at the pot. I'd completely forgotten about the tea. "How much do I owe you for it?"

"I don't want you to pay for it. I want you to sit down and drink it."

"We've done what we came here to do."

"Professor Rose, I made time for you this morning. In fact, I canceled an appointment so we could meet *and* I'm lending you a laptop. The least you can do is drink the tea I bought you."

I must admit, I did appreciate straightforward, forthright speaking, so I sat down again.

"And while you're here," he continued, smiling, "my department has a symposium coming up on ecotoxicology, and I've been asked to give the keynote talk. I'd love to pick your brain on the paper you wrote back in 2012 about the impact of plant toxins on ecosystems and their interactions with other organisms."

I distinctly remembered him saying he would help me, which

he'd just done. I did not remember him saying his offer of help came with conditions.

I sighed. "What do you want to know?"

18

AT THE BACK OF MY DESK DRAWER AT HOME WAS A SECRET COMpartment that required a key. Opening it was actually quite a convoluted process that required my getting to my knees and shining a flashlight at the keyhole. Once it was open, I felt around inside for a small black leather address book, held together with a piece of thick elastic. I removed this and flicked through the book until I found what I was looking for, then picked up the handset of my landline telephone and dialed the number. It took many rings for him to answer.

"Marco? It's the professor."

"Why are you calling me? We do not have conversations on the phone. I call, leave message. That is how we do business."

"I know...ordinarily, but I'd like you to make a special purchase for me using a different method to before."

"What different method?"

"I'd like you to buy me something from the dark web."

There was a pause. "The dark web?"

"Yes."

"No. I do not go near that place. That is not how I do business."

"It's just one purchase. One small sample of a synthetic toxin for an experiment, and I'm prepared to pay double your usual fee."

"No. I am a plant trader. I get you plant cuttings so you can grow a beautiful garden," he said. "I do not buy small samples of synthetic anything, and you should not buy synthetic anything either. You are a botanist."

"It's a synthetic substance made to replicate a toxin from a plant. It's not so far from what you do."

Silence.

"We've known each other for over twenty years," I continued. "We trust each other completely. Please make this small purchase for me just once; then I'll never ask you to do it again."

I heard sighing, tutting.

"If you want someone to buy you chemicals from the dark web, ask a drug dealer."

"How am I meant to do that? I don't know any drug dealers."

More loud breathing, more tutting.

I waited a moment. "Marco?"

"I am hanging up now. Do not call me again about this."

"No, wait. Wait." I didn't want to say this, but he was leaving me no choice. I inhaled. "I don't want to have to give your number to anyone…in authority."

Another silence. Much longer than the last one.

Eventually, he said, "After twenty years of a perfectly good business relationship, you are threatening me?"

Threatening was a strong word. I would have preferred *warning*.

"I said I *don't* want to have to do that. In fact, I'd like our relationship to stay the same as it's always been. Don't you want that as well? Honestly, this is just a one-off. It will never happen again."

I heard a deep sigh, then eventually, "Okay, okay. What is the web address?"

"Ah now…that's a bit complicated. Are you free this afternoon? I need to show you rather than tell you."

⚜

I cut across the traffic on Hampstead High Street and went into the bank to take out a thousand pounds in cash. Then with the envelope tucked safely in the inside pocket of my jacket, I re-crossed the road to the café where Marco was waiting for me. I was used to meeting him in the middle of the night in a secret location. In fact, I was so used to only ever seeing him in the half-light that I'd given him the nickname Moonflower. Latin name *Ipomoea alba*, a large white flower that blooms only at night and closes up at the first touch of morning dew. Seeing him now in the daylight, sitting in a café without his courier jacket, was so incongruous, I almost didn't recognize him.

He looked up as I approached but didn't stand, which was fine. There was no need for pleasantries.

"What happened?" he asked, waving a hand beside his own head. "Did someone hit you?"

"No. I had a small accident. It looks worse than it is."

He narrowed his eyes and shook his head as if he should be concerned, then decided he shouldn't be.

"There is something I want to say," he said as I sat down. "I did not like the way you threatened me on the telephone. It hurt my feelings."

I bowed my head. "I'm sorry about that."

"We worked well together for a very long time. There was no need for unpleasantness."

"You're right. I'm very sorry."

He inhaled deeply while he considered my apology then nodded. "Okay. That is done. You want coffee?"

"I don't drink coffee."

"Why? Because the caffeine toxin affects the central nervous system and can stimulate heart palpitations?"

"No. Because I don't like the taste."

He made a gesture with his mouth that made me think of a shrug. "You want something else then?"

"No, thank you." I took Professor Hutchins's laptop out of my satchel and put it on the table.

"You should have something. It is not right to sit in a café without buying anything."

I sighed. "Alright. If I have to, I'll have a small bottle of sparkling water."

I expected him to stand and go to the counter, but he didn't, so I flicked him a quick glance, and in return, he raised his eyebrows, looked at the counter then back to me, and I suddenly got it.

"Oh," I said, picking up his empty cup. "Shall I get you another?"

"I'll have a large flat white with oat milk and a sprinkle of chocolate. And two cookies. No, three cookies. The big ones."

I frowned, and he leaned back in his chair and folded his arms. We must have looked a strange couple, a strong, proud man with cropped hair, the sleeves of his T-shirt rolled up to show off his biceps, and me, a woman in her forties, in a man's suit and a large, now slightly grubby dressing taped over one side of my head.

"I'm doing you a massive favor," he added. "You buy the cookies."

When I returned, he'd moved seats so that his back was against the wall—I assumed to shield the laptop screen from view. I put the tray down and peered over the top; he'd already found the website and was scrolling through the pages.

"How did you do that?" I asked, genuinely impressed. I hadn't even given him the notebook.

"Browser history. You didn't delete the recent searches. Big mistake." He pushed a cookie into his mouth whole and spoke while he chewed. "Which one do you want to buy?"

"The *Datura*."

"You have that already. I got it for you years ago. Did you kill it?"

"Of course not," I said sharply, resenting the assumption that I would allow a plant to die. "I...lost it."

"Lost? How?"

I could feel him staring at me. "I don't like talking about it."

"Did you lose just that one?"

Inhaling deeply, I replied, "I lost them all."

"What?" he shouted, spraying me with a mouthful of crumbs. "I lost...them all."

He was silent for a long time. Long enough for me to glance at him and see the misery on his face.

"All that work," he said mournfully. "All those years of searching the globe for that one tiny root. All the negotiations, deals, delivery logistics. All the difficulties."

"I know. It's very sad."

"Not sad," he cried. "Criminal. Who did it? Did you catch them? Did you send them to prison?"

I made a noncommittal sound, and, patently very upset, he

fell silent again. Eventually he asked in a low voice, "Do you know how hard I worked for you?"

"Of course I do, Marco. I also know you're the best in the business, which is why I'm employing you again today."

He let out a humph of air. "You do not need me for this. There is no skill in this purchase. You just put in your card details and the postman delivers."

I looked at him. "You're correct—if all I was interested in was buying a toxin." I took the envelope of cash out of my pocket and slid it across the table. "But there's a little more to this job than that."

⟨⟩⟨⟩

Over the past year, I'd become accustomed to ignoring the red flashing light on my voicemail, but now I was expecting Marco's call, I checked it eagerly. After three days, I finally came home to the flashing light and pressed the play button with excitement.

Meet me at the café, same time tomorrow.

He was sitting at the same table, his back against the wall, his arms folded with his fists tucked under his biceps.

"You want a coffee?" he asked, obviously forgetting or ignoring my answer from the last time. He looked at his empty cup, and this time, I got the hint straight away.

"Same again?" I asked, picking it up.

When I returned, he was tapping a piece of paper on the tabletop.

"Is that the address of the lab?"

"Yes and no," he replied cryptically.

"What does that mean?" I asked, sitting down.

"It's just a kitchen."

"A kitchen?"

"Not a clean one. Dirty dishes piled up next to the sink. Floor filthy, rubbish bin overflowing."

This didn't sound right. Giant Hogweed had said the toxins were being manufactured with university-grade equipment, not in someone's kitchen.

"Are you sure you went to the right place?"

"It was the address I was given. They wanted to make the sale somewhere else at first, but I insisted on going to the lab. It didn't take much persuading, which made me think they were amateurs."

He put his hand over the piece of paper, moved it in front of me, and said in a low, deep voice, "Hold my hand."

I looked at him sharply. "I beg your pardon?"

"Cover my hand with yours."

I blinked, hesitated, then did it anyway and briefly saw how small my hand was in comparison before he pulled his out from under mine and I felt the object he'd just slipped me.

"*Datura*," he said quietly. "As instructed."

I wanted to look at it. Instead, I scooped it and the piece of paper into my satchel and handed him an envelope of cash under the table; payment for his services.

"Impressive scarring. What toxin was it?" he asked, slipping the envelope into his pocket.

"Urushiol. I brushed the back of my hand across a leaf last year. I was distracted. It was a stupid mistake."

He shrugged. "I've seen worse. You're a toxicologist. You should think of it as a badge of honor."

I lifted my ugly hand and turned it back and forth. The discolored, leather-like skin was so taut my fingers were permanently flexed. The nails were brown, the cuticles ragged, but Marco was right. One couldn't become a toxicologist without accepting the inevitable risk of accidents.

"Tell me everything," I said. "From the moment you first stepped through the door."

He took a mouthful of coffee. "I don't think I met the chemist, just some kid. Early twenties maybe. When he took the bottle out of the fridge, I saw all the food. Some way past the sell-by date. He didn't talk, just took the cash and gave me a bottle. As I was leaving, a woman was arriving. Very strange. It seemed like she was trying to hide her identity. Wide-brimmed hat, dark glasses. I wondered why she wanted toxins from this filthy place. It wasn't a respectable place for someone like her."

A thought struck me, making me stand up and turn for the door. Then, even though we didn't do pleasantries, I turned back.

"Thank you, Marco. You've been very helpful."

He nodded.

"I'll be in touch if I need you for anything else."

He nodded again and pushed a cookie into his mouth.

19

THE DUTY OFFICER INFORMED ME THAT DCI ROBERTS WASN'T at the station, which was annoying considering I'd rushed all the way there from Hampstead. What was even more irksome was his refusal to allow me into DCI Roberts's office in his absence. To be fair, I however, wasn't sure how to find what I was looking for even if he had. Luckily, as I was leaving, I caught sight of DS Chambers going through a door. The duty officer was distracted, so I slipped past him and followed her to an open-plan office full of desks and computers, low murmurs, and officers tapping keyboards. She sat at one of the desks and took out her notepad, so I dragged a chair across the office and positioned it next to hers.

"I need access to the CCTV footage of the night Charlie Simmonds was attacked."

She turned to me but said nothing.

I glanced at her. "I said I need access—"

"I heard what you said."

I waited.

"Eustacia…"

"Professor," I corrected.

"It's normal to say 'hello' or 'excuse me' as an opener."

And I waited.

"But I guess you don't do normal."

"I need access to the CCTV footage."

"Are we going to talk about what happened at the gym?"

What happened at the gym? If she meant me throwing her across the room, there was really nothing to talk about. I'd passed the point where I expected congratulations.

"I just need to see the CCTV footage." And I waited again then added, "Please."

With a head shake, she turned back to her computer. "There's footage from two different cameras. Which one do you want?"

"The one pointing toward Walker's Court."

She double-clicked a file on her monitor, and the footage filled the screen. It began with Simmonds entering the pub then the street fight. Simmonds writhing on the pavement. The men throwing punches. The shove that smashed the shop window.

"Rewind."

"How far?" she asked.

"To when Simmonds first goes into the pub."

There he was. I leaned closer, my face up against the screen. "Now then, let's see who follows him in."

"I've been thinking about you," she said. "To be honest, I've been a bit worried. You left the gym so abruptly. I've been wondering if I did something to upset you."

"Stop talking," I said sharply. "I need to concentrate."

Berwick Street was busy, the pavement crowded. The pub was popular because I counted at least twenty people enter after Simmonds. None of them the person I was looking for. I watched at double speed until he comically rolled out of the delivery hatch.

"Again."

DS Chambers didn't respond.

I glanced at her. "I need to watch this again."

"Are you asking me to rewind?"

I gave her the look I reserved for particularly dim students and repeated very slowly, "Could—you—go—back—to—the—same—place—but—play—it—at—normal—speed?"

She smiled, which was puzzling, but did as I asked. This time, I focused on the large group that had entered as one and shouted, "Stop! Pause!"

She clicked the mouse, and the image froze. I leaned even closer, squinted, and jumped up.

"What do you see?"

But I was already halfway across the office, marching toward the exit.

She was beside me in seconds, taking hold of my wrist and pulling me to a stop. "Wait. I need to talk to you."

"I'm very busy."

"It'll just take a minute."

Tutting with impatience, I lifted my eyes to the ceiling.

"Roberts asked me to trace a number plate for you," she continued.

At once, she had my full attention.

"I have an address." She took out her mobile. "Give me your number. I'll text it to you."

I gave her phone a side look and thought of Matilde. There were many things I may have been naïve about, but I wasn't born yesterday. "Write it down for me."

"You just said you're very busy. Give me your number. It won't take a second."

"Write it down and give it to DCI Roberts. I'll get it from him another time."

She was still holding my wrist. "Get it from *me* another time. Do you know Burnt Amber? The bar on Camden High Street? Meet me there tomorrow night at eight, and I'll give you the address."

KK

I'd never been to West London—apart from passing through it with Father on our countless visits to the science and natural history museums. It was a melting pot of contradictions, wide tree-lined roads with imposing houses right up against tower blocks. Designer shops and fine dining restaurants two steps away from market stalls. Gleaming Teslas parked next to filthy vans. I stood in front of a tired-looking low-rise flat building, holding the address Marco had given me, wondering if this was a mistake.

It took several rounds of knocking and many more doorbell rings before someone opened the front door. And when he finally did, he greeted me in a stained gray T-shirt that may once have been white and a pair of baggy boxer shorts the same color. His hair looked like it had been a while since it'd seen a hairbrush, and there was a large wad of sleep in the corner of one eye. He had the appearance of someone who'd been dragged from his bed by his ankles, even though it was two o'clock in the afternoon. I shook my head at the sight of him and ascended the front steps.

"I'm here to buy some *Psychotria viridis*," I said in a conspiratorial whisper.

"You what?"

"I'm here…" I began again. "I heard I could buy DMT here?"

"Oh…yeah. Come in."

He turned and walked along a hallway, and I stepped inside and closed the door behind me. Following him wasn't easy because of the three bikes, the mountain of shoes, the skateboards, and the traffic cone, but I finally arrived at the kitchen door as he was filling the kettle.

"I don't want a cup of tea," I said.

"Didn't offer you one."

He flicked on the switch and peeled back the lid of a tub of instant noodles and I looked around the room. Marco was right. It was filthy.

"Does the manufacturing take place in here?" I asked, my nostrils flaring in distaste.

He shrugged, which I took to be an affirmative.

"With what?"

He poured the boiling water over the noodles. "You what?"

"With what equipment?"

"I don't know. This isn't my side hustle. It's my pal's."

I had no idea what he was talking about, so I tried again. "Was laboratory equipment used in the manufacture or simple kitchen utensils?"

He rubbed his eye thoughtfully as if I'd asked a complicated question, found the wad of sleep, inspected it, and flicked it onto the floor. "You what?"

What was wrong with the man? Then I knew. He was a poison ivy, *Toxicodendron radicans*. A highly irritating individual.

"Are you hard of hearing?"

He glanced at me. "Rude."

"I beg your pardon?"

"You're rude." He stab-stirred the noodles with a fork. "Listen, I've got stuff to do. What d'you wanna buy?"

I didn't want to buy anything, but I couldn't tell him this.

"I'd like to know about the manufacturing process before I part with my money."

"Why?"

"Because." I wasn't sure what to say. "Because it's interesting."

He scooped a forkful of noodles into his mouth with a slurp and spoke through them. "You want to have a go at making this stuff yourself? You won't be able to. It's really complex, really difficult science." He slurped up another forkful. "So don't even think about stealing the recipe because you wouldn't be able to cook this shit, even if you had it. Now, stop wasting my time. Either buy the DMT or leave."

"I'm not sure I want DMT now. I'm still deciding. Can I see what else you have?"

He opened the fridge, revealing rows of small glass bottles packed into the door shelves. There must have been over a hundred. I couldn't help but gasp at the sight.

"What do you want? Poison? Or d'you just wanna get high?"

I glanced at him and saw boredom. He quite clearly had no idea what was being stored in his fridge right next to his food.

"I've changed my mind. I don't want to buy anything."

His eyes narrowed. "I knew you were a time waster," he said with a nasty edge to his voice. "I knew it the moment I opened the door." He threw the empty noodle pot in the general direction of the rubbish bin and added, "Off you go then, rude time waster."

I sniffed, resisting the urge to throw back a hygiene-related insult of my own, but something about his demeanor had changed. He was no longer the hapless friend who seemed not to truly know what was going on under his nose. He'd become the alpha, jealously guarding his territory and everything within it. He stepped forward, chest first, and I turned for the front door. But as I was negotiating my way past the clutter in the hall, I caught sight of something on the floor next to the wall. Something I thought I recognized. I slowed to study it, but he was right behind me, herding me forward with his body like a security guard.

"Keep moving," he said then shoved me aggressively in the small of the back, and almost instinctively, I spun round, grabbed him by a shoulder and an arm, kicked his legs out from under him, and threw him to the floor. It wasn't perfect. It wasn't what DS Chambers had taught me, and I certainly wasn't going to hang around to celebrate. But, in the chaos of the shouting and falling bikes, I bent down, grabbed the item from the floor, and dashed out the door.

20

THE FOLLOWING DAY, I HEADED WEST AGAIN. THIS TIME SO FAR west that I was no longer in London. But I knew Bourne End. It was between London and Oxford, and sometimes Father and I would stop en route for a walk beside the Thames and a pint of beer. I didn't have the beer, of course, but I liked making daisy chains in the pub garden while Father drank his pint and read the paper.

I got off the bus in the town center and took out my phone. Susan had shown me the ingenious trick of typing a destination into it to receive directions. I typed the address in now and followed the dotted line on the map to the end of the high street, down a private road, and along a profusely potholed single-track lane. After two hundred meters, I came across a house partially hidden behind a group of beech trees and, checking my phone, realized I'd arrived at Giant Hogweed's parents' house.

I walked further past the trees and saw that it wasn't a house. It was a manor, with a circular driveway lined with mature topiary yew trees. I thought again of him insisting he couldn't afford the synthetic toxins and let out a low whistle. This was a whole other level of wealth. Whatever Mr. Bennett had paid to build my lab was probably small change for him. Clicking my tongue, I crunched my way up the long, graveled driveway to the enormous front door.

At my very first knock, it opened instantly and violently to reveal Mr. Bennett, his huge bulk blocking my view of the interior. I admit, his sudden appearance made me stagger, but I righted myself quickly and nodded a hello.

"Come in, Professor. We've been expecting you."

Judging by the speed he'd opened the door, I expected he'd been expecting me very keenly indeed. He moved to one side so I could step past him into the hall, and I had to suppress a gasp because it was indeed a *hall*. A vast one, with a grand staircase snaking up and away in two directions and a mahogany fireplace as tall as Mr. Bennett himself.

"Coffee?"

"I don't drink coffee," I said, my eyes lifting above the fireplace to an imposing oil painting of a woman on horseback, an imperial expression on her face.

"My great-grandmother," Mr. Bennett said, following my gaze. "Now *she* was a woman. Tea then?"

I glanced at him. "Alright. I'll take a cup of Earl Gray. Black. Weak."

"Did you get that?"

Turning to see whom he was talking to, I found the diminutive Mrs. Bennett standing meekly against the opposite wall, and I instantly knew what she was. She was a touch-me-not, *Mimosa pudica*. The shy, creeping annual with sensitive compound leaves that fold inward when touched.

"Hello," I said, and she quickly disappeared down a dark corridor.

"Let's go to the orangery," Mr. Bennett said, crossing the hall with long, purposeful strides.

"The orangery?"

"Follow me. She'll bring the tea."

He moved rapidly across a huge sitting room that contained at least six sofas to a set of French doors that he threw open and passed through at speed, and I trotted along behind, trying to keep up. Outside, he crossed a Yorkstone terrace—planted with sedum, rosemary, and achilleas—and entered an impressive Victorian glasshouse that ran along the whole length of one side of the house. My jaw dropped as I followed him in. This wasn't only an orangery. It contained much more than citrus trees. It felt like I'd entered the national collection of rare and unusual pelargoniums. I'd never seen so many, and that smell—that particular hot, heady pelargonium-leaf smell—was so intense, it was hard to fill my lungs. I let out a sound that was intended to express surprise but that in fact sounded like a moan of ecstasy. I was truly awestruck.

Mr. Bennett spun to face me and waved a hand in the general direction of some white-painted Lloyd Loom chairs. "Take a seat."

I did as I was told because, frankly, I was feeling quite overwhelmed by my surroundings.

"I have so many questions," he said, pacing the length of the glasshouse, his body coiled tight. "But I promised I'd wait for her." He snapped his head to the door. "Where is she?"

"I'm sure she won't be long."

"She's so bloody slow. Always has been. It's enough to drive a man—" But he stopped as Mrs. Bennett entered the glasshouse carrying a tray. "At last! What took you so long?"

In my estimation, it had only been five minutes.

"I didn't steep the leaves," she said, handing me a cup and saucer. "I left the pot just one minute before I poured."

"That's kind of you." I took a sip and placed the cup on a side table. "It's perfect. Thank you."

"So? Have you found the bastard?" Mr. Bennett asked.

I turned to him. "Not yet."

"Why not?"

"Because these things take time, Mr. Bennett. This is a very complex case. There are many different leads to follow."

"Call us Ginny and Jonty," Mrs. Bennett said.

He shot her a look. "No, she bloody well may not call us Ginny and Jonty." Then he turned back to me. "Why are you here then, if it's not to tell us you've found the bastard?"

"I'm here to ask for your help." I took the photocopy of the plant list out of my pocket and handed it to him. "Does this mean anything to you?"

He gave it a cursory scan. "What is it?"

"A list of plant names. It was found with Aaron when…"

He threw the piece of paper at his wife. "Ask her. The garden's her department. Now, if you've nothing important to tell us, I have better things to be doing with my time."

I waited for him to leave, but he stayed where he was, glaring at me.

"Well? Do you have anything important to tell us?"

I shook my head. "I just want to know about the list."

He huffed, spun around, marched to a chair in the far corner of the orangery, and sat down heavily. I thought he wanted to leave to do the better things, but it appeared he still wanted to be part of the conversation.

Beside me, Mrs. Bennett sighed. "Mr. Bennett's very upset."

She stood, picked up the piece of paper, and moved her Lloyd Loom next to mine so we could look at the list together.

"These are common plant names, but you must know that already," she said. "None of them are poisonous. I thought his PhD was about poisonous plants?"

"It was."

"Then why did he write this?"

"I was hoping you'd tell me."

She ran a finger down the plant names slowly. "Cat's claw, snowbush rose, globe thistle...maybe it's a code? He used to love inventing codes with his little brother. They spent hours writing secret messages to each other. If his brother were here now, he'd crack this straight away."

I frowned. It hadn't occurred to me that Giant Hogweed would have siblings. He seemed too self-focused, too self-interested to have shared his childhood with another.

"Where is Aaron's brother?"

There was a pause before she answered. "He died. Last year."

From the corner of the orangery, Mr. Bennett's brooding presence was palpable. I glanced at him. His legs were crossed. His arms were folded. His hands were fists. He was staring through the glass roof at the sky, a muscle in his jaw clenching rhythmically.

"The police said he was larking about with friends at a building site; they were daring each other to climb the scaffold," Mrs. Bennett continued. "They said he slipped and fell."

"Rubbish," Mr. Bennett shouted, making me leap. "Those kids they said he was with weren't his friends. They lured him to that building site. They knew he was terrified of heights, and they forced him to climb the scaffold anyway. They must have done.

There's no way he would have climbed it of his own free will." His tone changed. "But he was too much like his mother... He didn't stand up to them."

So this explained their distrust of the police. This explained Mr. Bennett's bullish and Mrs. Bennett's meek behavior. In simple terms, he was angry, and she was sad that both of their sons were dead. It must also have been the darkness within Giant Hogweed that was not necessarily of his own making. The darkness within them all. A whole family of troubled souls.

The correct response should be *I'm sorry for your loss...losses.* But that seemed woefully inadequate. Instead, before I could stop myself, I said, "What rotten luck."

A silence descended that lasted until Mr. Bennett broke it by saying quietly, "Nothing to do with luck. Both our boys were murdered, but the police want nothing to do with it. They want nothing to do with us..."

I thought about this. "Do you know anyone who had a reason to kill Aaron?"

"The criminals behind the synthetic toxins," Mr. Bennett said. "I already told you that."

"Other than them?" I asked.

Mrs. Bennett shook her head. "Since his brother died, he developed—how can I put this—a prickly personality, unsociable traits, a brusque manner, which, understandably, people were wary of."

"Having a prickly personality isn't a reason for murder," Mr. Bennett cut in.

"No. But it meant he wasn't popular. He found making friends difficult at the best of times. So after…what happened…he stopped trying and threw all his energies into his studies instead. He'd fallen behind, what with everything that happened. He had to catch up. It made him a little insular. A little too focused on one thing. It also made him anxious, prone to insomnia. It was a very difficult time for him."

"Difficult enough for him to turn to drugs?" I asked. "Marijuana, say? To help with his anxiety?"

She looked at me sharply.

"Did he then progress onto something stronger?" I pushed.

Mr. Bennett let out a growl. "Aaron was not an addict. He wasn't interested in all that. He said drugs made him paranoid."

I turned to him. "How did he know they made him paranoid if he didn't take them?"

"Well, obviously, he tried them to know he didn't like them."

A thought struck me. I stood up and took the note out of Mrs. Bennett's hand. "I have to go."

Mr. Bennett stood as well and blocked the door. "Why? What are you thinking?"

I looked up at him then quickly away. "I don't know what I'm thinking."

It was true. I really didn't know. I was just having a feeling that

I couldn't yet explain.

"You must be thinking something, or you wouldn't have jumped up like that. You have to tell us."

"As soon as I have anything, you will be the first to know, Mr. Bennett."

He looked down at me, the muscle in his jaw clenching, but eventually stepped to one side. "Alright, but you can see how my poor wife's suffering. You have to keep us in the loop."

When I was thirteen, Father told me about something called a "demonstration of humanity," which he explained was an unexpected glimpse of vulnerability in a hard-hearted person. He was reading me *Wuthering Heights* at the time. He always read to me because I didn't have the attention to finish a whole novel by myself. He'd reached the part where Heathcliff was consumed by grief after Catherine's death. Father said Heathcliff was a hard-hearted man, but his despair demonstrated vulnerability through his intense longing for her. All these years later, I think I now had an inkling of what Father had meant, because behind Mr. Bennett's anger and bluster, I could definitely see a demonstration of humanity. I could see he was frightened... I suppose even bullies get scared sometimes.

Two hours later, I was walking up the stairs at the university, consumed by the thought that had struck me at the Bennetts' house. If the *Datura* injected into Charlie Simmonds's jugular—a major artery—hadn't killed him, how had Giant Hogweed died from exactly the same toxin being injected into a much smaller vein? Had there been something else in his system at the time the *Datura* had entered his body? There was a small amount of blood left in his test tube, and I intended to find out what it might be.

I left the stairwell and headed for the lab, wondering if Carla's and DS Chambers's observations about him had been right and his parents were wrong. Maybe he'd taken MDMA and followed it up with the synthetic *Datura,* and maybe it was this combination that'd killed him.

I took my lanyard and key card from my pocket but stopped when I saw the door to the lab was already open. I pushed it and found Carla standing behind the counter wearing a lab coat and protective glasses.

"Hello. What are you doing here?" I asked.

She looked up, smiled, and answered brightly, "Research."

"But it's the weekend."

"I know. You said I could use the lab the first Saturday of every month."

I frowned. I had absolutely no recollection of saying this, and I certainly wouldn't have agreed to student experimentation without supervision, even if they were a postgraduate.

"I don't think I did, Carla."

She took off the glasses and looked at me with an open expression. "You did, Professor. It's the reason I wanted to be your assistant. In my interview, I asked if I could use the lab on weekends."

I hesitated. There had been a great many interviews because a great many students had wanted to be my assistant, and I must admit, I didn't recollect every word that had been spoken. But still, it seemed highly unlikely.

"You said yes," she continued, interrupting the thought. "But only one Saturday a month because you needed the lab the rest of the non-teaching days for your own research. We agreed on the first Saturday of the month."

She waited for me to say something. When I didn't, she added, "Today's the first Saturday of the month."

Again, she waited, smiling, while I tried to recall the conversation.

"Anyway, I've been here all morning. I've done enough for today. I'll pack up and get out of your way."

"What have you been doing?"

"What?" she asked.

"What are you working on?"

I wasn't her supervisor, but I had a broad overview of the PhD subjects for that year.

"Plant hormones in root development. I've been treating the roots of my control plants with different hormone combinations, auxins, cytokines, gibberellins. The plants are all back in the cold frame now. Next time I'm going to check the effects of the hormones on root growth and architecture and compare them with the untreated plants."

"And the purpose of the study is?" I asked, suddenly interested.

"To analyze root morphology, gene expression, and hormone response pathways for the purpose of developing disease resistance."

"Sounds fascinating," I said, coming into the room and putting on a lab coat.

"So you're not angry with me?"

I shook my head. "I'm not angry, but I do need the lab."

While she was packing up, she asked, "I know you're not my supervisor, but if you have some time, could you check my results?"

I didn't hesitate. "I don't have time. I'm very busy." But when her expression turned crestfallen, I added, "Today. I don't have time today. I'll take a look soon," which was unusual, because ordinarily, I didn't respond to crestfallen expressions.

It turned out to be fiddly work running the test. There'd been so little blood left that I'd only been able to collect a trace sample, which all but disappeared in the drop of suspension fluid on the slide. It was enough, however, to confirm the absence of MDMA, or any other class A drug.

I moved my head away from the microscope. Either Carla and DS Chambers were mistaken about his drug use, or Giant Hogweed was serious about trying to change and had managed to stay clean since his expulsion. But if he didn't die from the synthetic *Datura* on its own, could there have been another substance in his body that had combined with it to kill him? I thought back to what else Mrs. Bennett had said. Something about anxiety... insomnia, then picked up the test tube and lifted it to the light. There was a smear of blood on one side of the lip. It wasn't much. Possibly not enough. But it would have to do.

It was a simple test, because I already had a notion of what to test for. As soon as it was done, I went to the Department of Pharmacology and asked a technician if they could spare a couple of pregabalin tablets. She was hesitant at first, but after I assured her it was for a controlled experiment, she agreed. While she was dispensing, she told me that although pregabalin was primarily used to treat epilepsy, it was also being prescribed by psychiatrists for anxiety and insomnia. I paused. This must have been what he'd meant when he'd said he was getting help. He was taking medication. She added that the pills must only be taken in the evening because they caused profound sleepiness.

"Profound sleepiness?" I asked.

"Yes, that's why they're an effective treatment for insomnia."

Another thought struck me. "What happens if you take too much?"

"You'll be knocked out. Most probably for hours."

"That's it," I cried. "That has to be it! Thank you. You've been very helpful."

I was suddenly eager to get back to the lab. So eager that halfway down the corridor, I broke into a flat-footed jog and didn't stop until I pushed open the lab door. I went straight to my satchel and took out the small bottle of synthetic *Datura* Marco had bought for me, placed it on the counter next to the pregabalin, and set to work.

21

I CHECKED MY WATCH. IT WAS EIGHT P.M. PRECISELY. THE BAR wasn't an establishment I would ordinarily enter; it was overly busy and playing the loud, discordant music that made me highly anxious. I much preferred the quiet place Matilde and I frequented, even with its abundance of toxic plants.

I was about to enter when I caught sight of my reflection in the bar's front window. The dressing on my head was in danger of coming loose. I could have attempted to reapply it; instead, I ripped it off and threw it into a street bin. I checked my reflection again, brushed my fringe the wrong way with my fingers to cover the Steri-Strips, and pushed open the door.

Inside, I scanned the space for DS Chambers and spotted her sitting on a tall stool at the crowded bar, her bag claiming the empty stool beside her. I took a deep breath to steady my nerves and threaded my way through the tables toward her.

"Do you have the address?" I shouted when I arrived.

She turned to face me, smiled, and shouted back, "Hey, babe. I like what you've done with your hair."

I frowned and brushed my fringe the wrong way again, trying to ignore how uncomfortable it felt. "The address?"

"I promised you a cocktail." She picked up one of two brightly colored drinks that were on the bar in front of her. "Here—it's got strawberries in it."

"I told you: I don't drink."

"There's no alcohol. Take it."

I eyed it with suspicion. "No, thank you. Do you have the address?"

She put the glass back down. "You're not good in social settings, are you?"

I ignored the irrelevant observation. "It's too loud. Just give me the address so I can leave."

She turned away, took a sip of her orange drink, and said something I couldn't hear.

I stepped closer. "What did you say?"

Again, I didn't hear so moved closer still. "What—"

"I said," she said, turning to face me, "let's sit at the bar and have a drink together. Let's watch the cocktails being made. Let's have some fun. You know what fun is, right?"

I thought about the thrill of going to the secret rendezvous in the dead of night to purchase a new root cutting, the rush of slowly peeling open the package to see if it had survived the journey, the excitement of the potting and propagating process, the ecstasy when a new shoot appeared through the surface of the compost. Yes, I knew what fun was. I also knew watching stressed bar staff slopping alcohol and sugar syrup into glasses filled to the brim with crushed ice then squashing in fruit was not it.

"I don't feel comfortable here. I'm leaving."

Straight away, her hand was on my arm, stopping me. She scanned the bar and nodded to an empty table at the back.

"Okay. Let's move over there. It'll be quieter." She handed me the bright pink drink. "Carry this."

I had no intention of touching one drop of it, but I put it down on the marginally quieter table and sat. She was sitting beside me, watching other people, so I took the opportunity to give her a brief, appraising look. She wasn't in her usual floral-print blouse and sensible dark blue trousers. Instead, she was wearing a moss-green silk dress that made her eyes appear very blue. And her hair wasn't tied back in a tight ponytail. It was loose and wavy and soft. I looked quickly away.

"Can I have the address now?"

She sipped her drink, taking her time. "Sure. But first, I want your opinion on something."

"My opinion?"

She turned her chair to face me. "What do you think of Roberts?"

"Detective Chief Inspector Roberts," I corrected. "I don't have an opinion about him, so if you'll just give me the address, I'll be on my way."

It wasn't true. I had very strong opinions about DCI Roberts, but I wasn't going to share them with her because I suspected she might use them as a weapon.

"I do," she said. "He's a cleaner."

I frowned. "A cleaner?"

"Yeah. A bad one. All he does is sweep everything under the rug. So many of his cases didn't go to trial because he couldn't be bothered to get enough evidence for the CPS." She took a sip of her cocktail. "You know, he's absolutely fuming I read those case files, and it's obvious why. He doesn't want me to know about his lazy policing, his mistakes."

There were many words I could use to describe DCI Roberts's policing methods, manipulating, cunning, obfuscating, nebulous, illogical...but lazy was not among them. I knew what time he left his office every night. I knew the off-duty hours he put in, and I doubted DS Chambers came anywhere close to his level of commitment.

"He's doing it again with Aaron Bennett," she continued. "Sweeping everything under the rug. Did you know his parents came to see me?"

I didn't, and I have to admit I was surprised. Why would they do that when I'd already told them I'd help? "Why?"

"Because they were furious with Roberts's decision to close the case, of course."

My heart sank. The last thing I needed was DS Chambers elbowing her way into my investigation.

"It wasn't his decision," I said. "It was the superintendent's."

She made an expression that clearly indicated she already knew this.

"What did you say to them?"

"I told them I couldn't do anything because the case was closed."

My shoulders sagged with relief.

"Anyway," she added, "I'm not interested in some junkie accidentally overdosing because he was an idiot."

I frowned. Giant Hogweed was many things but certainly not an idiot.

She must have seen my displeasure because she abruptly changed the subject. "So, tell me. Do you prefer on-duty or off-duty Barberry?"

"I beg your pardon?"

"Do you like me more as a police officer or a civilian? I like you in the old-man suit, but when I saw you in your lab, wearing that white coat… What can I say? You looked hot."

I shook my head at this obvious inaccuracy. "The temperature in the lab is meticulously regulated to be beneficial to the storage of the phials. At no point does the lab ever get hot."

For some unfathomable reason, this made her laugh.

"You're hilarious," she said when she'd calmed down. "Funny and clever. That's an intoxicating combination."

Her laugh subsided into a smile and a head tilt. "Your tiny girlfriend with the loud voice—what's her name?"

I didn't reply. It was none of her business.

"What's her name?" she asked again.

"Matilde."

"*Matilde*. Sounds foreign. She sounded foreign as well. Where's she from?"

This was absolutely none of her business. "Portugal."

"Portuguese, petite, and pretty. How's a sporty girl from the valleys ever going to compete with that?"

I flicked her a quick glance, not one hundred percent sure I understood what she was saying, but then she surprised me by adding, "You're not as into her as she's into you."

It wasn't a question. At least I don't think it was because I heard no upward inflection at the end, which meant she was making an assumption. An offensive one.

I sniffed with disapproval. "Matilde is my person. Our affections are mutual."

She let out a snort. "Didn't look that way to me."

"What's that supposed to mean?"

"You wiped your cheek after she kissed you."

"That's..." I began, suddenly flustered. "That's no indication of my lack of affection. I simply cannot abide other people's bodily fluids."

She was silent a moment. "Then how do you…"

I flicked her a quick look. Her brow was furrowed, her eyes narrowed.

"How do I what?" I asked.

Her eyes narrowed even more. "Never mind. It's none of my business."

I stood up. "No. It most certainly is not. Now, give me the address before you say something else to offend me."

DS Chambers stood as well. "I'm sorry. I can be quite direct sometimes. That's something we have in common." She took a piece of paper out of her bag, and I looked at it expectantly. "To be honest, I invited you for a drink to see if there was anything going on between us. If there was a spark. Even a tiny one. You see, I've been a bit confused."

I held my hand out for the piece of paper. She kept hold of it. "But I guess there isn't anything. Not for you anyway. Besides, even if you're not so into her, I can see you're never going to leave your tiny girlfriend."

This was becoming tedious. "Are you going to give me that address, or what?"

This made her laugh again. Not the happy laugh like before—a joyless one that didn't involve her eyes.

"My God, you can be cruel."

Cruel? I blinked at her. I truly had no idea what she was expecting from me. She'd told me to meet her at the bar so she could give me the address, and it was right there in her hand.

"DS Chambers—"

"Helen. My name's Helen. Or Barberry. You choose."

"DS Chambers. I'm very tired. My head hurts. I feel dizzy. I don't like crowded, noisy places, and I don't drink. Not even *mock*tails. I really just want to go home. So please…may I have that address?"

ƙƙ

It was past ten o'clock. I was exhausted, but there was no way I would sleep with this racing mind. I let myself into my building and silently climbed the stairs. Inside the flat, I went to my desk and sat down. What I didn't understand was, whereas Simmonds had been attacked in public, Giant Hogweed had been at home. Everything pointed to him injecting himself and overdosing, except for the fact that I'd now established he had double the amount of pregabalin in his system than he should have had. Which meant he could have been deeply asleep, making it easy for someone to sneak in, inject him, then make it look like he'd done it himself. The tourniquet was a nice touch. Clever.

If he was murdered, did the killer know he'd taken too much pregabalin, or did they just get lucky? And how did they get in?

It wasn't the easiest flat to access. Had they hung around outside his building waiting for someone to come out so they could slip in, like I had? Had he conveniently left his front door open for them? I shook my head. There were too many obstacles for this to have been done by someone he didn't know. I doubted Giant Hogweed invited friends back to his flat, though, because he didn't have any. I picked up a pen and tapped it against my teeth, then let out a growl of frustration, took off my glasses, and rubbed my eyes. I wasn't getting anywhere.

The address DS Chambers had given me was in my jacket pocket. I took it out, unfolded the paper, and typed the postcode into my phone. The location was close to where Pascal Martineaux lived. I checked my watch. I'd hardly slept for days. I should go to bed and wait until morning, but Father always said there was no time like the present.

22

THE FLAT WAS IN THE BASEMENT OF A LARGE VICTORIAN house, the front door down a narrow-stepped passage to one side of the building that lit up with a motion-sensing security light as soon as I descended the first step. I knocked on the pale blue door then retreated up a couple of the steps while I waited. It could only have been a small flat because the door opened almost immediately by the woman with long white hair—Jessica Parks.

"Eustacia! How did you find me?"

"Your car registration."

"Ah…that was very clever of you."

I could have told her it was a police database that found her, not my intellect, but for some reason it felt important not to disappoint her.

She smiled and stepped backward. "Come on in then, you clever thing."

The flat really was tiny. The front door opened directly into a lounge that was only able to accommodate an armchair and small coffee table. Beside that was a bedroom with a single bed. Off the lounge, a galley kitchen. I hovered by the front door because the space felt too small for both of us.

"Wait there a minute," she said, limping across the room and pulling a folding canvas chair out from under the coffee table. "The space is a bit tight. Serena wanted me to live with her. She's got plenty of empty rooms, but I felt I should keep some distance. It's important to have a place of one's own, don't you think? I know the apartment's small, but I have simple needs."

I'd long since stopped listening because I was staring at the canvas chair. It was the same as the one I kept on my roof. The one that had belonged to Father.

"I have a chair like that," I said.

"Do you? I'm not surprised. They were a very popular design in the seventies. I imagine there're still a lot of them in junk shops. Come in. Sit down. You can have the armchair. Would you like a tea? I have cinnamon buns. They're from the bakery next to the station. They're really rather good."

I was experiencing a very peculiar sensation: a mixture of strangeness and familiarity. I turned to her.

"Why did you tell me to stay away from Pascal?"

She sat down on the canvas chair, abandoning her offer of tea and buns. "Could we spend a few moments together before we launch into that?"

"Why?"

"So we can get to know each other."

"Why?"

"Because it's been a very long time."

I frowned. "Since?"

"Since we last saw each other. In fact, it's been over forty years."

My frown deepened. "You knew me when I was a child?"

"I did," she said, smiling. "I knew you very well."

It was actually a relief to hear this. It explained the feelings of familiarity, the memories. The canvas chair. It made sense now. She was a family friend.

"You knew my parents," I said, sitting in the armchair. "What a coincidence to run into each other after all this time. Did you come to the Oxford house often?" *Did you give me strawberries? Did you teach me about mayflower?*

The smile wavered, but she quickly reinstated it. "No. I never went to the Oxford house. I saw you in my flat."

This was puzzling.

"Were you a childminder then? Did you look after me while my parents were at work?"

She maintained the smile. "Something like that. Pascal tells me you're a professor of botanical toxicology. He says you're the head of your department at University College London."

I paused, wondering how Pascal would know this.

"Your father must be very proud to have another professor in the family."

"Must have been," I corrected.

"Must have been?" She inhaled, short and sharp. "Oh...I'm very sorry to hear that."

I looked at her with curiosity. "You say you were a family friend?"

"I didn't say that."

"An employee then?"

"I didn't say that either."

I took a moment to try to make sense of what she was saying.

"Well, whatever you were, I think I have memories of you."

She leaned forward in the chair. "You do?"

"Yes, I think so, but only from when I was very young. Did you go somewhere?"

"America. I've been there for forty years."

"Aha." I leaned back, satisfied that everything was now explained and we could move on to the reason I was there.

I repeated my question. "Why did you tell me to stay away from Pascal?"

She smiled again. "You like everything to be in its place, don't you? Everything precisely arranged. All the loose ends tied up.

Like the chair I'm sitting on now. I could tell it disturbed you the moment you saw it. Why would a complete stranger own a chair like yours?"

She was silent a moment, as if I was meant to say something, but before I could think what that might be, she added, "Are you okay now? Did I answer all your questions correctly?"

I tilted my head and said, "That was sarcasm."

And for a reason that was totally beyond me, she burst into a peal of laughter that lasted a very long time and made her cry.

"Oh, Eustacia," she said, wiping away the tears, "I have missed you."

I took a breath and asked again. "Why did you tell me to stay away from Pascal?"

It was a moment before she spoke, and when she did, all the laughter had gone.

"Because bad things happen to people he takes a liking to."

"Then why should *I* stay away from him?"

"Because he's taken a liking to you, Eustacia."

"I doubt that very much," I said with a snort.

"Believe me, he has. He let you into his home. He locked himself away in his studio to paint your portrait. He approached you at his opening. Pascal does not approach people. People have to go to him."

Why would a famous American artist be interested in a botanical toxicology professor? I wasn't interesting. Far from it. I was a nobody. But then I remembered what he'd said to me in his studio. He'd invited me in because he liked the way I spoke, the way I dressed, the way it looked as if I'd stepped out of another time.

"What bad things happen?" I asked.

She didn't speak for a long time. Long enough for me to look at her. She was hunched forward in the chair, her hands clasped tightly between her knees, her mouth a thin line, her eyes fixed on me. "Accidents."

"Accidents?" A shiver ran from my scalp to my heels. "What kind of accidents?"

"Unexplained ones."

※※

It was a relief to be outside. In the end, I couldn't leave the tiny flat fast enough. It had become oppressively small, Jessica Parks's warning stiflingly intense. I needed to breathe, to think because my mind was reeling. However, I wasn't given the chance because as soon as I walked through the gate, DCI Roberts surprised me by stepping into my path.

"Thought I'd find you here. Let's grab a cup of tea. I know a place."

I could have refused. Said I needed to go home. To sleep. Instead, I followed behind as he led the way across London Fields toward Broadway Market.

He went into a Japanese restaurant, chose from the tea menu, and found a quiet table. After a momentary hesitation, I sat down opposite him.

"Why were you hanging around outside?" I asked.

"I was investigating."

"Investigating what?"

"You."

"Me?" I asked, surprised. "Why?"

"Because I've learned from experience, Professor, that you have maverick tendencies. You keep things to yourself. Important things. Which made me wonder why you disappeared from the hospital without telling anyone. Not even your girlfriend. She was very upset, by the way. Then it made me wonder whose number plate you wanted me to trace. Turns out it belongs to a woman with long white hair. You asked me if I'd seen a woman with long white hair at Pascal Martineaux's opening." His thick, untidy eyebrows lifted. "Is it the same woman?"

I have to admit to being highly annoyed by this intrusion. I'd just received an unsettling warning. I certainly didn't need DCI Roberts sticking his nose in before I'd had the chance to process it. So why I didn't refuse his suggestion of a cup of tea, I have no idea.

"Yes."

"Is she something to do with the case?"

"Which one?"

"Simmonds's. She was at Pascal's opening. Pascal knew about the syringe in Simmonds's neck—ergo…"

"You're making assumptions."

"No. I'm investigating. Is she something to do with the case?"

A waiter placed a wooden board on the table, upon which was arranged a small earthen teapot and two equally small cups. I'd seen something similar in Pascal's enormous kitchen.

When the waiter had gone, I lifted the lid to reveal dried flowers slowly unfurling in the hot water. "What's this?"

"Cherry blossom."

"I know that. Why are we drinking it?"

"It's called *sakura*. The cherry blossom's salt-pickled."

"Again, why are we drinking it?"

"My daughters drink it. It tastes like spring. Apparently."

I put the lid back on and pushed the pot to his side of the table, and he poured some into his cup, took a sip, and made a face.

"Is she something to do with the case?" he asked for the third time. "Come on. We're meant to be working together."

I gave him a cool look. I had to give him something, but not yet. "Let's talk tomorrow. I've got a busy teaching day, but I'll ring you in the evening."

"Tomorrow's Sunday."

"Is it?"

He made the humming sound, folded his arms, and rested them on his large belly. "You're at it again, aren't you?"

I stood to leave. "I've got to go."

"Withholding information."

"I'll speak to you tomorrow."

"Obstructing an investigation. That's a crime, you know."

23

SUNDAY MORNING, WHEN PEOPLE LIE IN BED LONGER THAN necessary, or put on Lycra and go on long bike rides, or cook huge breakfasts, or visit a place of worship. When I still had my collection, Sunday morning was just like any other day. I donned my overalls, shoe protectors, and gloves and went up to my roof to tend to the plants. Since losing it I must admit, I haven't really known what to do with the day, because Matilde's plants took barely any tending at all. She did once suggest we go for a Sunday roast at a pub. I don't know why. She knew I didn't like to eat food I hadn't prepared myself. In all honesty, I would have preferred to go to the lab, but she told me Sunday was a day of rest.

Ordinarily, I would have listened, but my mind was turning and turning over a possibility that made me reach for my landline telephone.

"Marco? It's the professor."

"I know who it is. You do not call on the weekend, okay? Goodbye."

"Wait, don't hang up. I just have a very quick question. Did you tell me everything from when you went to buy the *Datura*? Isn't there anything else?"

"No."

"Please try to remember. Isn't there anything?"

"This is not a quick question. It is Sunday. I am at the park with my son. Call tomorrow."

"Please, Marco. You said something about a woman as you were leaving?"

He sighed. "Big hat, dark glasses. I wondered why she would want toxins, then I thought maybe she was after the hallucinogens. But why would a woman in her condition want hallucinogens? Maybe to ease the pain? *Stefan!* Get down!"

I jerked the phone away from my ear at his shout.

"I have to go. My son—*Stefan!*"

"Wait. What do you mean, 'in her condition'? What condition was she in? Did she walk with a limp? Did she have a cane?"

"*Stef*—" And he was gone.

I tried calling back but was sent to voicemail. I tried again and again and eventually put the telephone back in its cradle. I thought of the CCTV footage I'd watched with DS Chambers and remembered the woman following Simmonds into the pub. The woman with her face obscured by a wide-brimmed hat. I could have been on a completely wrong track, but maybe when Marco saw her, it wasn't the first time she'd been to the chemist. Maybe she'd bought from there before.

My mobile started to ring. I snatched it up, thinking Marco might have somehow got hold of its number, but immediately deflated when I saw it was Matilde. I didn't need another offer of a Sunday roast. I needed to be alone to think, so I switched it off and took Giant Hogweed's notebook out of my satchel. Tucked between the pages was the photocopy of the plant list. I pulled it out and stared at it as I had stared at it a hundred times before. Whichever way I looked at it, I couldn't fathom what it could mean. If his mother hadn't told me he and his brother were obsessed with code-breaking, I would doubt this was anything other than what it was: a list of plants.

I sighed, rubbed my eyes, folded it, and tucked it into the inside pocket of my jacket, thinking that if I took it for a walk, it might miraculously reveal its secret.

I wandered around the neighborhood for an hour, with no particular destination, until I found myself outside Susan's house. It hadn't been my intention to visit Susan, and I certainly wasn't the sort of person who turned up at someone's house unannounced, but as I'd unexpectedly found myself there, I thought I may as well see if she was home.

I descended the steps to her door and found that it was once again unlocked. Tutting, I pushed it open and discovered her in her garden, tying sweet peas to a tripod of bamboo canes.

"Alright, lovely?" she asked.

"Not really," I replied, sitting on her garden chair.

"That don't sound good. What's up?"

"I've been trying to solve a puzzle for days, but whatever I try, whomever I ask, I keep drawing a blank."

"You ain't asked me yet."

This was true. She'd been so helpful last time. I don't know why I hadn't come to her straight away. I took the list out of my pocket and handed it to her.

"These are plant names," she said. "I've got a couple of 'em in my garden. Let's see… I've got globe thistle, sage. Never heard of the rest of them."

"That's just it. Some are well known; others are obscure. And I can find absolutely nothing that connects them. So how can I break the code?"

"You sure it's a code?"

"Not a hundred percent."

"So it might not be?" She stared at the list again then added, "Back in a tick."

I watched her shuffle into her kitchen then leaned back in my chair and lifted my eyes to my roof garden, remembering all the plants that had once been hidden behind the vine and feeling the cruel pang of their loss.

"Here we go," Susan said, putting a battered copy of *The RHS Gardeners' Encyclopedia of Plants and Flowers*, a notebook, and a pencil on the table. "Give us the first plant name."

I'd looked at the list so many times, I knew it off by heart. "Cat's claw, but I've already checked if there's a taxonomy connection."

"A what?"

"Taxonomy connection."

"Sounds complicated."

"This list was written by a PhD student. The solution isn't going to be simple."

She turned to the common-names index at the back of the encyclopedia and ran her finger down the page. "Maybe that's where you're going wrong. Maybe simple was what they were aiming for. Now then...cat's claw, page one seventy-four."

She flipped to the page and found the picture of the pretty yellow flower with its description underneath. "*Macfadyena unguis-cati*," she read, laboring over the pronunciation. "What's a Macfadyena?"

"James Macfadyen. He was a nineteenth-century Scottish plant collector. He named this plant after himself."

She took her time to write the plant's Latin name into the notebook in large capital letters then asked, "What's the next one?"

"Snowbush rose. Are you planning on looking up and writing down all the Latin names?"

"I am," she said, finding the plant in the index.

"But I can just tell you what they are. Besides, I already looked for an etymological connection and didn't find one."

"Just let me do it my way, will you?" she said, turning to the page. "*Rosa 'dupontii.'* Dupontii. Sounds like a name 'n' all."

"It is. Dupont was a French nurseryman. Again, in the 1800s."

"He named a rose after 'imself?"

"He did."

She tutted. "All these vain Victorian men, naming stuff after themselves as if those things didn't exist before they came along."

Again, she wrote the Latin name into her notebook in the large, shaky capital letters, and the sight of it made me shift uncomfortably in my chair.

"There's a correct way to write plant names, and that isn't it."

"No?"

"No."

"What does it matter?"

I let out a small cry. "It matters a great deal, Susan. The taxonomy of a plant helps with its identification. The name is divided into two, sometimes three orders. The genus, the species, and sometimes the variety. The genus always begins with a capital letter, the species always lower case. You're using all capitals."

"What does it matter?" she asked again.

"Here let me show you." I took the pencil out of her hand and wrote down the Latin names for a few more plants. Globe thistle—*Echinops ritro*. Mayflower—*Epigaea repens*. "See? The first letters are very important."

"I can see it's important for an obsessive compulsive," she said, taking the pencil back and correcting the two plant names she'd written. "Happy now?"

And I was. I was ecstatic. I was euphoric—because I finally saw what Giant Hogweed was trying to tell me, and I couldn't have done that without her.

"Susan! You're a genius!" I cried.

Then I did something I'd never done before. I leaped to my feet, ran around the table, and flung my arms around her.

"Oi! Get off me, you daft muppet," she said, laughing as she rested her head on my shoulder and patted my hand.

Back at my desk, it was swift work to decode the list, although landing on the meaning less so. In my notebook, I wrote out the common names and their Latin names beside them.

Cat's claw—*Macfadyena unguis-cati*
Snowbush rose—*Rosa "dupontii"*
Globe thistle—*Echinops ritro*
Mayflower—*Epigaea repens*
Scarlet sage—*Salvia*
King's spear—*Eremurus robustus*
Blue sage—*Eranthemum nervosum*
Knife-leaf wattle—*Acacia cultriformis*

Next I took the first letters of the Latin names and wrote them underneath.

MURDERERSERENAC

I stared at the string of letters, trying to make sense of them, until, like a fog lifting, they became clear.

MURDERER SERENA C

Serena C? C? My mind flashed back to the first time I went to Pascal's studio. To the monologue he'd given about Serena's charmed, privileged life. I was sure he'd said her father was called Carmichael. How on earth could Giant Hogweed know Serena? He couldn't. It was impossible. I rubbed my face vigorously with both hands, trying to recall what he'd said to me on the phone the day he died.

I know who's making the synthetic toxins.

Had he accidentally stumbled into something that may have cost him his life? And did it have something to do with Serena? I let out a heavy exhalation then pulled out my mobile and called DCI Roberts.

᯾᯾

"It's good to see you've decided to stop being the maverick,

Professor," he said as I walked into his office. "I assume you're ready to share now? And on a Sunday, no less. What have you got for me?"

"I'm not a hundred percent sure." I took the notebook out of my satchel. "But I've decoded the list, at least."

DCI Roberts smiled. "I knew you would. What does it say?"

I opened the notebook and handed it to him.

"MURDERER SERENA C," he read. "Who's Serena C?"

"Pascal Martineaux's wife."

"The pregnant woman with all the face metal at his opening? She's our murderer?"

"Aaron seemed to think so. I'm not so sure."

"Why not?"

"I don't know. A feeling maybe."

His eyebrows lifted. "Don't tell me you're having another hunch? At this rate, I might start thinking you're after my job as well."

I glanced at him. He was smiling. Which meant he didn't really believe I wanted his job.

"Let's get her in for a chat, shall we? Then maybe we'll find out if your hunch is right."

I doubted Serena would voluntarily come to the station for a chat. "Probably be better if we went to see her."

He stood up. "Alright then. Are you free now?"

"Now?"

"Unless you have plans?"

I thought of Matilde's missed call. "I have no plans."

I wasn't the best at judging moods, but I could tell DCI Roberts's was off as we drove up Kentish Town High Street. I suppose I could have asked him what the matter was, but to be honest, I didn't really care.

"I have some news," he said at last.

I glanced at him. "Oh?"

"Simmonds is dead. The poison finally stopped his heart. Which means, now you've confirmed the substance that killed him was the same as the one that killed Aaron Bennett—"

"You have a double murder to solve," I finished for him.

"Indeed."

We fell silent while we considered this.

"We need to establish a connection between these two deaths other than the weapon," he said.

"Not the same weapon. The syringes were different."

"True. We know Aaron Bennett was struggling with his mental health, so we can't assume his code is the evidence that will wrap this up. What I'm trying to say is"—he glanced at me—"we can't go to Serena Carmichael all guns blazing. We'll have a gentle conversation and feel our way to some kind of understanding of why Aaron is accusing her of murder."

"We're not going to ask her straight out if she killed him?" I asked.

"No. We're not. Is that understood?"

This was when I should have told him everything I had so far—finding the lethal combination of *Datura* and anti-anxiety medication in his blood, tracing the manufacturer behind the dark website, visiting their lab, spotting the person with the wide-brimmed hat following Simmonds into the pub on the CCTV… but these could just be random jigsaw pieces, and the code one more piece that may not even belong in the same puzzle. I needed more time to fit everything together, which meant DCI Roberts would have to wait.

"Of course. I'm assisting with the case. I'll follow your lead."

The gate to Serena and Pascal's building was locked when we arrived, and nobody was answering the intercom. We were about to give up when a van pulled into the curb and a man unloaded several large bags of laundry. He nodded at us as he punched a code into the keypad that opened the gate and didn't comment when we followed him through it. We also followed him through the main entrance, along the corridor, and up the stairs to Pascal's front door, and only then did he turn round to give us a question-ing look.

"We're here for Serena Carmichael?" DCI Roberts said.

He nodded again, rang the doorbell, and stepped back until he was standing beside us. Soon after, the huge door was opened by a woman in a smart gray uniform. She looked at us in turn, signed the delivery sheet then bent to drag the bags into the flat.

"We're here for Serena Carmichael?" DCI Roberts repeated. The woman ignored him.

"My name's DCI Roberts. I'm a police officer. May we come in?"

She stopped dragging the bags and straightened. "She's not here. She's at a silent retreat."

"When will she be home?"

"Next week."

"Is Pascal Martineaux home?"

"He's walking the dog."

"On London Fields?"

"I don't know. He goes all over. Sometimes Victoria Park, sometimes Hackney Marshes. He often takes the dog to Hampstead Heath. He could be hours."

The woman bent to the laundry bags again.

"Are you the housekeeper?" I asked.

"Yes."

I bent down as well and picked one up. "Here, let me give you a hand." Then I stepped through the door. "Where do you want it?"

She watched me but didn't try to stop me, so I carried the bag to the kitchen island and put it down. An ironing board and iron were set next to a drying rack of putty-colored clothes. Delivery boxes were piled up on the kitchen counter. A floor mop stood in a bucket of brown water, chemical-free cleaning products beside the sink. A dustpan full of dog hair. I remembered Pascal saying that the housekeeper waited until they weren't at home before she came out to clean. This must have been her opportunity, these the prosaic tools to maintain this bastion of perfection.

"We're sorry to disturb you when you're so busy, but we really need to speak with Serena. Could you call her mobile for us?" I asked.

"She's at a silent retreat. She won't answer."

"Then perhaps you can help us," DCI Roberts said.

The housekeeper froze, her eyes suddenly very wide. Unexpectedly, she blurted, "I don't know anything."

I exchanged a glance with DCI Roberts.

"You don't know anything about what?" he asked gently.

"I don't know." She wiped her hands down her thighs once, twice. "I don't know anything about anything. I just work here."

"So you haven't seen some small bottles with a clear liquid inside them?" I asked. "Small bottles?"

I took the bottle of *Datura* out of my satchel. I hadn't planned to reveal it in front of DCI Roberts, but I had no choice.

"Like this one? Does Serena have some bottles like this?"

She shot a look at the wall that was a cupboard, then at me before fixing them on the floor.

"Does Jessica?" I tried.

She frowned. "Who?"

"Pan...Pan...Serena's shaman."

"I don't know."

DCI Roberts let out a sigh. "This isn't getting us anywhere.

Let's leave this young lady to get on with her work in peace and head back to the station."

"One moment," I said, walking around the island and pressing the wall to open the cupboard door.

"I don't think you're allowed to do that," the housekeeper said hesitantly.

But after a short rummage, I found what I was looking for, held it up, and cried, "Bingo!"

24

I WAS UNDER THE IMPRESSION IT TOOK TIME TO APPLY FOR A search warrant, but DCI Roberts and his team of officers were ready to go the very next morning and, in fact, were already waiting around the corner from the address in West London when I arrived.

"Will that be necessary?" I asked, waving a hand at the officer holding a battering ram.

"Only if they don't open the door."

The chances of that were highly likely, I thought, as I waited behind while they approached the flat. Especially as it was eight o'clock in the morning. To be fair, DCI Roberts did knock several times and even shouted through the letterbox before the officer was called forward to ram the door, but once we were inside, there were too many people, too many bikes in the narrow hall, so I waited for everyone to sort themselves out before I followed.

The kitchen was as much of a mess as the last time I was there. Perhaps even more so. And the young man, when he was dragged downstairs from his bed, just as disheveled. He took one look at me and let out a roar of anger.

"I knew it," he shouted. "I knew the moment I opened the door you were a filthy grass." He twisted round to the officer who was holding his arms behind his back. "She's the one you should be arresting. She attacked me in my own home. I've got the bruises to prove it. Look." He lifted an elbow to look down at his side.

"She did?" DCI Roberts asked. "What did she do?"

"She grabbed me and threw me. I think I cracked a couple of ribs. Look at the bruises. Take a photo."

DCI Roberts turned to me with a grin. "You took DS Chambers up on her offer of a self-defense lesson?"

I wasn't sure it could be called a lesson, but I nodded anyway.

"Glad to hear it. Now, what are we looking at here?"

"In the fridge door," I replied.

He opened it, whistled through his teeth, and turned to the young man. "What's all this then?"

"It's not mine. It's my pal's. It's nothing to do with me."

That was most likely true, but it didn't change the fact that he was prepared to act as the salesman.

"And where is this pal?" DCI Roberts asked.

The young man shrugged. "Cleared out after I told them

about you," he said, looking at me. "They said I could sell the gear in the fridge and keep the money. Haven't seen them since."

"When was that?"

"The same day she attacked me," he said, jutting his chin. "Look, that isn't my gear. I didn't cook it. I'm not the chemist. So take it. Take it all. It's yours."

"Where was it made?" I asked. "Clearly not in here."

He looked at the back door. "Out there. There's a gate at the back of the garden that leads to some derelict land beside the railway track. They set up their kitchen there."

"Why don't you lead the way?" DCI Roberts asked.

"Can I get dressed first?"

While we waited, I stood by as an officer emptied the small bottles from the fridge door into evidence bags. I was sorely tempted to ask if I could take some, but I knew the answer would be no.

Soon after, the young man came downstairs dressed in jeans and a T-shirt and stepped into a pair of filthy sneakers. We crossed the small garden and went through a gate into wilderness. Obviously, no one had tended this patch of land for years. All about was broad-leaved dock, couch grass, bindweed, chickweed, nettles, save for a narrow path made from someone repeatedly pushing through it all to a small shed twenty meters away. The door was locked but flimsy. It took only one kick, and when it flew open, I gasped.

I couldn't believe my eyes. The outside may have looked like a dilapidated garden shed, but inside was a sophisticated laboratory, as well equipped as some of the best I'd ever seen, but in miniature. There was one centrifuge, one microscope, a burner, trays of test tubes, shelves of flasks containing variously colored solutions, overalls, a box of latex gloves, and a full-face mask with filtration units and respirator. And there, by the window, was Giant Hogweed's laptop with its cartoon cover, which meant either he'd left it here or someone was hiding it.

A label on the microscope caught my attention. I reached out, but before I could touch it, DCI Roberts ushered me back through the door with his belly and a "Don't touch anything." Then he turned to an officer and said, "Get on to forensics. Tell them they'll need hazmats."

Outside the shed, I could hear a freight train approaching, the *thu-thunk, thu-thunk* moving closer and closer until the noise was thunderous.

"Too loud," I moaned, covering my ears and crouching down, and it was in this position that I saw a small footprint. Not mine. Certainly not DCI Roberts's or any of the other officers'. I lifted my head. There were more footprints heading to a path less obvious than the one to the shed. I glanced behind me. Everyone was busy, so I pushed through the overhanging branches of an elder tree and stepped onto this new path.

Another twenty meters or so into the wilderness, I came

across an old glasshouse in a state of disrepair, many of its dirty panes broken or missing. I cupped my eyes and peered through the murky glass. There were plants inside. Marijuana. Nicotiana. I forced my way through chest-high cow parsley and goose grass that skirted the outside of the glasshouse until I found the door, and when I opened it and saw what was nestled in amongst the plants, my jaw fell open.

༺༻

We were sitting in DCI Roberts's office. No. He was sitting; I was standing, pacing, thumping things.

"But it's mine," I shouted.

"It's evidence."

"It was stolen from my roof garden last year. It's mine. I want it back."

"It'll stay here until we find and arrest the chemist."

"Where? In your dark basement? With all the other evidence?" I cried. "It's already in a perilous condition. If it's not given attention immediately, it'll die."

"Is that such a problem?"

"YES!" I shouted, thumping the desk. "That most definitely *is* such a problem!"

I began to fast pace the room, swinging my arms erratically. "Have you any idea how much effort went into raising that plant?

How much energy and dedication? Do you even know how much it's worth?"

DCI Roberts stood up. "Calm down, Professor."

"No. I will not calm down. You have *no* idea, do you?"

He let out a mighty sigh. "Tell you what. Why don't you ask your university to apply for a custody permit. If it's granted, you can look after all the plants until we need them."

"I don't want all the plants. I want my plant."

"You'll still need a custody permit."

"How long will that take?"

"Two or three weeks."

In a rage, I picked up a folder from his desk and threw it across the room, making pages flutter in all directions. "Good God, man! It'll be dead by then."

"Professor...you're not helping your cause right now. Please...sit down."

I rounded on him. "I will not sit down until you see how critical this situation is. I need to take it away today. It needs my urgent attention."

"It's not within my power to allow you to take it without a permit."

"Then whose power is it within?"

He made the humming sound. "The superintendent's."

"Ring him then. Ring him now."

"I'd rather not."

I glared at him, and he glared back.

Eventually, his shoulders dropped, and he sighed. "There is another way, but it takes a lot of time, which I don't have."

"What is it?"

"I said I don't have the time."

"What is it?" I asked, louder.

Another sigh. "We'll need to go through the emergency release of organic evidence procedure. We'll need to document the evidence in detail with descriptions and photographs. We'll need to set up a chain of custody to maintain the security of the evidence. We'll need to get the legal permissions, the warrants, etc. We'll need to open a channel of communication with forensics to regularly report the condition of the evidence."

"Excellent. Let's do it," I said in my lecturer's voice.

"It could take all afternoon."

"Can I get you anything from the vending machine?"

Five hours later, a porter was unloading the plant from a police van onto a trolley and wheeling it to one of the university glass-houses, and I trailed anxiously behind. I was excited. I don't deny it. It was like being reunited with a child that had been snatched away and held in captivity for a year. My *Datura stramonium.* Common name, Hell's Bells. And by the looks of it, not only kidnapped but also horribly mistreated. It was barely alive.

I thought back to the theft the year before, and I'll admit, I experienced a momentary crisis of conscience. I knew full well the dangers of my plants being out in the world. I'd warned DCI Roberts about it several times, and here was the evidence, because it was highly likely the chemist had synthesized the toxins using this plant as the base structure. This plant that I'd propagated and brought to maturity myself. This plant that had contributed to Charlie Simmonds's and Giant Hogweed's deaths.

An image of Mr. and Mrs. Bennett in the dean's office came to mind. Their rage, their desperation. Followed by another of Charlie Simmonds lying in the hospital bed, his eyes behind his closed lids flicking from side to side as he watched whatever terrifying hallucination he was having. I shook my head vigorously, trying to dislodge them, but they stubbornly refused to leave, so, inhaling deeply, I set to work.

The first step was to remove the dead wood then prune back the remaining stems to three inches above soil level. All those years of growth sacrificed to the secateurs. It seemed brutal. But it was the only way to save the plant. I took it from its pot, murmuring soothingly, telling it everything was going to be okay, teased out the roots and repotted it in fresh nutrient-rich compost, fed and watered it, and placed it in the cold frame. Then I cut the discarded stems into four-inch lengths, sealed them in airtight bags, and put them in my satchel. Waste not, want not.

I could have done with some assistance. The root ball was huge and backbreakingly heavy, but I'd tasked Carla with the job of preparing the lab for the afternoon plant genetics lesson. Besides,

I'd nurtured this plant from a tiny cutting alone, tended to its every need, helped it weather every storm, alone. It seemed appropriate that I should now be saving its life on my own.

When all the tasks were complete, I documented what I'd done, took photographs, and sent everything to forensics, and then I disposed of my gloves and headed for the lab to give the genetics lesson. I was in a buoyant mood. It had been a successful day. The synthetic toxin factory had been shut down, as had the possibility of someone else being hurt. Now, I just needed to find the person behind it all. I needed to track down the chemist.

25

THE FOLLOWING AFTERNOON, DCI ROBERTS CALLED BECAUSE not only had he located Serena's silent retreat, he'd also picked her up and she was now sitting in the interview room at the police station. Twenty minutes later, I ducked past Pascal and Jessica Parks in reception and headed for the monitor room. On the other side of the mirror, Serena was calm and composed, as if she didn't expect to be there for long.

"Morning," DCI Roberts said as he joined me. "I'll be in here with you today. DS Chambers is going to do the interview. We thought a lower-ranking officer would be less formal and a woman officer more approachable."

I considered telling him that Serena was not the kind of person to be intimidated by rank.

"Why did you bring her here? Why not just talk to her at the retreat?"

"She insisted."

I frowned, scarcely believing anyone would enter that room voluntarily. "Whatever for?"

"She won't talk to us without her lawyer. We're waiting for him now." He took a breath. "Interesting she's insisting on a lawyer when we only want a chat."

"She's an heiress. Her father's a billionaire."

"Ah…that explains it."

Soon after, the door to the interview room opened for DS Chambers and the lawyer. They took their places, and each put a file on the table. Serena briefly glanced at DS Chambers then, with a blank expression, looked away.

"Good morning, Ms. Carmichael. Thank you for agreeing to talk to us."

"My client hasn't agreed to anything," the lawyer replied.

DS Chambers smiled and took two photographs out of her file. "I wonder if you know either of these men?"

Serena ignored the question.

"If you wouldn't mind looking at the photographs, Ms. Carmichael?"

She glanced at them then, with the same blank expression, looked away.

"Do you recognize them?"

Again, she ignored the question.

DS Chambers glanced at the mirror. "I believe we interrupted your stay at a silent retreat. Are you still abiding by your vow of silence, or are you just refusing to answer?"

"My client has the right to remain silent."

"Yes, that's quite correct—if she's been arrested. But Ms. Carmichael hasn't been arrested. We would just like her to help us with our investigation. Two men have died, you see, and we believe Ms. Carmichael may have known one of them, while the other may have known Ms. Carmichael."

I had my eyes glued to Serena's impassive face, and when DS Chambers said the word "died," I could have sworn there was a flicker of a reaction.

"This is just one of many lines of inquiry," DS Chambers continued when neither of them spoke. "If Ms. Carmichael doesn't know these men, we can close this line and concentrate on the others. So if you wouldn't mind suggesting to your client that she answer the question, that would be greatly appreciated."

Silence.

DS Chambers glanced at the mirror again, then took Giant Hogweed's plant list out of the file, put it on the table, and tapped his photograph. "This piece of paper was found in the pocket of this young man. It's a list of plant names. The list was actually quite a clever code. He was a botany student, you see, so he used his plant knowledge to tell us something. Do you want to know what that was?"

Not even a glance from Serena this time. She kept her eyes firmly fixed on the floor.

DS Chambers took another piece of paper from the file. On it was printed in large, bold capital letters:

MURDERER SERENA C

I looked at DCI Roberts, surprised by the theatrics. He was smiling.

Finally, Serena couldn't resist a quick glance then couldn't contain her gasp. "I'm not a murderer," she cried, standing. "How dare you!"

She walked to the door, tried the handle, and found it was locked. DS Chambers stood as well, and so did the lawyer.

"Please sit down, Ms. Carmichael."

"Why's the door locked? I'm not under arrest."

"The door locks automatically."

"Open it immediately!" Serena shouted.

"Ms. Carmichael…"

"This is false imprisonment," Serena yelled, cradling her belly with one hand and thumping the door with the other. "Open it now, or I'll sue."

"Dear, dear," DCI Roberts said, but I wasn't interested in the histrionics because I was too busy staring at the plant list on the table. I'd made a blinding error.

I spun round to DCI Roberts. "Stop the interview. I've made a mistake with the code."

"What?" he said, his voice rising.

"I've made a mistake with the code."

"That's what I thought you said. Should I let her go?"

"Yes, let her go."

He picked up his radio and spoke to the officer outside the door; then when Serena had been escorted out of the interview room, he turned to me. "What mistake?"

"I'll tell you as soon as I've fixed it," I said. "I'll need that plant list."

DCI Roberts looked through the mirror at the piece of paper still lying on the table.

"You can't have it. It's evidence."

"But I need it. Besides, it's mine. He wrote it for me."

"Nevertheless...you can't have it."

I glared at him, or rather, I glared at his chest, which after a moment, he rubbed with a hand as if I were causing him physical pain.

"If you don't give me that plant list, Inspector, I won't be as forthcoming with my findings as you would like."

I heard the humming sound.

"Nothing new there then."

With the original of Giant Hogweed's plant list safely in my pocket, I hurried out of the custody suite. It was a basic mistake for a botany professor to make. So remiss it was embarrassing.

As I descended the station's front steps, I was surprised to see Pascal on the other side of the road, sitting on a wall smoking a cigarette. He gestured for me to join him, and I remembered Jessica Parks's comment that people had to go to Pascal Martineaux. I didn't want to go to Pascal Martineaux. I wanted to go to my office.

"What're you doing here?" he asked as I crossed the road.

"I'm assisting the police with a case."

"Oh yeah. The Soho poisoning."

"The Soho *murder*," I corrected. "He died."

"Did he?"

"Didn't Serena tell you?"

"Tell me what?"

"That the man died?"

"What's it got to do with her?"

I paused. "That's what we're trying to find out."

We looked at each other, neither speaking while we tried to read each other's thoughts.

He took a drag of the cigarette. "Serena didn't tell me anything. She came charging out just now, grabbed the witch's hand, and jumped straight in a cab. She didn't have a single word to say to me…which isn't unusual. She much prefers the witch." He screwed the cigarette into the pavement with his heel. "To be honest, their relationship is driving me a bit nuts. I'm not sure how much longer I can stick it. It's getting to the stage where I'm thinking either she goes, or I go."

Suddenly a memory crashed into my mind so violently that my whole body jolted.

Either she goes, or I go.

I blinked rapidly. I'd heard those words before. I was sure of it. And I was also sure they'd been spoken by my mother. My beautiful, tall, glamorous, missing mother.

"Are you okay?"

I shook my head, trying to push the memory aside.

"I'm fine. I should go. I'm giving a lecture in an hour. I'll need time to collect my thoughts."

I didn't need to collect my thoughts. I knew all of my lectures off by heart, but there was an urgent matter I needed to attend to. I turned away then immediately back again.

"Just one thing," I said.

He lifted his eyebrows questioningly.

"In my portrait, why did you paint a syringe next to my neck?"

The eyebrows came down again. "I didn't paint a syringe next to your neck."

"You did, on the right, pointing at my jugular."

"You're mistaken. I painted it so it was partially hidden in the leaves. I hide a syringe in all of my paintings. But you know that. You know what it represents as well. You've done your homework, haven't you?"

His assumption was presumptuous, but also correct. I nodded. "But why right next to my neck?"

"I hadn't realized it was right next to your neck."

"You painted the tip of the needle a millimeter away. How could you not realize what you were doing?"

He shrugged. "I don't have an answer."

"I told you the Soho poison victim was stabbed in the neck with a syringe."

"You did? When?"

"The first time I went to your studio. Don't tell me you don't remember."

"I don't remember."

I let out a snort.

"I guess it went into my subconscious?" he ventured. "What's the word? Subliminal? Suggestion? Whatever, I didn't intend it to look like it was aiming for your neck."

Adder's-tongue, I thought and let out a louder, more forceful snort. "I don't believe that for a second."

He tilted his head and regarded me before saying, "You're sounding paranoid, Professor."

With a huff, I walked away. Famous artist or not, I didn't have time to play his mind games. I had a code to fix.

But before I was out of earshot, he added, "Should I be worried about you?"

⁂

When I reached my office, I placed the list on my desk, opened my notebook at the page where I'd written the plants' Latin names, and added one word—*splendens*, because I'd neglected to add the species for the scarlet sage the first time—*Salvia splendens*. Then I wrote the code out again.

MURDERERSSERENAC

MURDERERS SERENA C

Murderers…did that mean Giant Hogweed thought there was more than one? Did he believe Serena hadn't acted alone?

Looking closer at the list, I noticed a rough edge at the bottom, as if a strip had been torn off. I took Giant Hogweed's notebook from my satchel, opened it to a fresh page, and laid his list on top. It was the same width. The lines the same distance apart. He had written his list on a page from this book. The only difference being, his list was about five lines shorter. I frowned. Why had he ripped off the bottom of the page? And what did he do with that small strip of paper? It wasn't in his pocket. Forensics would have found it. Did he eat it?

I inhaled deeply then carefully opened and ran my fingers down every page of the notebook, looking for the place the list had been torn from and feeling for indentations.

26

It was time to tell DCI Roberts everything. But first I had to go to the lab because there was something I needed to check. It took a while because I wasn't responsible for this particular task, but eventually, I found it tucked in a drawer underneath a year's worth of tutorial notes. I opened it, scanned the pages then, as instructed, went to the assigned cupboard, opened the door, and counted the contents.

"What've you got for me?" he asked when I arrived at his office.

It was difficult to know where to start. I sat opposite him and took a moment to order my thoughts. I suppose it was a long moment because he interrupted by prompting, "Well?"

"I have several things for you. I'm just trying to decide in which order to give them."

"Don't worry about the order."

I was a little anxious about this first part, but there was no getting around it.

"When I found Aaron in his flat, I...borrowed his notebook, fully intending to pass it on to you once I'd looked at it."

DCI Roberts sat bolt upright. "You did what?"

I took the notebook out of my satchel. "I borrowed—"

"I heard you," he shouted, then took a deep breath and ran his hands over his head.

I flicked him a quick glance. His eyebrows were bunched. His head was shaking. I placed the notebook on the desk in front of him.

"You didn't borrow it; you withheld evidence," he said, his voice strained. "You're meant to be assisting with the case, Eustacia, not sabotaging it."

"I'm not sabotaging it."

"When I arrived at the scene, I caught you interfering with evidence."

"I wasn't interfering. I was simply reading his PhD proposal while I waited for you."

I could feel his eyes on me. It didn't feel good.

"You can't keep doing this. It's illegal."

"Do you want to know what I have, or are you just going to chastise me?" I interrupted. "I haven't got all day. I'm very busy."

There was a silence—I assumed while he was deciding whether or not to continue chastising me.

He tapped the notebook. "How do I know you haven't tampered with it?"

I gasped with indignation. "Of course I haven't tampered with it. What do you take me for?"

It was several seconds before he answered.

"You know what I take you for. You're a maverick. A well-meaning one, but still a thorn in my side. If this gets out, it could scupper a trial."

I sat straighter in my chair. "I've done nothing more than you would've done had you found the book before me. I haven't written in it or deleted anything from it. All I've done is act on its contents. Just give me retrospective evidence-handling authorization, or whatever it's called, and let's be done with it."

He made the humming sound.

"Do you want to know what I have? Or not?"

The humming sound turned into a sigh. "Go ahead."

"You already know I traced the synthetic toxins manufacturing lab and purchased one of their products. You also know I found that bottle in Serena's kitchen cupboard."

"Ah, yes...that reminds me."

He opened his drawer, pulled out an evidence bag, and shook it open, and I took Serena's bottle out of my satchel and dropped it in.

"And the other one," he said.

I hesitated. I didn't want to give him my bottle. Not only

because it'd cost me a thousand pounds, plus Marco's fee, but also because I wanted to test it. I wanted to separate its component parts then put it back together again. But I could tell by his eyebrows he wasn't going to let me do that, so I took it out of my jacket pocket and handed it over.

"When we were at the lab, I noticed a label on the microscope. But then I was distracted by the excitement of finding my stolen plant and it slipped my mind."

I stopped. This wasn't the right order.

"Wait a moment. I should mention the woman with the wide-brimmed hat and dark glasses who had some kind of condition. She went to the lab as well."

DCI Roberts was slowly shaking his head.

"Bear with me," I said, inhaling. "I had another look at the CCTV of Simmonds going into the pub, and there was a woman with a wide-brimmed hat following him in."

He held up a hand. "Stop. When did you have another look at the CCTV?"

"Last week."

"Why didn't you tell me?"

"DS Chambers was with me. I assumed she would."

His eyebrows bunched together. "She didn't. What was the woman's condition?"

"I don't know. I didn't see her. Someone else did."

"Who?"

I paused. It was probably best not to drag Marco into this. "I'd rather not say."

"Why not?" he asked, leaning forward.

"I'm protecting my source."

"Your *source*?" he cried.

"Anyway," I continued, ignoring this, "we have a possible suspect who was seen at the West London lab and also at the place Charlie Simmonds was attacked."

He opened a file on his desk and took out the piece of paper with the solution to the code written in the large bold letters:

MURDERER SERENA C

"Could the condition be *pregnancy*?"

My eyes flew open. "Oh!"

"I think we need to invite Ms. Carmichael in for another chat." He picked up his telephone.

"Before we do that..." I took one of his pens and added the missing S to the end of MURDERER. "My mistake with the code. I neglected to add the species. It was a silly mistake. Well, not silly—embarrassing. It should have been *Salvia splendens*. I can't believe I—"

"Are you saying there's another murderer?" he interrupted.

"Yes. Exactly that. Aaron was trying to tell us Serena didn't act alone." I opened his notebook and took out the list of plants.

"I believe his list was longer, but for some reason, he ripped off the bottom."

DCI Roberts picked it up.

"I found the place in his notebook where he tore it out," I said, opening it to the right page. "And there are indentations on the page underneath. See? But they're too light to read with the naked eye."

He took the notebook and held the page in its original place.

"Does your department have an imaging light document scanner so we can read the missing words?"

"Imaging light document scanner?" he muttered, rummaging in his desk drawer for a pencil then lightly shading the page until white words appeared. I couldn't believe what I was seeing. It was like a magic trick.

I clapped my hands with delight. "What a simple solution! Ingenious!"

DCI Roberts paused the shading to look up at me. "I'd think you were being sarcastic if I didn't know you better. Did you not do this as a kid?"

"Never!"

He shook his head and continued shading. "Did your old man teach you nothing?"

"Certainly he did. Plant identification, Latin and common names, plant folklore, medicinal and herbal properties."

"That was a rhetorical question."

I closed my mouth.

"There you go."

He passed the notebook back to me, and I read the white words at the bottom of the page—the words Giant Hogweed had torn off the list. Windflower and English lavender. I wrote out the Latin names—*Anemone rivularis* and *Lavandula angustifolia*—then added their first letters to the solution.

MURDERERS SERENA CARLA

A sinking feeling filled my chest, fell to my stomach, and tumbled down into my legs.

DCI Roberts's brow furrowed. "Carla?"

"A student on the same botany PhD program as Aaron Bennett. Also...my lab assistant."

I met his eyes and sensed he could tell how upsetting this was for me.

"But...this is just confirmation of what I already suspected," I continued. "Because the microscope in the synthetic toxins lab was stolen from the university. I recognized the label and checked the laboratory inventory before I came here. The microscope was missing. Probably other equipment is missing as well. I'll need to check. But I think we can assume the chemist is Carla. There's also this."

I placed the small item I'd snatched from the hall floor of the flat in West London on the desk.

"It's a personal attack alarm. I found it in the flat we raided. Carla had it attached to her bag. She used it to warn off Aaron one time when he was intimidating me."

DCI Roberts shook open another evidence bag and put the alarm inside. "This is enough to call Carla in for questioning, but we'll need more for an arrest. Let's see what forensics come back with."

"You won't find any prints in that shed. She won't have gone in without protective overalls and gloves. Perhaps in the house, but I'm sure she would've been careful. I'm also sure she didn't intend to leave the personal attack alarm. It must've got caught on one of the bicycle handlebars without her noticing. Have you asked the friend who the chemist is?"

DCI Roberts nodded. "He won't say a word...worried he'll be implicated."

"He is implicated. He was the salesman. He said so himself, remember? He said the chemist told him he could sell the stuff in the fridge and keep the money."

"But we didn't actually catch him doing it."

I thought of Marco then quietly pushed the thought aside.

DCI Roberts leaned back, laced his fingers behind his head, and lifted his eyes to the ceiling. "So we have two victims and two perpetrators, two syringes but one toxin. What we don't have is a motive. We can't even assume the perpetrators knew each other."

"Aaron thought they did."

"Not necessarily. He just told us there were two of them."

He sighed, opened his arms wide, stretched, checked his watch, and stood up. "It's late. Let's grab some food. I'm not good at thinking on an empty stomach."

"I don't like eating food I haven't prepared myself."

"Oh, yes. I forgot. Let's go to a pub for a drink then, and I'll grab something from the bar menu."

"I don't drink, and I don't like pubs."

He paused to think. "I know one you'll like. I'll buy you a pint of soda water, and if you're lucky, I'll even stretch to some ice cubes and a slice of lime."

"Is soda water the same as sparkling water?"

He smiled and took his jacket off the back of his chair. "It's close enough."

⋊⋉

He took me to a pub beside Hampstead Heath that I'd walked past many times but had never entered. I chose a table in the garden, in amongst the tasteful pale green, gray, white, and blue planting, all with differing levels of toxicity. It was a pleasantly warm evening. Not many tables were occupied, and I began to relax. Presently, DCI Roberts joined me with our drinks and sat down with a sigh.

"I've ordered a pizza. If you can put your food phobia aside for today, you can share it with me."

Ignoring the impertinent suggestion, I turned away and fixed my gaze on the giant oaks at the entrance to the heath.

"I have some news," he said after taking a long draft of his pint and wiping the froth from his upper lip.

"Oh?"

"DS Chambers has transferred back to Cardiff. Apparently, London wasn't what she'd hoped for. She said there wasn't anything here for her. Can't say I'm too upset. She was a particularly thorny person. The station will be a much happier place without her."

He lifted his beer again then fell silent, probably because he was waiting for me to say something, but I had nothing to say.

"I was expecting a reaction," he said at last. "I thought you two had become friends."

"I don't know what gave you that idea."

"You don't mind that she's gone?"

"Not in the slightest."

He took another gulp, and I sipped the soda then pushed the glass away. He was wrong. It was nothing like sparkling water.

"There's something else. Something that's been nagging at me."

I glanced at him. "Oh?"

"The woman with long white hair you've been so interested in. What's she got to do with all of this?"

After a moment of consideration, I said, "I don't think she has anything to do with it. She's just part of Serena's entourage."

"You must have thought she was involved at one point; otherwise you wouldn't have asked for her plate to be traced."

I nodded. "I thought she might be the woman with the wide-brimmed hat and dark glasses, because she walks with a cane. I thought that was her condition."

"Who is she?"

Strawberries in a bowl, a peony-pink duvet, mayflower.

"I really have no idea."

27

The following evening, I was enjoying the therapeutic task of watering Matilde's plants when my mobile screen lit up with the word *Dickie*. We were working on a case, but I'd had a busy teaching day, I was tired, and his constant calls on my time were becoming irksome. I let his call run out then looped the hose over to the chrysanthemums.

Less than a minute later, he called again, and, with a groan, I picked it up. "Yes."

"Do you have a minute?"

"No. I'm watering the garden. I'll call you back when I've finished."

"Put me on speakerphone."

"On what?"

"Press the speaker icon on the keypad."

I looked at the screen. "I don't see, oh…wait…there, done."

"Can you hear me?"

"Loud and clear," I said, wincing at the volume.

"Okay, now, leave your phone somewhere close by and you can carry on watering while we talk."

"Remarkable," I said, propping the phone up against a plant pot. "What do you want?"

"To fill you in. Pascal Martineaux came to see me today."

I glanced at the phone. "Oh?"

"We had a long conversation. Or rather, he spoke; I listened. I got the feeling he needed to offload."

"What did he say?"

"Plenty. It turns out Serena's the jealous type. She can't stand him taking an interest in anyone other than her. It drives her crazy. He also told me his sister and mother had accidents before he and Serena moved to the UK. His sister was hit by a car, his mother was badly scolded by a pan of boiling water, but neither could remember what happened."

At once, Jessica Parks's warning rushed into my head—*Stay away from Pascal. Because bad things happen to people he takes a liking to.* But perhaps it wasn't Pascal doing the bad things.

"Unexplained accidents." I dragged the hose over to the other side of the garden to water the pots of annuals. "Does he think Serena caused them?"

"He wouldn't say. Even when I pushed, he wouldn't say. He did say they'd had an on/off relationship for years. He'd tried to end it many times because Serena was clingy, unreasonable about his friends, but she always managed to win him back. It was when his friends started having accidents they couldn't remember as well that he tried to break up with her once and for all. That's when she told him she was pregnant."

A thought occurred to me. "The green eyes in his portraits. I asked Pascal if the green eyes represented envy. I wondered if the people were jealous of him, but now I think they were the people Serena was jealous of. Including Charlie Simmonds."

"Was Charlie Simmonds in the exhibition?"

"He was the man in silhouette, sitting in front of the window. I recognized him at the time but couldn't think how. I guess he was in the exhibition because he'd also suffered an unexplained accident. Perhaps he'd worked out it was caused by Serena and was trying to see Pascal to tell him."

DCI Roberts whistled and added, "And Serena had to stop him."

I turned off the tap and sat down with the phone in my lap.

"You were in the exhibition as well," he said after a moment. "I thought he'd included you as a threat, what with the syringe against your neck. But now it's obvious it was a warning. He was warning you about Serena. Don't know why he didn't just come straight out and tell us his wife was a crazy person."

I wondered this as well. Then it came to me. "Because he couldn't be the one to say it. She's carrying his child. What would she have done if he'd openly accused her of attacking his family, his friends, his ex-lovers? What might she have done to his child? No. He needed someone else to say it for him."

"And he chose you."

I thought back to the first time we'd met outside his building. The way he'd looked me up and down as if he was assessing me. Was that when he'd made his decision? Or was it later, in his studio, just before he abruptly told me to leave?

"In my opinion, he chose well." He cleared his throat noisily. "Listen. We might have something here. Let me make some calls. If I can get statements from a few of the other people in the exhibition, we might have enough for an arrest."

28

DCI ROBERTS PRESSED THE RED BUTTON ON THE RECORDER.
"The time is eight p.m. This interview is being recorded and may
be used as evidence if this case goes to trial. Present are Ms. Serena
Carmichael and DCI Roberts. The assisting expert is…"

"Eustacia Rose, professor of botanical toxicology."

"Also present is…"

"David Hargreaves, lawyer."

"Good. Then let's begin." DCI Roberts cleared his throat.
"Ms. Carmichael, you've been charged with the murder of Mr.
Charlie Simmonds and are suspected of being involved in the
murder of Mr. Aaron Bennett. Is there anything you would like
to say to these charges?"

Diagonally opposite me, Serena was sitting with her head
bowed, her cuffed hands on the tabletop, her fingers linked as if

in prayer. She'd been crying steadily the entire time she'd been in the interview room, her tears falling onto her hands.

"Ms. Carmichael has the right to remain silent," her lawyer said. "However, she's already told me she would like to speak so that she can clear her name."

I looked at her expectantly, but she stayed silent. I looked at the lawyer; his head was also bowed. Then I looked at DCI Roberts. He glanced at me and made the *slow down* gesture with his hand, telling me to wait. I lifted my eyes to the ceiling and counted to one hundred then asked, "Well? We haven't got all day. She said she'd like to speak."

Serena took a deep, wavering inhalation and spoke on the out breath. "Everything I have done, I did for Pascal...for love."

I almost let out a guffaw at the idea she would do anything for anyone other than herself.

"Did what?" I asked impatiently, which made DCI Roberts shoot me a look I instantly understood to mean *shut up*.

"What did you do, Ms. Carmichael?" he asked gently.

I tutted. Why he was treating her with kid gloves, I had no idea.

She took another wavering breath and lifted her head. Her face was covered with tears and mucus, so DCI Roberts handed her his handkerchief, and we had to wait again for her to blow her nose.

"For God's sake!" I cried.

"Interview paused," DCI Roberts said, pressing the red button and turning to face me.

"Professor."

"Yes, Inspector?"

"Everything said in this room is being recorded. It will become the official transcript of this interview. It will be the transcript used in court if this case goes to trial. Our job here today—*your* job—is to listen to what is said without interruption. Is that clear?"

"Perfectly," I said, straightening my spine.

"Good. Then let's continue." He pressed the button again. "Interview resumed. Please go ahead, Ms. Carmichael. What did you do?"

She took another wavering breath. "A couple of months back, I found out a friend of Pascal's was in London. I say 'friend,' but he wasn't really. He was just some guy Pascal knew from New York. He wanted to see Pascal while he was here, but Pascal doesn't see anyone when he's painting—he was working on the exhibition and hadn't come out of his studio for days. Anyway, the guy kept calling and coming to our home, trying to see Pascal. He just wouldn't take no for an answer."

"This friend was Charlie Simmonds," DCI Roberts stated.

Serena paused. "May I have some water?"

DCI Roberts nodded at the mirror. "Certainly."

"Anyway. He kept coming back, and eventually I told him Pascal had agreed to meet him at a pub in Soho. Pascal hadn't agreed to anything because I hadn't told him anything, but it was the only way I could get rid of the guy."

An officer tapped the door, came in, and placed a paper cup of water on the table.

"Why was Charlie Simmonds being so persistent?" DCI Roberts asked.

Serena began to cry again. "Because he hated me."

My eyebrows lifted, but I kept my mouth firmly shut.

"Why's that?"

"Because...he wasn't just some guy... He was Pascal's lover before me, and he thought I'd stolen Pascal from him. He blamed me for their breakup. He blamed me for our move to London. He blamed me for everything."

I remembered what Pascal had said about Serena the first time I met him—if she saw something she wanted, she got it. If she saw some*one* she wanted, she got them.

Serena took a sip of water. "I thought if only I could make him forget about Pascal, he'd go back to New York and leave us alone. We'd never have to deal with him again."

I frowned. "How were you planning on making him forget?"

She glanced at me. "There's a drug called Hell's Bells, but you can't buy it in this country, at least not real Hell's Bells."

"You can buy synthetic *Datura stramonium* though," I said.

She nodded.

DCI Roberts opened his box file, took out an evidence bag,

and said, "This small bottle was found in your kitchen cupboard. It's been tested, and the results show it contained the hallucinogen that killed Charlie Simmonds. Did you purchase this hallucinogen from the dark web?"

After a hesitation, she nodded again.

"To be clear," DCI Roberts said, "you purchased synthetic *Datura stramonium* from an illegal supplier, with the intention of making Charlie Simmonds lose his memory?"

She shook her head. "Not completely. I only wanted him to lose his memories of Pascal. Hell's Bells makes you highly suggestible. A bit like hypnosis. I was going to drug him then suggest he forget he ever met Pascal."

"Did Pascal know what you were doing?"

"No. No one knew. I didn't tell a soul."

DCI Roberts made the humming sound, letting me know he didn't believe her either. We'd both seen the syringe Pascal had painted in my portrait.

"We have CCTV of you following Charlie Simmonds into a pub on Berwick Street the night he was found," DCI Roberts said.

This wasn't strictly accurate. We had no way of confirming the woman in the wide-brimmed hat was her, but although my understanding of hunches and gut feelings was still imprecise, I was beginning to understand their role in the interview room— they were a weapon in the game player's armory, a gambit.

"Could you tell us what happened in the pub?" he added.

She took another sip of water. "The pub has a toilet in the basement."

I glanced at DCI Roberts and saw the single satisfied nod. The gambit had worked.

"I waited until he needed to use it," she continued, "then I followed him and emptied the syringe of Hell's Bells into him. I'd intended to stab his arm, but he turned around unexpectedly at the bottom of the stairs, and the needle went into his neck. I knew I shouldn't pull it out. I knew he'd die if I did…"

Serena's sentence trailed off, as if she'd run out of steam, and her head lowered again.

"What happened next?"

"He was touching the syringe real gentle, as if he knew not to pull it out as well. Then he looked up at me…" She covered her face with her hands and let out a sob. "God…the look in his eyes… I couldn't stand it. He was walking backward, stumbling from me, trying to get away, I guess. He found an open door and fell through it, and I just turned and ran."

DCI Roberts gave her a moment to compose herself before asking, "So you weren't aiming for his neck?"

"No, his arm."

"And your intention was not to kill him but to make him lose his memories of Pascal?"

"Yes."

"When you realized the needle was in his jugular, why didn't you tell the bar staff or call an ambulance?"

She let out a sob. "I was panicking... I was scared... I needed to get out of there."

Serena's lawyer lifted a hand. "Perhaps my client would like to take a break?"

DCI Roberts took a whistling inbreath through his nose. "Would you?"

She closed her eyes and said in a small voice, "No. I'll continue."

He nodded, laced his fingers, and put his hands on the table, mirroring hers. "I can see this is upsetting for you, Ms. Carmichael. Let's move on to something else. Tell us about the synthetic toxin. How you found it. From whom you bought it."

Serena's eyes flew open and landed on me, as if I were the one who'd sold it to her. "I found a website, but I didn't want to buy directly from it, because I could have been buying anything."

I nodded in enthusiastic agreement.

"I insisted I meet the manufacturer in person." She looked at me again. "And, eventually, they agreed. We met at University College London, in a botany lab."

DCI Roberts's head jerked toward me.

"She seemed a sweet girl. Very smiley. She made me coffee, gave me cookies."

"Carla Oliver?" I asked.

"Carla, yes. I never knew her family name. She said the

synthetic toxins were part of her PhD research. She said her supervisor knew all about it. I liked her, so I believed her."

I thought of the dirty cups, the biscuit crumbs, and gritted my teeth. But no. That was some time after Charlie Simmonds had been attacked.

"How many times did you meet her at the laboratory?" I asked.

"Several. I liked her a lot. She was a cute little thing, you know? I loved her energy. I enjoyed hanging with her."

In my *lab*, I thought. *In* my *space,* my *domain.* She would have known the lab was mine. Carla would have told her. It was like inviting someone into my flat then finding they'd already sat at my table, slept in my bed, and used my bathroom many times in my absence. Not only that, but she probably already knew who I was the first time I went to her flat. She probably knew and still didn't give me the *Monstera.* My muscles clenched tight. I turned my face away, forcing myself to remain in the chair.

"Did she sell you the toxin in the lab?" DCI Roberts asked.

"No. She gave me an address, some dismal place in the butt-end of nowhere with some creepy guy selling the stuff in his boxer shorts." She shuddered. "When I saw him that first time, I almost turned right around again."

"So you bought the *Datura,* filled a syringe, and went to Soho."

"Yes."

"Where did you get the syringe?"

Serena ducked her head. "I took it from Pascal's studio. It's like his talisman. He keeps it in a wooden box with a glass lid and looks at it now and then to remind him of all the friends he's lost to addiction. To remind himself that he was almost lost as well. I bought some needles and filled it with the Hell's Bells. I was going to put it back, but when the needle went into Charlie's jugular...I had to leave it behind."

It occurred to me I must have been the one who'd alerted him to the missing syringe that first day I went to see him. That day I'd questioned him about his trademark then told him someone had been stabbed with a syringe full of poison in Soho. Perhaps when he'd stood up and turned his back on me, he'd been looking at the empty wooden box...then set to work on a portrait of me, with the syringe next to my neck.

"Did you go home afterward?"

"I couldn't. I was too upset. I needed someone to talk to, but it couldn't be Pascal—or Pandita. I really, really needed a friendly face." She glanced at me. "I called Carla and asked if we could meet at the lab."

My whole body jolted. That's why Carla was in the lab so late the night she'd scared Giant Hogweed away with her personal attack alarm. She was there to meet Serena. She must have walked me to the bus stop, seen me on to my bus, then gone back to the lab. I felt my jaw drop, my eyes widen, the blood rush to my ears.

"I'll take that break now," Serena said, standing up. "The baby's kicking my bladder. I need to pee."

As soon as Serena had been escorted out of the interview room, I sprang out of my chair, swung my arms wildly, and fast paced the room, much to the lawyer's alarm.

"In my lab!" I shouted. "Carla was schmoozing her customers in *my* lab! The cheek of it! The bloody cheek. And not only that"—I thumped the table, making the lawyer jump—"she was stealing my equipment! When I get my hands on her…"

"That might be a problem," DCI Roberts said slowly, "because she left the country. She emptied her bank account, ditched her phone, and caught the Eurostar to Paris. We think she's still somewhere on mainland Europe, but we don't know where."

I blinked at him. "Surely you have friends in Europe who could help you look?"

He blinked at me. "Friends?"

"Police officer friends. In the different countries?"

For some reason, this made him smile, which was infuriating.

"I could make some calls, but let's calm down and find out what happened to Aaron Bennett first."

I was furious. In fact, I can't ever remember feeling such rage. "We have to find her, Richard. And when we do, I'm going to give her a piece of my mind. My lab! Mine!" I yelled. "Under my very nose!"

DCI Roberts raised his hands. "Please sit down, Professor. You're scaring Mr. Hargreaves."

29

SERENA MUST HAVE SPLASHED HER FACE WITH WATER BECAUSE when she returned, she looked brighter, her cheeks pinker. Back in control, she sat straighter, her aloof superiority reinstated.

DCI Roberts pressed the record button. "Interview resumed. How're you feeling, Ms. Carmichael? Are you okay to continue?"

She glanced at her lawyer and nodded.

"Good. Then I'd like to move on, if I may, to Mr. Aaron Bennett. The PhD student whose deceased body was found in his flat, having been injected with the same toxin that killed Charlie Simmonds. Were you acquainted with Mr. Bennett?"

"It was Carla's idea," she said with calm authority.

"What was?"

"She said we should do it to make him forget. He snuck into the lab while we were chatting."

"Who was chatting?"

"Me and Carla. He heard some stuff he shouldn't have about Charlie and Hell's Bells and…he found out Carla was making the synthetic toxins. He got super excited about this and demanded she give them to him for free in exchange for not exposing her operation." She looked at me. "He kept saying he'd tell the professor if she didn't do as he said. Carla refused, but he was right in her face, really intimidating, so I jumped in and said I was sure we could come to some kind of arrangement. But Carla kept saying no. She obviously hated him. It looked like they had some kind of history. Anyway, he took out his phone and made to call you," she said, addressing me. "So I stepped in again and asked if Carla and I could have a moment. He went out for a minute, and I told her she should do as he asked because this wasn't just about her. He'd heard us talking about Charlie. I couldn't be involved in whatever he might do. I just couldn't. That's when she suggested we make him forget, like with Charlie."

She took a sip of water.

"You're saying it was Carla Oliver who first suggested you inject Mr. Bennett with synthetic *Datura*?" DCI Roberts asked.

"I didn't inject him. Carla did."

"But you were with her?"

She nodded. "We went to his apartment together because she didn't want to go on her own. She thought he might attack her or something."

DCI Roberts cleared his throat. "Let's take a step back. You were in the lab. Aaron Bennett was waiting outside. You had the conversation about making him forget. What happened next?"

"Carla told him to come back in. She agreed to his demands; she said she'd bring all the toxins he wanted to his home that same day, in exchange for his silence. She made a big thing of the silence bit, of how important it was he didn't tell anyone; then he gave us his address and left."

He left then immediately rang me. And if I hadn't been busy that afternoon, I may have got to him sooner...

"So, that same day, you and Carla Oliver went to Mr. Bennett's flat."

"Yeah, with five bottles of different-colored saline."

"What I don't understand is why he let Carla empty a syringe into his arm," DCI Roberts said.

"There were three syringes. She took them from the lab. She'd filled one with Hell's Bells and two with the saline. Carla told him if we were going to enter this new relationship, there must be trust between us. She said we should sample one of the hallucinogens together, get high together, share our visions when we came down. He didn't want to. He said he didn't do drugs anymore. And he didn't want me to take it. He kept saying, 'She's pregnant. She's pregnant.' So Carla put the syringes and bottles back in her bag and made to leave, and he jumped up and said, 'Okay, okay, but not her. She can be the monitor in case anything goes wrong.'"

"'In case anything goes wrong,'" DCI Roberts repeated. "What happened next?"

"Carla tied a thing around her arm—"

"A tourniquet," I said.

"—and injected herself with saline; then she tied it around his arm and injected him with the Hell's Bells. Then we waited."

Serena lowered her head, as if powering down again.

"Go on," DCI Roberts urged.

She took a breath. "After a while, he got really sleepy. Carla kept trying to wake him up, but he couldn't keep his eyes open. She seemed worried. She said it shouldn't be affecting him like that. It shouldn't make him fall asleep."

I waited five seconds.

"Aaron had mistakenly taken two doses of his anti-anxiety medication pregabalin. It has a side effect of profound sleepiness. The *Datura* reacted with the pregabalin. It was the reaction that caused his death."

I could feel DCI Roberts's eyes on me. I pictured his brow furrowed, the corners of his mouth turned down. I imagined him silently chastising me for keeping this piece of information to myself.

DCI Roberts's weight shifted. I heard a heavy exhalation. "Please continue, Ms. Carmichael."

Serena had started crying again. "We didn't know he was on medication. I swear. If we did, we would never have given him the Hell's Bells. You have to believe me. We would never…never…"

But she couldn't continue because of the sobbing. I lifted my eyes to the ceiling and bit my tongue.

"You didn't give him anything, Ms. Carmichael; Carla Oliver was the one with the syringe," DCI Roberts said gently, leaning forward and patting her hands.

He straightened and took a key out of his pocket. "Let's get those cuffs off, shall we? They must be very uncomfortable."

"Now hold on one minute," I said forcefully, but he shot me a look, and I clamped my mouth shut.

"Would you like a cup of tea?"

"What do you have?" she asked through a snivel.

DCI Roberts paused, as if confused by the question. "Tea. From the vending machine. Or coffee? I think it does hot chocolate?"

She pursed her lips. "I'll pass."

I couldn't help myself—I let out a guffaw then clapped a hand over my mouth. Another glare from DCI Roberts.

"More water then?" he asked in his irritating gentle voice.

"Yes, I'll take another cup of water."

He nodded at the mirror.

"So then. Mr. Bennett was feeling sleepy. What happened next?"

"He said he was going to bed. He told Carla to leave the bottles on the table. He said we should let ourselves out. He said he'd be fine."

"And you left."

"Yes. It didn't feel right, but we left. I kept saying, 'This doesn't feel right. This doesn't feel right,' but Carla flagged down a cab for me, put me in it, and sent me home."

Serena fell silent.

"Then what happened?" I asked.

She looked at me. "I went home."

"No. What happened with Aaron?"

"I don't know. I went home."

"You didn't ask Carla?"

"I haven't spoken to her since that day. And I don't want to."

I frowned with suspicion but said nothing.

"You're saying you haven't spoken to Carla Oliver since the day Aaron Bennett died?" DCI Roberts asked.

"Yes."

"Are you sure?"

Her cheeks flushed red with anger, and she stood up. "How many times do I have to say it? Oh…there's no air in here. I can't breathe." She covered her eyes with a hand, swaying dangerously, and the lawyer jumped up and caught her by an arm.

"I think it's time for a break. It's late and my client's tired."

DCI Roberts leaned back in his chair and checked his watch. "You're right. It's late. Let's stop for the day. Interview paused." He pressed the red button. "Ms. Carmichael, you'll be escorted to the holding cell now, and if everyone's in agreement, we'll reconvene here at nine o'clock tomorrow morning."

It was a fast and frantic march on a sweltering evening from the police station, along Prince of Wales Road and up the hill to home. To say I was upset would not do justice to what I was feeling. I couldn't believe the extent of Carla's betrayal. Not only to me but also to herself. She was an excellent student. She'd achieved a first in her bachelor's and also her master's. During her interview to be my lab assistant, her PhD supervisor had told me she was a diligent student, who, although slightly behind with her research, was making great strides toward a good result. Why she'd then chosen to jeopardize her education, her future career, her reputation by synthesizing illegal toxins and hallucinogens was utterly beyond me.

I thought of that Saturday I'd found her working in the lab. On reflection, I'm positive I wouldn't have given her permission to undertake research without supervision. This was a hard and fast rule I've never once broken. I couldn't believe she may have begun the synthesizing experiments in my lab, maybe made the breakthrough there, perhaps even manufactured the first batch there. Or was she just using the lab as a shopfront for her clients: a world-class laboratory to inspire confidence in the product before the purchase? I shuddered at the thought of the type of people she may have invited into the lab and also at what they were planning to do with whatever they were buying. They must have been sorely disappointed when they turned up at that filthy kitchen in West London.

As soon as I got through my front door, I threw off my jacket, dropped my satchel, and went straight up to the roof. I wheeled the telescope out, opened the canvas chair, settled against the eyepiece, and slowed my breathing. Breathe, one. Breathe, two. Gradually, as I panned across the Milky Way, the healing power of our small galaxy seeped into me, soothing away my anger like a celestial elixir, and I was finally able to think rationally. To form the questions calmly. Why did Carla feel it necessary to risk everything she'd worked so hard for by building an illegal lab? For money? Was she struggling financially? What was her family situation? Could they not support her? I made a mental note to check with student admin and pulled in the telescope's focus until I could see Lyra. My favorite constellation. And how on earth did she come into the possession of my *Datura stramonium*?

Unexpectedly, I heard a peal of laughter I instantly recognized. I stood up and looked down into the neighboring gardens. They were empty, but a light was on in Susan's kitchen and the back door was open. I sat down again and lowered the telescope until I could see into the room. There was Susan sitting at the kitchen table with her back to me. Opposite her was Matilde. It was a cozy scene. Matilde looked happy.

I frowned. It was the first time I'd seen her at Susan's house, but I shouldn't have been surprised. I knew they'd become friends.

Susan had told me Matilde visited often. It was just strange to see these two people from different parts of my life, enjoying each other's company without me. I looked at the dishes on the table between them, the home-cooked meal they must have prepared together, and felt a pang of an emotion I couldn't quite grasp. All I knew was it made me sad. Sad that I was so inflexible, I couldn't eat a meal I hadn't prepared myself. Sad that I couldn't sit at someone else's table and enjoy food with friends.

Very slowly, I increased the focus until I was looking only at Matilde's beautiful face, and I saw the pleasure in her dark-brown eyes, the curl of her soft lips as she smiled at whatever Susan had just said. Then there was that laugh again. That unaffected, pure sound that usually brought me absolute joy but which at the moment only served to increase the sadness.

I moved back from the eyepiece, questioning what I was doing sitting up here alone. Surely if I made an effort, I could spend an hour or two listening to nonsensical chatter about inconsequential matters? I wasn't a misanthrope after all. I just found social interaction exhausting.

Then a thought struck me, making me jump up, climb down the ladder, hurry along the hallway to my desk, and pick up my landline telephone.

"Marco? Do you still have that laptop?"

30

"SHALL I TELL YOU WHAT I THINK HAPPENED?" I ASKED.

We were back in the interview room the following morning. DCI Roberts was in his usual place beside me. Serena was diagonally opposite, her lawyer David Hargreaves beside her. She didn't answer.

I turned to DCI Roberts. "Should I tell her what I think happened?"

He nodded. "Go ahead."

"Carla knew Aaron wasn't reacting to the drug as he should have. When you left his flat, she left the door unlocked because she had every intention of going back after she put you in the taxi. However, she forgot to lock it again when she left the second time, because it was still open when I went to his flat later that evening."

I couldn't tell if Serena was nodding or rocking. In fact, I wasn't sure she was listening at all, but I pushed on.

"Once you were on your way home, she went back, let herself in, and found him on the floor of his bedroom. He may already have been dead, but whether he was or not, she had to cover her tracks. She placed the tourniquet under his arm, cleaned the syringe of prints then pushed it into the same hole she'd made when she gave him the *Datura*. She then left the flat, forgetting to lock the door."

Serena covered her face with both hands. "I don't understand. If she found him lying on the floor like that, why didn't she do something? He could've still been alive. Why didn't she call an ambulance or something? What kind of person would just leave someone lying there and walk away?"

DCI Roberts shifted his chair forward. "Did you ask her?"

She lowered her hands. "Excuse me?"

"Did you ask her why she didn't call an ambulance?"

Before she could reply, he asked, "Where is Carla Oliver?"

Serena lifted her eyes to the ceiling. "I don't know. I told you, I haven't spoken to her since that day."

There was the hum. "I've had a chat with your husband."

At these words, she shot her lawyer a look. Then the sobs returned, noisily, messily.

"My *husband*? He isn't my husband anymore. He's leaving me. He's going back to New York with the dog. The ungrateful bastard." She clasped her belly. "After all I did for him. After all the support, the love, the encouragement. All the *money* I spent on him. I changed his life. I saved him. And now I'm stuck in this shithole with his baby inside me. The absolute bastard."

DCI Roberts cleared his throat. "As I was saying, your husband very kindly came in for a chat. We had a long talk about his friends and family back in the States. And accidents...and memory loss."

He paused for a reaction. She didn't give one.

"He told me that for some time now, you've been regularly speaking with Carla Oliver on the phone. He also said you gave her a substantial sum of money. So I repeat the question: Where is she?"

An unguarded expression flashed across her face. I was familiar with the obvious ones. Anger, joy, hate, love. Smiles, frowns, tears, pain. But this one—this one was a flash of truth. A glimpse of the real Serena—Wolfsbane, *Aconitum napellus*, the wolf in sheep's clothing—and all at once, I had a whole other theory of what happened the day Giant Hogweed died.

"Carla didn't put you in a taxi to send you home," I said. "It was you. You put Carla into a taxi. You kept his front door unlocked, and you returned to his flat. It was you who set the scene to make it look like he'd overdosed, not Carla. Then you walked away without calling an ambulance...just like you did with Charlie Simmonds."

She threw me a nasty look. "Everything coming out of your mouth is total garbage. You can't possibly know what happened that night."

"Ah…but I do because Aaron told me."

Serena looked at her lawyer, at DCI Roberts, and then back to me. "What are you talking about?"

I took Aaron's plant list out of my pocket and placed it on the table. "This is the piece of paper found in Aaron's pocket. The list of plant names that turned out to be a code. You've seen it before. The solution to the code spelled the words MURDERER SERENA C. Words you so vociferously objected to. He rang me after he left the lab."

"He what?" Serena gasped.

"He rang to tell me he knew who was manufacturing the synthetic toxins, but he wouldn't say who it was over the phone. He wanted to meet me straight away, and I very much regret that I couldn't because I was busy. So he wrote me a note instead because he suspected he was in danger. He needed me to know the truth in case something happened to him, and the note had to be in code in case you found it and destroyed it. However, there was more to the code than we first thought. There were two more plants on the list, which changed the solution to MURDERERS SERENA CARLA. Aaron was telling me he knew you were both involved in Charlie Simmonds's murder. You by sticking him with the syringe and Carla by supplying the toxin. However…" I took a breath. "However, something must have happened while you and Carla were visiting him. Something that made him go to his bedroom to rip off the last two plants that spelled out the rest of Carla's name.

Something that exonerated her and put the blame fully on you. He must have been terrified, barely lucid, hardly able to stand, but he managed this final act before he collapsed."

Serena was glaring at me. Her pale eyes bored into me. If I was a different kind of person, I might have been intimidated.

"I believe it was your idea to make Aaron forget what he'd overheard in the lab," I continued. "And I believe it was you who injected him with the *Datura*. I believe it was you and you alone who murdered Aaron Bennett so that he couldn't tell anyone you killed Charlie Simmonds."

Serena's head was moving very slowly from side to side, her eyes still fixed on me. When she eventually opened her mouth to speak, she was silenced by the sound of the lawyer's mobile pinging a text alert. He picked it up, opened the message, and made a point of reading it to himself with deliberate intent.

"Very good. He's arrived."

"Who's arrived?" DCI Roberts asked.

"Jarvis Carmichael. Ms. Carmichael's father. He and his attorney flew over from New York this morning." He looked up at DCI Roberts. "He's outside in the lobby. He says he wants to speak with you."

DCI Roberts pulled his brows so low, his eyes disappeared; then he reached for the red button.

"Wait," I said. "I have one more question."

He lowered his arm.

"When you talked about going to the West London flat to buy the *Datura*, you said 'that first time.'"

Finally, Serena's gaze shifted from me back to the floor.

"But you went back. You disguised yourself with a wide-brimmed hat and dark glasses and went back to buy a second bottle." I paused. "Who was the second bottle for?"

There. Right there. The sheep's clothing slipped again, revealing that shrewd, intelligent, terrifying glint of truth as her eyes flicked to me and flicked away. A cold shiver ran across my scalp as DCI Roberts and I turned to each other. I didn't say a word. I didn't need to, because he'd seen the wolf as well.

31

WHILE SERENA WAS ESCORTED BACK TO THE HOLDING CELL, I took the opportunity to leave because my duties as an assisting expert were over, and, quite frankly, I didn't want to remain in that station longer than was absolutely necessary. However, halfway across reception, I was waylaid by Jessica Parks. She was with a tall, distinguished-looking man with swept-back silver hair and an expensive suit, and a slim woman in a smart pinstriped dress, carrying a black briefcase. The father and the attorney, I presumed.

"Eustacia, I'm glad I caught you. Come and meet Jarvis Carmichael, Serena's father."

I stayed where I was.

"Jarvis, this is Eustacia Rose, the botanical toxicologist I was telling you about."

"Why yes. The brilliant professor. I've heard so much about

you," he said, striding toward me. "In fact, Jessie won't stop talking about you."

I took a backward step and another. Why on earth would she be talking to this man about me? He didn't stop striding until he was right in front of me. I fixed my eyes on the exit doors, trying to judge how quickly I could reach them if I made a run for it. He put out his hand for me to shake. I ignored it.

"David Hargreaves tells me you're also a bit of a wizard when it comes to sleuthing. You certainly put paid to my daughter's shenanigans. And a good thing, too. I want to thank you."

I glanced at him. He was smiling but not in the happy way.

"Serena is… How can I put this…extremely intelligent but also a wild card. She's unpredictable, obsessive, prone to misadventure, sometimes dangerously so." He turned back to the others. "Jessie here's been keeping an eye on her for me for years. Trying to keep her on the straight and narrow. Making sure her mind's occupied with all sorts of strange and wonderful things. What've you covered recently? Shamanism? Buddhism?"

Jessica nodded. "We've explored many spiritual teachings over the years. Many philosophical ideas."

I frowned. "You're not a shaman?"

"No," he answered for her. "She's Serena's babysitter."

"I prefer *surrogate mother*," Jessica said. "Keeping watch."

"You work for him?" I asked.

"She does. Since Serena was little. Serena's mother died when she was seven, and I couldn't raise her on my own. I needed help. Nannies didn't work—Serena made sure of that. I think the longest any of them stayed was four months. Then I thought of Jessie. We go way back. We were at Magdalen College together, oh, it must be over forty years ago now. I was a Fulbright student. Jessie was reading English literature."

I snapped to attention. That was Father's college. Father's subject.

"We were great friends. We did everything together. Everyone called us The Js." He put on an English accent. "Where are The Js? Here come The Js. *Oh no*, it's The Js."

They both laughed at this. I don't know why.

"So I called her up and straight out asked her to help me raise my daughter, and as it happens, she's turned out to be a pretty good mom."

Questions began to form, but before I could ask them, DCI Roberts appeared at my side.

"Mr. Carmichael? I'm DCI Roberts, the lead investigator on your daughter's case. Will you come this way? Mr. Hargreaves is waiting for you, and then I believe you'd like to speak to me?"

He held out a hand in the direction he wanted them to walk and took a couple of steps.

Serena's father looked back at me. "It's been a real pleasure to meet you, Professor. I hope we meet again very soon."

Then he and the attorney followed DCI Roberts, and I

was left alone with Jessica Parks. I glanced at her. Who was this woman? She'd been so many people—the woman with long white hair; for a while, the woman with the wide-brimmed hat and dark glasses; Pandita-vaggo, Serena's shaman; the witch. The woman who was always trying to tell me something. The woman who had awakened long-forgotten memories. *Either she goes, or I go.*

She was looking at me with an open expression, a slight smile on her lips, and I finally asked the question I'd wanted to ask for weeks.

"Who are you?"

She took a step toward me. "Do you really not know?"

"Patently not."

"Eustacia... I'm your mother."

For a split second, I felt a pulse of excitement then let out a derisory snort. "I'd've thought you'd have enough on your plate with Serena. Besides, I don't need a surrogate mother, thank you very much. I'm perfectly fine as I am."

She took another step forward and said softly, "Eustacia, I'm your *real* mother."

I snorted again, louder this time, and shook my head vigorously. "Well, I happen to know that's not true because I have photographs of my real mother, and I can assure you, you are nothing like her. Nothing at all."

She took one more step. "That woman..." She paused to take

a breath. "That woman was your father's wife, not the mother of his child."

⁂

It was after this that I made that dash for the exit and didn't stop to look behind me until I was halfway along Prince of Wales Road. She was nowhere in sight of course. She probably hadn't even followed me out of the station.

With a sigh of relief, I pulled out my handkerchief, took off my glasses, wiped my sweating face, and continued home at a more reasonable pace, but as I turned the corner into my road, I stopped in my tracks, because there, leaning against the front door of my building, was Pascal Martineaux, an enormous rectangular package leaning against the door beside him. My steps faltered. I wasn't in the mood for more of his mind games, but I couldn't help feeling curious.

He was so engrossed in whatever he was reading on his phone that I was right in front of him before he noticed me.

"Professor. I was hoping I'd catch you before I left for New York."

There was the white-teeth smile.

"What can I do for you?"

"You've already done it."

I frowned. "What have I done?"

"You followed the clues and caught the culprit. You did the thing I couldn't do. I knew you would."

My frown deepened. "How did you know I would?"

"From the way you dress. The attention to detail. The fact that you had no idea who I was. Also, the way you got angry about the plant. The way you stood up to Serena. The way you didn't bat an eyelid when I told you who her father was."

I shook my head at this bizarre logic, but he smiled again and tapped the package beside him.

"I'm here to thank you and to give you a gift."

"A gift?"

"Your portrait."

I shuddered at the thought of the unnerving eyes, the needle at my neck, and shook my head vigorously. "No, thank you very much. I don't want it. You can keep it."

For some reason this made him laugh. "If you don't want it, sell it. It's valued at ninety thousand dollars, but you'll get more at auction."

I couldn't suppress a gasp.

"You want me to carry it into your apartment?"

"Yes, please," I said immediately. "Top floor."

He looked past me. "Ten minutes max." And I turned to see a sleek black car parked outside my building with a uniformed man sitting at the wheel and the Great Dane taking up all three back seats.

Once I'd opened the door for him, he leaned the painting

against the wall and looked up and down the hall, taking in the front room at one end and the kitchen at the other; then his eyes came to rest on the photograph of Father. He stepped closer and studied it for some time, taking in every detail.

"This old guy's wearing your suit," he said. "Is he your pa?"

"He is."

"You look just like him. That's one crowded table. What is all that stuff?"

"Educational aids. I was home-schooled."

"By him?"

"Yes."

"The table looks as chaotic as my studio. I like his style. Where's your mom?"

That woman was your father's wife, not the mother of his child.

"I... I..." But I couldn't continue because it suddenly felt as if I'd been hit by a juggernaut. I sat down abruptly. Directly where I'd been standing.

"You okay?"

"Not really."

He squatted beside me. "Anything I can do? You want some water?"

Embarrassed, I clambered to my feet and even attempted something like a smile.

"Don't mind me. It's been a busy few days. Lots of rather staggering revelations. I must admit to feeling a bit bewildered."

"You've been interviewing Serena," he said with an understanding nod. "I had a call from her father earlier. He flew in from the States this morning. He's here with the family attorney. They're going to push for her trial to be held in New York, what with Charlie being an American citizen. They'll plead for leniency, as she's pregnant. I expect there'll be a huge out-of-court settlement with his family. Serena will be bailed out, yet again, by her father." He shook his head, adding, "Story of her life."

I looked at him. "And what about you?"

"What about me?"

"Serena said you're leaving her and the baby."

He let out a growl. "Did she now? Well, she's half right, I am leaving her. But not my child. I plan to be a very big part of his life. In fact, Jarvis and I are discussing custody later today. I'm mean, she's a crazy person, right? She shouldn't be allowed to look after a baby. Not after what she did to Charlie, and all the others…"

"All the people in your exhibition," I clarified.

He glanced at me. "Yeah, all those accidents. I know she didn't mean to kill Charlie but…poor guy. He didn't deserve that. And my mom… Those burns… She's scarred for life." He paused a moment. "I think Serena might actually be insane. They say highly intelligent people can tip over, don't they?"

A thought occurred to me. "Why didn't she stop the exhibition? She would've recognized all the people you'd chosen to paint. She would've known what you were doing. You told me if she wanted something, she got it. If she'd wanted the exhibition canceled, would it not have been canceled?"

"She didn't see the paintings until the opening. She won't set foot inside my studio because it stinks of ash trays."

"And you smoke in there to keep her out?"

He smiled and inclined his head. "She sure was furious at the opening, but what could she do? Challenging me would've been an admission of guilt. So she sat there silently seething the whole night. It was actually kinda satisfying to watch."

He let out a laugh that didn't sound happy and squared his shoulders. "Anyway, I'd better scoot. I'm meeting Jarvis and the attorney at the apartment. You want me to unwrap the painting before I go?"

"No, thank you," I replied curtly. "But perhaps you could tuck it behind that door?"

He nodded, then stopped and pulled a paper bag out of his pocket. "Oh, I almost forgot. I found this in Serena's bedside cabinet."

I opened the bag and found a small bottle and a syringe still in its sealed sterile packaging. I glanced up at him. He was looking at me keenly and added, "I can't pretend I don't know who it was intended for."

32

THE FOLLOWING MORNING, I LEFT THE BANK WITH A FAT ENVE-
lope of cash and crossed the road to the café where Marco was
waiting for me. I didn't even stop to say hello but went straight
to the counter to buy him coffee and cookies. He hadn't wanted
the job at first, but my offer to triple his rate had finally persuaded
him to delve into the murkiest parts of the dark web that no law-
abiding person should go anywhere near. And that's where he
found it—the site that had sold Carla my *Datura stramonium*.
He didn't stay long. Just enough time to screenshot the plant's
photograph, make spurious inquiries, and find out the *Datura*
had already been sold. Enough time also to express an interest in
buying, for a very generous price, any other mature toxic plants
that may come into their possession. He'd cast the line. Now I just
had to sit back and wait for a bite.

As I was heading down the hill toward home afterward, my

mobile vibrated a text message—*We have Carla*—and my heart almost leaped out of my chest. I spun round, looking up and down the hill, then for the second time in my life, flung out an arm to flag down a taxi.

At the station, DCI Roberts was waiting for me in the reception, ostensibly to prevent me storming into the interview room to confront her. I admit to attempting a dash toward the door as he accompanied me to the monitor room, but he blocked it with his large body and ushered me on. However, when I looked through the one-way mirror, the interview room was empty, so why he'd made that song and dance about keeping me out of it, I have no idea.

"How did you find her?" I asked as he pulled out a chair and positioned it in front of the mirror for me.

"There'd been a few sightings of her in the south of France. The French police were keeping an eye out but never caught up with her. It appears she was enjoying Serena Carmichael's money. Mostly at five-star hotels in Nice, Saint-Jean-Cap-Ferrat, and Beaulieu-sur-Mer, until it ran out. Border control informed us she returned to the UK yesterday." He rested his rear on the monitor table in front of me, held its edge with both hands, and stretched out his legs. "Her parents weren't very forthcoming to begin with but eventually told us she was staying at a friend's flat in Kilburn. We picked her up half an hour ago. She's being processed now."

I leaned sideways to try to see past him. He shifted his bulk to block me.

"Why can't I be in the room?"

"Because it's likely this case will go to trial, and we don't want the recording littered with your strong opinions."

"I'll keep my mouth shut."

"No, you won't. You don't know how, and even if you manage to, your dagger looks will make her clam up."

"But what if I have questions?"

"This interview isn't about you, Eustacia. Whatever charges of betrayal you want to fling at her, whatever accusations or remonstrations you've been brewing…now isn't the time or place to bring them up."

I inhaled deeply through my nose. "Alright. But please ask her one question on my behalf."

"Depends what it is."

"Serena said she thought there was some kind of history between Carla and Aaron. I sensed there was something more than dislike between them as well. I'm wondering if there was more to this than Carla simply wanting to stop him exposing her operation. It feels like her grievances with him were much longer held."

"There you go with those feelings again."

I glanced at him. "I beg your pardon?"

"Those *feelings*. Those illogical notions and irrational conclusions you complain so bitterly about."

"Does that mean you will ask my question?"

He glanced behind him and stood up. "Maybe. Okay. Looks like we're ready to start. You sit tight in here and enjoy the show."

I wasn't alone in the monitor room. There were two other officers sitting at their desks politely ignoring our conversation. I glanced at them, and they quickly looked away, busying themselves with their keyboards. However, our attentions were quickly diverted as Carla entered the interview room with her lawyer, closely followed by DCI Roberts. They took their seats, and the red button was pressed, but, frustratingly, Carla opted for the "no comment" position and refused to answer a single question. I must admit, as the clock ticked, I was becoming more and more annoyed with her behavior. I was due an explanation, an apology—even if it was through a pane of mirrored glass.

I stood up. "Perhaps she'd like some water?" And I left the room.

The officer at the door hesitated when I approached with the paper cup but let me in when I said I had a vital message for DCI Roberts from the monitor room. Once inside, the first thing I did was march up to Carla and hurl the water at her face, because in my opinion, she needed waking up. She let out a cry.

DCI Roberts and the lawyer jumped up, and I folded my arms and said in my sternest lecturer's voice, "I think it's high time you explained yourself, young lady."

To which she burst into tears, and DCI Roberts slammed

down the red button and shouted, "What the hell do you think you're doing?"

"I'm waking her up. She's half asleep. Look at her."

"Profe—"

"Carla," I said sternly, "you're a very diligent and determined student. You're on track to get an excellent PhD. You've been an exceptional lab assistant. I don't know what I would've done without you this past year. So why, oh why, risk it all by synthesizing illegal toxins?"

Carla was sobbing now, her chin on her chest, but she managed to get out the words, "Because of Aaron."

DCI Roberts immediately pressed *Record*.

"What do you mean because of Aaron?" I asked.

She took a shuddering breath and leaned toward me, as if finally impelled to talk.

"We were put together as research partners at the start of our PhDs last year. I didn't want to be with him. He gave me the creeps, but even though our subjects were different, I wasn't allowed to switch with anyone else because we were on the same academic path. We were about eighty percent along with our research. All our samples were growing well. I headed off to the European Conference on Biodiversity, and Aaron stayed behind to tend our samples because, as you know, they needed attention every day."

I nodded, and she nodded back.

"Anyway, I was due to start collating results as soon as I got back from the conference, but when I went to the cold frames, all our samples were dead. Aaron hadn't been in to tend them the whole time I'd been away. He just let them die. A whole year's worth of research gone. I was devastated. I wanted to kill him!"

Carla's lawyer cleared his throat.

"Metaphorically speaking," she added, glancing at him. "But Aaron had disappeared. No one had seen him for ages, and when he did finally show up, he was off his head on drugs. He couldn't even string a simple sentence together, let alone explain why he'd destroyed our research. I was raging, but he couldn't care less that we were back to the beginning when we were so close to finishing. He didn't give a toss that I'd have to extend my PhD and start all over again. He was so high he didn't care about anything."

I inhaled. This explained why he'd spent the year hounding me for the cuttings. He was racing to catch up.

"Thing is, Professor, I couldn't afford to extend for another year. I needed money. Not a part-time hospitality job, money. Real money. The synthetic toxins lab was the only way I could afford to finish my PhD. Being your assistant and having access to the lab on the weekends was the only way I could catch up."

She leaned further forward, her cuffed hands palms down on the table, her chin thrust out, her eyes wide open, pleading with every sinew for me to understand. "You get it, don't you?"

"Aaron disappeared because his younger brother was pushed off some scaffolding by schoolboy bullies and he died."

She continued to stare at me, wide-eyed, as if my words hadn't yet reached her brain.

"He didn't take it well," I added. "In fact, I'd go so far as to say he took it very badly indeed."

Still, she was staring but also opening and closing her mouth as she was editing what would come out of it next.

"I…didn't know that," she said at last and slumped back in the chair.

"So now his parents have lost both of their children."

I thought she would say something more to defend herself, but she simply put her hands in her lap, lay her cheek on the table, and closed her eyes.

DCI Roberts cleared his throat. "Miss Oliver, we would like you to give us your account of what happened on the afternoon Aaron Bennett died. We already have Ms. Carmichael's statement. We'd like to hear your side of the story." He shifted his weight. "Let's begin at the lab in University College London after Aaron Bennett overheard your conversation about Charlie Simmonds. Was it Serena Carmichael's idea to inject him with the *Datura*?"

She stayed where she was, her head resting on the table, her eyes closed; then she took a ragged breath and on the exhalation said, "Yes."

And I turned for the door because there was nothing more she could say that I didn't already know.

33

I WAS KEEN TO SEE MATILDE. I HADN'T SEEN HER FOR QUITE
some time, and I have to admit, I was missing her terribly. Missing
her joyful laugh, her tight embraces, her kisses on the cheek, her
beautiful deep-brown eyes, her ridiculously loud voice. But before
I could do that, I had to make a stop at Bedford Avenue where I'd
arranged to meet Mr. and Mrs. Bennett.

I climbed the grand steps to the building's front door, pressed
the bell for Giant Hogweed's flat, and instantly a voice I recognized as Mr. Bennett's crackled out of the intercom.

It wasn't a pleasant feeling to be back standing outside Giant
Hogweed's door. The memory of finding his body was still too
vivid, but I made myself knock and even managed a short nod
when the door swung open to reveal Mr. Bennett, so tall and wide
that he filled the door frame.

"Come in," he said, moving into the kitchen so I could pass him.

Mrs. Bennett was standing in the lounge doorway, smiling weakly. "It's good of you to come, Professor Rose." She gestured toward the lounge. "Would you like a cup of Earl Gray?"

"That's kind of you," I said, following her in and sitting in one of the armchairs. "But no. I can't stay. I just wanted to bring you up to date with Aaron's case."

"Aaron's case," Mr. Bennett repeated. "You don't know how relieved we were when we heard it had been reopened, and I believe we have you to thank for that."

I inclined my head in acknowledgment. "We now have the perpetrators. Forensics made a second sweep and have placed both Carla Oliver and Serena Carmichael here. They're currently both in custody."

Mrs. Bennett sank onto the ornate two-seater sofa, and Mr. Bennett squeezed down next to her and took both her hands.

"You must know, they didn't intend to kill him," I continued. "Their intention was to make him forget a conversation he'd overheard. The hallucinogen they injected him with has a side effect that causes amnesia. They just wanted him to lose one day. However, they didn't know the toxin would react with his medication, or that the combination of the two would kill him."

Mrs. Bennett straightened. "Medication?"

"His anti-anxiety medication. Pregabalin."

She turned to her husband. "Did you know he was taking anti-anxiety medication?"

"No," he replied, shaking his head.

They both seemed so different from the last time I'd seen them. He'd lost his volume, his arrogance. She appeared to have collapsed in on herself, as if she just didn't care anymore. I looked at them both in turn, really looked at them, and saw two pitiful people ravaged by grief, propping each other up, exhausted, neglected, bewildered, barely alive themselves, and I inhaled deeply and decisively through my nose.

"I spoke to him on the phone the day he died."

They looked up. "You did?"

"Do you know the reason he was expelled?"

They nodded.

"He attacked you," Mr. Bennett said softly. "We're truly sorry about that."

I waved a hand; I wasn't looking for an apology. "When we spoke, he told me that since he was expelled, he'd been seeing a therapist to help him manage his anger. He was brave enough to ask for help. You can be very proud of him for doing that, can't you?"

Mrs. Bennett began to cry. Then Mr. Bennett began to cry, and after a moment, I added, "I know I am."

I wasn't sure where Matilde would be, but my guess was the library, as that's where she spent most of her time. I didn't mind going to the library because it was inside Senate House, and Senate House was by far my favorite building in the whole university complex, because its towering Art Deco simplicity never ceased to fill me with awe. I paused to gaze up at it now, appreciating its stark beauty, then hoisted my satchel and walked toward the entrance doors, determined to follow every word of Susan's advice.

As expected, I heard her long before I saw her, which meant all I had to do was follow her voice to a wood-paneled side room, where she was sitting at a table, working with a student. When she spotted me standing in the doorway, she seemed surprised then shook her head and frowned, which was confusing because usually she rushed to me, wrapped her arms around me, and kissed my cheek. Perhaps she felt that would be inappropriate in front of the student, and I suppose that was fair enough.

"I'll be with you in five minutes, Professor. Don't you think you'd be more comfortable waiting outside?"

I leaned against the door frame and smiled at her. "No. I'm perfectly comfortable here."

And I was. I'd never observed Matilde teaching. I was interested to see her methods.

She was still looking at me, her lips pulled in. I glanced at the student. He was also looking at me. I got the feeling they were waiting for something.

"You'll be more comfortable outside, Eustacia."

I took my weight off the doorpost and stepped backward through the door. "Okay, then."

It wasn't five minutes. It was seventeen, but I didn't mind because I was in my favorite building, sitting in a deep leather sofa, surrounded by books. I had one open on my lap now. *Wuthering Heights*. I'd just read the first page, although I couldn't recall a word of what I'd read.

"Sorry to keep you waiting. You should've texted to let me know you were coming," Matilde said, sitting next to me.

I smiled at her. "I wanted to surprise you."

She lifted her eyebrows expectantly, which was the cue for me to explain myself, but first, I needed to inquire about her life.

"How is your life?"

"What?"

"Your life? How is your life going? Good, I hope?"

She exhaled heavily and shook her head. "I'm actually very sad at the moment."

I frowned. This wasn't what I was expecting. I thought she would say everything was great, and we could move on to other subjects.

She glanced at me. "Don't you want to know why?"

I didn't really. I widened my smile and picked up the carrier bag. "Well, maybe this will cheer you up."

She looked at the bag. "What is it?"

"A cake."

Her brown eyes widened. "You bought me a cake?"

"I bought *us* a cake. I thought we could celebrate—"

"Eustacia," she said, cutting me off, "I'm glad you're here because there's something I've been wanting to tell you. In fact, I've been trying to contact you for days, but you haven't been answering my calls or texts." She paused and looked away. "I've made the decision to go back to Portugal."

I tilted my head. "For a holiday?"

"No, my darling. I've accepted a teaching position at Universidade de Lisboa. I leave at the end of the month. I'm leaving London forever."

I stared at her as a strange sensation crept into my chest, a sensation of being lassoed. Of being dragged behind a horse, in the dust, scarcely able to breathe.

"But...I thought you were my person."

She took my hand. "Oh, Eustacia. I wanted to be your person. I wanted it with all my heart, but it just didn't work out for us, did it?"

"Didn't it?"

"I'm so very sorry to say...no. It didn't. But I've learned something important about you these past months. You are an extraordinary human being. It's just...you have a problem with hyperfixation. Once you become fixated on something, everything else becomes irrelevant. Every*one* else becomes irrelevant."

"That's not strictly true," I said, thinking I should at least make an effort to defend myself.

"It is, my darling. You've been fixated—obsessed—with that case, and only now that you've solved it have you got time for me. But I don't want to be the person you only have time for when you don't have anything else to think about. I want to be the person who's in your life every day. Who you think about every day. Who you miss when you aren't with me. Who you text *goodnight, sweet dreams* before you fall asleep. Who you think of when you first wake up in the morning."

I shifted my eyes to the bookshelves behind her. "I've never really been that kind of person."

She let go of my hand. "Yes. I know that now."

When I was a child, Father once said most things that are beautiful disappear. However, I didn't always have to listen to Father.

"But I want to be. And I'm going to be. From now on," I said brightly, forcing myself to meet her eyes. "So you can call Lisbon and tell them you've changed your mind." I held up the bag with the cake in it. "I know I missed Susan's birthday, and I'm very, very sorry about that. But I've come to pick you up so we can go to hers together for a belated celebration."

I smiled at her, and she stared at me, her eyes glistening.

"Eustacia..."

"Yes?" I asked, still smiling.

"It's too late."

"Oh, I'm sure she won't mind if the celebration's a few days late."

"No. It's too late...for us."

34

THE NUMBERS ON MY DIGITAL CLOCK CLICKED OVER TO SIX A.M.
I saw this because I'd been staring at it for hours. With effort, I
raised my upper body, turned sideways, and sat on the edge of the
bed. The light behind the curtains was sharp and clear that morning, which meant summer was reaching its mid-point. Summer.
I'd barely noticed it. I'd been so—what did Matilde call it?—
hyperfixated on the case that I hadn't noticed much of anything.
Certainly not what was going on in the lives of my friends, my
acquaintances, my loved ones. My person…my beautiful Sweet
Alyssum… I was still not completely confident about what I'd
done wrong.

People come and go from one's life. Father told me one should
be pragmatic about such things and never sentimental. So many
students had passed through my life that I should have become
accustomed to transience, but I hadn't. It took work for me to

connect with others. Hard work. And when they moved on, I believe I felt their absence more keenly than most. It was like a betrayal of all the effort I'd put in.

I stood and walked woodenly to the bathroom. There was no need to rise so early. Term had ended the week before, but old habits die hard.

In the mirror, I tilted my head and parted my hair to look at the wound. The doctor had been right—the shaved area had grown back faster than the Steri-Strips had peeled away. There was only one strip left, which I pinched between finger and thumb and pulled to give it a helping hand. The gash was clean and still slightly raised but the swelling had mostly subsided, which was a relief. The last thing I wanted was to hunt down a prescription for a course of antibiotics. I shook my head and my hair fell back to cover the wound.

I looked different without the Brylcreem and the side parting. No. I looked how I used to *before* the Brylcreem and the side parting. I sighed, turned on the bath taps then went to the kitchen to prepare porridge, wondering how on earth I was going to fill my day.

It had been a long time since I'd ventured onto the heath. Exploring the solitary paths through the ancient woodland had been my way of clearing my head when I was upset, or angry, or frustrated, or, as Father called it, "in need of a restoration of equilibrium," but since I'd been back at the university, my time was no longer my own to indulge in this pastime. In fact, when I wasn't teaching, I was either grading, taking tutorials, or planning coursework. There was no time left to simply go for a walk. But term had finished, so too had my teaching commitments, for a few weeks at least, so, my time was once again my own to fill as I pleased.

I left the porridge to simmer and walked back along the hall to the bathroom, stopping in front of the photograph of Father. There he was, sitting at the long table in our Oxford kitchen, reading his ancient paperback as if he didn't have a care in the world, and I wished I could be a child again, playing with his Kodak camera, accidentally taking this photograph, living my charmed life as if I didn't have a care in the world.

I took a deep breath, deciding that after my bath and breakfast, I would head out to the heath for a morning stroll.

I didn't get as far as the heath, however, because before I knew it, I was standing outside Susan's door. I couldn't even remember how I got there.

I gave it a push, expecting it to be on the latch, but it didn't move, which was puzzling. There was no response to my knock and no movement inside when I peered through the window either, which was also puzzling because Susan was always at home. It crossed my mind to force entry so I could check on her welfare, and after knocking again and rattling the door and shouting her name through her letterbox, I admit, my current level of emotional upset was taking me to an unnecessarily high level of panic. But then I heard her voice from the pavement above me.

"What'cha think you're doing? You'll break the bloomin' door if you keep that up."

"Susan! You're alright," I cried, sniffing and wiping my eyes.

"Course I am," she said, carefully descending the steps. "Just had to get a few bits and bobs from the shops."

I rushed forward to take her shopper as she fished for her keys in her bulging housecoat pocket.

"Was it you what left the cake on my doorstep?"

"Yes."

"Thought so. Why didn't you bring it in? We could've had a slice together."

"I…was a bit upset. I just wanted to go home."

She opened the door but turned to face me before she went through it. "About Matilde? She rang last night. She was ever so upset. Come on, lovely. Let's have a cuppa tea."

"I don't know what I did wrong," I said, sinking onto a kitchen chair.

"Don'tcha? Want me to enlighten you?" she asked, putting her hands on her hips.

I hesitated to answer, because by the look on Susan's face, I could see she wasn't going to be easy on me.

"You didn't follow my advice, did you?" she went on without waiting for a reply. "You didn't make a fuss of her, you didn't appreciate her, compliment her. You stayed your same old cur-mudgeonly self, and she got sick of it."

"Curmudgeonly," I repeated. "Father used to call me that sometimes."

"That's because you can be...sometimes." She put the cake and two side plates on the table and gave me a knife. "And sometimes you can be lovely. You just need to show Matilde a bit more of the lovely."

I stared at the knife then lay it on the table. "It's too late."

"No, it ain't. She ain't left for Portugal yet. You two just need some alone time to sit down, have a chat, and sort things out."

"But she said it was over."

"D'you want it to be over?"

"No! Absolutely not. No, no, no."

"Did you tell her that?"

I hadn't told her anything. I'd been so busy blindly hurrying away, I hadn't even said goodbye.

"You didn't, did you?"

I covered my face with my hands. "I have to admit, Susan, I've never been lucky with love. In fact, I can honestly say, I've been decidedly unlucky. Everyone always leaves in the end."

But then behind my hands, I saw Father shaking his head as if to say, *Pull yourself together. We'll have no self-pity in this house, thank you very much,* and I sniffed loudly, straightened my shoulders, and added, "But it's alright. I've been perfectly fine on my own for the past twenty years. I enjoy my own company. I'm very busy at work. I have my research. I don't need anyone else in my life."

Susan didn't speak for a long time, which was unlike her. I glanced at her and caught an expression that could have been disbelief or pity or annoyance.

Eventually, she opened her mouth and said, "Twenty years… Lordy. You know what your problem is?" I shrugged.

"You've been on your own so long, you don't even know you're lonely. Now, I suggest you pull your socks up and fix this mess."

"I already told you. She said it was over."

She pulled her mobile out of her housecoat pocket and checked the time. "I know, but lucky for you, you can tell her it ain't. I invited her for brunch. She'll be here any minute."

My heart skipped a beat, and I let out a gasp. I stood up, sat down again, stood up, cast around, expecting her to walk in at any second. And then she did, right on cue.

She looked from me to Susan, back to me and asked, "Susie? What are you playing at?"

"This ain't nothing to do with me, dear. I come back from the shops and found her trying to break my door down. But as you're both here, I might as well pop out and get me nails done."

And with that, she was out of the door and gone, and I was left standing there, staring at Matilde, my Sweet Alyssum, my throat closed, my mouth dry, my pulse racing, without the first idea of what to do next.

"Eustacia…"

But then my body took over, or perhaps it was my heart, and I rushed forward, pulled her into my arms and kissed her mouth. And I felt the shock of this, the first kiss I'd ever instigated, surge through her before she relaxed, her arms wrapped around me, and she began to laugh.

"Eustacia," she said, my name a muffled giggle.

"Mmm?"

"You're standing on my foot."

ONE MONTH LATER

PROFESSOR HUTCHINS'S KEYNOTE SPEECH AT THE IMPERIAL College London Ecotoxicology Symposium went well, I think. There was certainly a lot of nodding in the vast auditorium, but I wasn't particularly following because I was engaged in an emoji battle on my mobile phone with Matilde. In the end, she did decide to go to Lisbon but only during term time. We'd agreed that during the holidays, she'd come back and stay with me at the flat in Hampstead.

I wasn't altogether sure about sharing my flat with another person, even if it was for only a few weeks at a time, but if my choice was suffering the inconvenience of Matilde's magazines and newspapers littering every room, of her post-cooking chaos, of her long baths and wet towels on the floor, of her make-up smudges on my collar…or losing her altogether, I chose the former.

After a hilarious combination of emojis from Matilde elicited a particularly loud guffaw from me at a highly inappropriate moment during Professor Hutchins's talk, I thought it best I leave. I wasn't one to linger or network at events like this anyway—there was no one I wanted to collaborate on research with or write a paper with. I was far too busy for that. So I slipped out and headed for the bus stop toward home.

Halfway up Haverstock Hill, I was getting off the bus when I spotted her on a bench outside the underground station, and the sight of her sitting where she should not be sitting stopped me in my tracks. Of all the people in the world, she was the last person I wanted to talk to, but the only way to get home would be to walk past her. I considered jumping back on the bus just to get away from her. In the end, I crossed the road and turned down a street that led to the heath. If I couldn't go home, I may as well go for a walk.

I was a fair distance along the road before I heard her.

"Eustacia, wait."

I quickened my pace, but there was no need to hurry. She would never catch up with that bad leg.

When I reached the entrance to heath, I slowed beside the ponds to watch a very old woman feeding the swans and geese and ducks and coots that were crowding and snapping at her feet. So much so that it looked as if she was in danger of being knocked over by two particularly aggressive geese. I was at the point of wondering whether I should intervene when she gave them both a stern word and a sharp tap on the head, and they retreated like naughty children.

"She's obviously done that many times before. They'd peck her if they didn't know her."

I turned sharply to find her standing next to me. How she'd managed to catch up so quickly, I had no idea.

"Let's have a cup of tea. There's a café over there."

"No, thank you. I'm going for a walk."

"To restore equilibrium?"

I flinched. "I beg your pardon?"

"You must be upset, Eustacia. Confused. Maybe even angry. You probably have a ton of questions but don't want to ask them. You don't want anything to do with me. You wish I'd go away. And all of this has upset your equilibrium."

I blinked at the ground, at the sky.

"The old man told me he used to take you for walks when you were upset. He said it was the only way to calm you down."

I blinked harder and harder because it felt like there was something in my eye.

"Come on—let's have a cup of tea."

The café was just across the road. I insisted we take an outside table so I could walk away whenever I wanted. She was smiling. I knew this even though I wasn't looking at her. It was an eternity before the waiter brought our order.

"Shall I be mother?" she asked, picking up the teapot.

Straight away a memory rushed into my head of me asking that same question in a café the year before to the young woman I'd nicknamed Psycho. I don't know why I'd said it then. I'd never said it before, and I don't recall Father saying it either. I glanced at her while she poured the tea.

"You loved me asking that when you were little. Every time, you had to point out the joke because I was already your mother. Every single time." She took a sip of tea and asked, "Do you have any questions for me? I'll answer with honesty and good intention."

She waited for my reply. When none came, she added, "I don't want anything from you, Eustacia. I'm not trying to force my way back into your life. Although it would be lovely to see you every now and again."

My eyes stayed fixed on the horizon. She was sitting right there, so why not ask her a question? I flicked her a quick glance. "Did you abandon me?"

A moment passed.

"Did you feel abandoned?"

I considered this. "I don't think so. I must have been too young to remember you leaving. I certainly have no recollections of thoughts or emotions about abandonment. Besides, I thought another woman was my mother."

"Do you have any thoughts or emotions now?"

I picked up my teacup. "Not particularly."

This made her laugh, although it wasn't clear why.

"Would you like to know why I left?"

I supposed it could be interesting, so I shrugged.

"When I was a student, your father and I had a brief affair, but I ended it when I fell pregnant with you."

"While he was married?"

"Yes, while he was married, which is why I didn't tell him I was pregnant. I thought I could have you on my own *and* finish my degree. I thought I could do it all, but it was a struggle. I was struggling. Because... Well, because you turned out to be a very special little girl who needed a lot of care and attention, and time and energy. And I was so, so tired." She took a breath. "In the end...I did the thing I vowed I would never do. Just before your third birthday, I asked your father for help."

She took a sip of tea. "I didn't expect his reaction when I told him about you. I didn't expect him to be ecstatic. He was literally jumping for joy. His wife...not so much. She was furious. She wouldn't allow us to come to the house. She forbade him from seeing us. She made all sorts of threats."

Either she goes, or I go.

This must have been when she'd said these words. These words I now distinctly remember her saying. This must have been when she left him.

"We never went to his house, but he came to our flat. Often. In fact, he couldn't stay away. He was besotted with you because you were so bright. You picked things up so quickly. He loved that about you, and you were different with him. You were calm, relaxed; his voice soothed you. You understood his boundaries; you didn't get upset like you did with me. He was an older man— you were the child he thought he'd left it too late to have. The arrangement turned out to be perfect because when he was with you, I was able to study and finally finish my degree."

She paused to refill our cups. "That's when Jarvis—Serena's father—suggested you and I move to New York so I could do a master's at Columbia University. He said we could stay in his apartment for the two years it would take, and he'd help with the childcare costs. His family was loaded. His apartment was a three-bedroom apartment on the Upper West Side overlooking Central Park. How could I turn down such an offer? So I applied for the master's and was accepted onto a scholarship program. I got you a passport, ended the tenancy on our little flat, and packed our bags."

She paused again, long enough for me to glance at her. She was gazing away toward the heath, her eyes unfocused as if she was lost in some other time. Then something brought her back, and with a small head shake and a smile, she continued, "But your father wouldn't let you go. Even when I told him about the apartment and Central Park just across the road and the childcare. He said you'd be better off with him in the Oxfordshire countryside than in another country with a stranger who didn't understand you. He even said he'd give up teaching to be with you."

She leaned back in her chair with a finality that I understood to mean she'd said what she had to say, and it was now my turn to speak. I took a slow breath. "You left me behind."

"I did. I left you with your father. Who loved you. Very much."

"You left me alone to live with a man I didn't know when I was only three."

"You did know him. You'd spent time with him at the flat. I think you even liked him. Besides, his wife was there. It wasn't just the two of you."

I shook my head. "No. She'd left him."

"You're right. She did leave him. But not until you were four. She stuck around for a year."

"No. That's not right. I distinctly remember her saying to Father, 'Either she goes, or I go.' We were in the kitchen in the Oxford house. I was playing on the floor in front of the fireplace. Father was wiping my hands and face and sweeping ash off the floor, back into the grate. She was standing next to us, and she said, 'Either she goes, or I go.'"

Jessica Parks didn't speak for a long time; then she leaned forward, placed her hands on the tabletop and said, "She was talking about you, Eustacia."

To discover the person I'd always thought of as Mother had turned out not to be was upsetting. To then discover she'd given Father the ultimatum to choose either her or me was more upsetting. To go on to discover that the woman who was my mother

had left me when I was three and hadn't come back was…well…
beyond upsetting. But that wasn't strictly true. I now remembered
she had visited once or twice when I was a child, but she was just
another one of the faces that turned our house into Piccadilly
Circus. What I meant was, she hadn't come back to collect me.

I stood up, deciding that whoever this never-present, non-
mother person was, I had no need for her. I was perfectly fine on
my own. I'd also found my plant nickname for her—Bittersweet,
Solanum dulcamara. A woody vine that scrambles over other
plants, suffocating them. Toxic to children.

"Wait a moment," she said when I turned to leave. "I have
something for you."

She rummaged in her bag, pulled out an envelope, and handed
it to me. "You don't have to open it now."

So I put it into my jacket pocket and walked away.

As soon as I got through my front door, I went to the bathroom, pulled up in front of the mirror, and gave myself a long hard
stare. My father. My *father*, so gentile that he could have stepped
out of the Regency period, had had an *affair*. With a *student*! I
shook my head. Not only had my father had an affair with a student, but that affair had resulted in a *child*. But the horror didn't
end there, because to make a bad story worse, that child had
destroyed his marriage. I let out a groan and covered my face with
my hands because it was all my fault. All of it.

In my torment, I heard Father's voice next to my ear.

Can't be helped, Eyebright. What's done is done. Best not to dwell on the past. Onwards and upwards.

Sniffing deeply, I uncovered my face. Perhaps he was right. None of it could be helped. Not by me anyway.

Another sniff and I opened the jar of Brylcreem, took Father's tortoiseshell comb, slicked back my hair, and made a very precise parting. And when I was done, I looked at myself and nodded because there before me was Professor Eustacia Amelia Rose, Head of Botanical Toxicology at University College London.

"Onwards and upwards, Eyebright. Onwards and upwards."

Then I went to my desk, took out a fresh notebook, picked up my pen, and began to write.

꘍꘍

I wrote all afternoon and all evening, detailing the twists and turns in Charlie Simmonds's and Giant Hogweed's sad demises, and was beginning my case conclusion when I was startled by the buzz of the intercom. I checked my watch—it was just after eleven thirty. For a moment, I wondered who it could be, but it could only be one person. The person I'd vowed never to answer the door or phone to this close to midnight ever again.

I sighed, stood, and went to the intercom. "Yes."

"It's Richard. May I come in?"

"It's very late."

"No, it's not. It's perfect. It'll start soon."

"What will?"

"The Perseids. Shall we watch it on your roof?"

The Perseids! With all that had been happening, I'd completely forgotten about this meteor shower, the most spectacular of the year, with hundreds of shooting stars per hour. But did I want to watch it with DCI Roberts? Yes, I most certainly did.

Without another word, I pressed the door-release button, opened my front door, and leaned over the banister. "Hurry up, man. It'll be starting in a minute."

As I was waiting for his inordinately slow ascent, I glanced at the notebook on my desk then at the answering machine, because, although I'd been sitting next to it for hours, I hadn't noticed the light was flashing. I looked down the stairs and caught DCI Roberts's bald patch approaching the second flight, so I dashed to the machine, pressed the play button, and the deep voice sent a thrill through me.

"We've had a bite. I await your instructions."

To say I was excited would not do justice to what I was feeling, but now was not the time to be talking with Marco. Not with a police inspector at my door.

I went back to the door and found that he'd finally reached the half landing, and I could see why it had taken him so long.

"I come bearing gifts," he said holding aloft a bottle of whisky and a very sick-looking *Ficus benjamina*. "Nice to see you looking more like your old self, Professor."

"Why on earth would you bring me a plant that's quite patently dead?"

He looked at the plant. "It's not completely dead."

"Ninety percent. Maybe even ninety-seven," I replied.

He began his slow ascent of the final flight. "It's from the sec-retaries' office. I saw it as I was leaving work and thought if anyone can bring it back to life, it's you."

"And how do you propose I do that?"

"I don't know. You're the botanist. Do your magic in that greenhouse of yours on the roof." He stopped walking. "Which, come to think of it, was full of cuttings that you said weren't mature enough to have developed toxicity when I came to inspect your destroyed garden last year."

I looked down at him. He was looking up at me.

"Correct me if I'm wrong," he added.

I didn't hesitate. "You're wrong. Here, give me the *Ficus*. I'll see what I can do."

He handed it to me, and I took it through to the kitchen, dumped it on the table, and all the leaves fell off.

"I bought a bottle of whisky as well," he said, following me in. "As a replacement for the whisky I drank last time."

"Why bring a replacement for something I won't drink?" I asked.

"It's not for you."

I blinked at the bottle, totally confused by this bewildering logic, and looked up to find him smiling broadly, which was puzzling.

"Where do you keep your glasses?"

Drink in hand, he was about to attempt the ladder when something caught his eye. I followed his gaze to Pascal Martineaux's wrapped package, tucked behind the kitchen door.

"What's that?"

"A painting."

"Don't tell me it's a Martineaux?"

So I didn't.

"How can you possibly afford a Martineaux?"

"It was a gift."

"A gift?" he boomed, putting down his drink and marching over to it. "Can I have a look?"

"I'd rather it stayed wrapped."

But he was already untying the string.

"You've been receiving bribes from Pascal Martineaux? What else haven't you told me?"

I let out a guffaw, and he shot me a look.

"I'm serious, Eustacia." But then he smiled and continued with the unwrapping. "No, I'm not. My God, I can't believe he gave you a painting. You've won the lottery."

When the last of the paper peeled away, he stood back, and we both studied my portrait.

"Oh…" I said.

"Indeed," he said.

Pascal had made some very pleasing alterations. Gone were the unnerving green eyes, and gone was the syringe next to my neck.

"Well, that's a relief," I said. "Can't say I was a fan of the hidden syringe cipher."

"It's still there. He just moved it."

I glanced at him. "Where to?"

There was that smile again. "I'm not going to tell you."

I turned back to the painting and scanned it from top to bottom, three times, but I couldn't find it anywhere.

"Where is it?"

"I'm not telling you."

"Come on, man."

"Relax your eyes and you'll see it."

I tried to do as he instructed, then let out an annoyed huff and went to the ladder. "The Perseids is much more interesting than this."

Luckily the moon wasn't bright, which meant we'd have a clearer view of the meteor shower when it began. It also meant the roof garden was in darkness so, although we were sitting close, I could scarcely see DCI Roberts at the telescope. I could hear him though, his whistling nose breathing, the slurps as he took a mouthful of whisky.

"Do you have to be so loud?"

I felt him look in my direction. "I haven't said a word."

"You don't have to speak to be loud."

"Well, pardon me for breathing," he said, slurping another mouthful of whisky and swallowing it loudly.

I tutted and pushed my hands into my pockets…and found the envelope. I'd completely forgotten about it. I pulled it out and turned it over in my hands.

"What's that?" DCI Roberts asked.

"I don't know. I can't see."

He turned on his phone flashlight and shone it in my direction, and I ripped open the envelope and pulled out a birthday card.

"I didn't know it was your birthday."

"It isn't," I said, opening it.

Inside, the handwritten words read, *For all the birthdays I have missed, I send you my best wishes. Happy Birthday, my dear, darling daughter, Love Mum x*

I stared at the words, these small marks made with a pen, and didn't understand why my eyes were pricking, welling.

DCI Roberts was sitting close enough to have read them as well. He inhaled deeply. "The woman with long white hair?"

I nodded and sniveled and heard a grunt as he stood up, then another as he knelt down beside me and circled his arm around my shoulders.

"You know what?" he asked gently, "I believe you have quite a few wishes to make tonight, for all those missed birthdays with your mother." He turned off the phone flashlight. "Look up, Eustacia."

And I looked up to see a hundred bright trails of light streaking across the sky, some white, some yellow, some blue. Intellectually, I knew they were small meteor particles entering the earth's atmosphere at high speed and burning up to create the brief but spectacular display, but emotionally, it felt like I'd never seen anything so beautiful in all my life. Fresh tears stung, but I let them fall because it was too dark for anyone to see. Then I made a wish, and another, and another, and another.

All the wishes for those motherless years. All the wishes for the childhood I could have had.

"Richard?"

"Yes, Eustacia?"

"There's one last thing. One last question that's been worrying me for a while now."

"What's that then?"

"What do hipsters do?"

"Eh?"

"The night Charlie Simmonds was found, you said in the café that clubbers go clubbing. If clubbers go clubbing, what do hipsters do?"

PLANT GLOSSARY

HELL'S BELLS: DATURA STRAMONIUM

* Family: Solanaceae
* Genus: *Datura*
* A weed native to Central America, used in medicines and drug abuse as a hallucinogen.
* Fatal

EYEBRIGHT: EUPHRASIA NEMOROSA

* Family: Orobanchaceae
* Genus: *Euphrasia*
* A small herbaceous flowering herb used in traditional medicines to treat eye infections.
* Nonfatal

GIANT HOGWEED: HERACLEUM MANTEGAZZIANUM

* Family: Apiaceae
* Genus: *Heracleum*
* A phototoxic flowering perennial, causing blisters and scarring; a dangerous irritant, if ingested.
* Fatal

RAGWEED: AMBROSIA ARTEMISIIFOLIA

* Family: Asteraceae
* Genus: *Ambrosia*
* A common weed native to Europe with a huge pollen count; highly allergenic, severe irritant.
* Nonfatal

BLACK-EYED SUSAN: RUDBECKIA HIRTA

* Family: Asteraceae
* Genus: *Rudbeckia*
* A flowering perennial native to North and Central America; coarse hairs are a mild irritant.
* Nonfatal

SWEET ALYSSUM: LOBULARIA MARITINA

- Family: Brassicaceae
- Genus: *Lobularia*
- A low-growing, small annual with sweet-smelling flowers; habitat of sandy beaches and dunes.
- Nonfatal

WOLFSBANE: ACONITUM VAREIGATUM

- Family: Ranunculaceae
- Genus: *Aconitum*
- A herbaceous perennial flowering plant native to the Northern Hemisphere. All parts are highly toxic.
- Fatal

ADDER'S-TONGUE: OPHIOGLOSSUM VULGATUM

- Family: Ophioglossaceae
- Genus: *Ophioglossum*
- A fern with a spore-bearing stalk loosely representing a snake's tongue. Native to tropical and subtropical habitats.
- Nonfatal

TOUCH-ME-NOT: MIMOSA PUDICA

- Family: Fabaceae
- Genus: *Mimosa*
- A creeping annual with sensitive compound leaves that fold inward when touched or shaken. Native to the Caribbean, as well as South and Central America.
- Nonfatal

BITTERSWEET: SOLANUM DULCAMARA

- Family: Solanaceae
- Genus: *Solanum*
- A woody vine, the stems of which have been used medicinally to treat eczema in adults. The whole plant is toxic to children.
- Fatal

BARBERRY: BERBERIS THUNBERGII F. ATROPURPUREA

- Family: Berberidaceae
- Genus: *Berberis*
- A deciduous shrub with spiny branches, small purple leaves, and bright red fruits. Avoided by deer. Native to Japan and East Asia.
- Nonfatal

MOONFLOWER: IPOMOEA ALBA

* Family: Convolvulaceae

* Genus: *Ipomoea*

* A species of night-blooming morning glory, native to tropical and subtropical regions, the flowers opening in the evening, staying open through the night, and closing only with the first touch of morning dew.

* Nonfatal

READING GROUP GUIDE

————

1. Despite not wanting to be involved in another police investigation, Eustacia agrees to help with a new case involving plant poisons. Have you ever been dragged into something you didn't want to join? How did that end up going for you?

2. Eustacia has a unique way of remembering people—by nicknaming them using plants. Do you have trouble with names, faces, or even places? If so, is there anything you like to do to help you remember?

3. DCI Roberts and DS Chambers butt heads over generational differences and stances on misogyny and sexism throughout the novel. Discuss some of the issues that they bring up and how they are poignant to our current times. Do you think either of them are right, or if not, where do you think they have yet to grow?

4. Eustacia is frustrated by her inability to defend herself when she is accosted by her student. What did you make of her decision not to press charges? What might this circumstance reveal about power dynamics, especially on school campuses?

5. The same syringe found at the scene of the crime is connected to the famous American artist Pascal Martineaux. Why does Pascal use the syringe as a trademark in his paintings? Do you know any artists who use repeated symbolism in their work?

6. Who is Jessica Parks, and how is she connected to both Eustacia and Eustacia's father? How did this twist affect Eustacia emotionally? Were you surprised by the reveal?

7. This story is filled with toxic plants from around the world, and one is even used as the main murder weapon. Did you learn anything new about plants and their potential uses? If so, what did you learn?

8. The poison that put the first victim in intensive care was the same poison that killed Eustacia's student Aaron, and yet the police close his case for lack of evidence. How does Eustacia plan to prove Aaron's death was a murder, and why would she do this, considering their complicated past?

9. Did you guess the identity of the chemist and the murderer before the end of the book, and if so, what clues led to your conclusion? When reading mysteries, do you like to try to

solve the case before the book ends, or do you let yourself be surprised?

10. This latest mystery following Eustacia Rose is filled with twists and turns as the evidence and connections begin to stack up. What was your favorite twist, and why? Did you see any of them coming?

A CONVERSATION WITH THE AUTHOR

————

This next installment in the Professor Eustacia Rose series is so much fun! Where did the inspiration for this story come from?

Thank you! It was fun to write as well. This is a bit dark, but the inspiration came from a news item I was listening to on the radio about the growing problem of synthetic drug addiction. It made me think about an addict I knew in the past. How the disease destroyed his life and also how he managed to recover. He had a talisman that he looked at every now and again to remind him to keep going with his recovery. He was the inspiration for Pascal Martineaux. The writing challenge—and also joy—was to then turn that dark theme into a fun story.

As always, your novel is filled with plants of all sorts. How do you choose the plants you feature in your stories?

The plants that feature in both Professor Eustacia Rose mysteries were chosen while I was plotting *The Woman in the Garden* because these are the plants that were stolen from Eustacia's illicit collection of poisonous plants when her garden was vandalized. The hallucinogenic plant *Datura stramonium* is featured in *The Poison Grove* but not in its true form. Its base chemical structure has been synthesized and multiplied to sell on the dark web by an unscrupulous chemist…and it is Eustacia's mission to find out who that chemist is.

There is another plant I enjoyed including in the novel, a very rare ten-foot tall *Monstera obliqua*, one of the most expensive plants in the world. I included it because I knew Eustacia would want it desperately. But Eustacia doesn't always get what she wants.

This story has an incredible cast of characters. Did you have a favorite character to write in this novel, aside from Eustacia?

I really enjoyed writing Aaron Bennett (Giant Hogweed), although he's not my favorite character. Creating an intimidating, desperate, unpredictable character who will stop at nothing to get what he wants, and then delving into his back story to explore the reasons he is the way he is, was an interesting process. I also enjoyed playing with Eustacia's reactions to him. I knew I didn't want her responses to his behavior to be common because Eustacia has a different way of seeing the world and the people within it. In fact, I wanted her reactions to be the complete opposite to most people's. By the way, aside from Eustacia, my favorite character will always be Susan.

What would you like readers to take away from Eustacia's experiences in this particular story?

My intention is for Eustacia to grow in each of the books. She had an unusual and very insular upbringing, which made her an unusual and insular adult. But gradually, as her world opens up and she lets more people in, she begins to accept that her unique way of thinking is actually rather useful when it comes to solving murders. I suppose I would like readers to take away the thought that we are all unique and unusual in our own way and these aspects of ourselves can be our superpower.

What was it like to write a sequel as opposed to the first book in a series? What kinds of new challenges did you experience?

I loved writing the sequel because it meant I got to spend more time with Eustacia and watch her character develop. I say "watch" because it feels like she has become a real person and she's telling me what to write! I have the story arc for the mystery series in my head, so I know broadly what's going to happen in the next book when I'm writing the one before. I've found that with writing sequels, the work I put into setting up the next book in the previous one is hugely important. The challenge is that if a mistake is made in one book, it's tricky to fix later in the series. Luckily, that hasn't happened to me yet, and fingers crossed it never will.

What are you working on nowadays?

I've just finished writing the third Professor Eustacia Rose mystery. Once again, it has the core group of returning characters, along with some new ones, and again, there are plant poison murders for Eustacia to solve, along with her long-suffering sidekick DCI Roberts. Oh…and I don't think it's too much of a spoiler to mention that there's also a little romance.

ACKNOWLEDGMENTS

I am indebted to my first reader, Casper Palmano, who always has the most insightful comments and advice…and sometimes appears to know Professor Rose better than I do!

Huge thanks to the team at Black & White: Campbell Brown, Ali McBride, Thomas Ross, Clem Flanagan, Rachel Morrell, Tonje Hefte, Hannah Walker, Lizzie Hayes, Leo, Pip, Freyja, and Beans.

Thank you also to the incredible agents at Pontas Literary and Film agency: Clara Rosell-Castells, Carolina Martínez, Anna Soler-Pont, and, in particular, Carla Briner, for your unflinching belief in and heartfelt support for my writing. Carla, you are a marvel.

Thank you, and thank you again to the hugely talented illustrator Lucy Cartwright for another stunning cover.

Once again, I have to acknowledge my very old and very tatty copy of *The RHS Encyclopedia of Plants and Flowers. The Poison Grove* couldn't have been written without it. And a newbie, *Breverton's Complete Herbal* by Terry Breverton. What a joy of a book to dip into.

And finally, my loved ones: Casper, Paris, Belle, Su, Siobhán, Bill, and Alison. Thank you for your limitless support and love.

ABOUT THE AUTHOR

———

Jill Johnson has lived in southeast Asia, Europe, and New Zealand. She obtained a BA degree in landscape design. She has previously owned an editorial cartoon gallery and a comic shop and has been involved in a graphic novel publishing house. She is a Faber Academy graduate and now lives in Brighton with her children. Jill's writing is inspired by her Maori heritage.